A ROYAL SCANDALS CHRISTMAS

THREE HOLIDAY NOVELLAS

NICOLE BURNHAM

A Royal Scandals Christmas: Three Holiday Novellas

Christmas With a Prince
Christmas on the Royal Yacht
Christmas With a Palace Thief

Copyright 2013-2015 by Nicole Burnham

Cover design by Patricia Schmitt

Edition: November 2015
ISBN: 978-1-941828-08-3 (paperback)
ISBN: 978-1-941828-07-6 (ebook)

For more information or to subscribe to Nicole's newsletter, visit nicoleburnham.com.

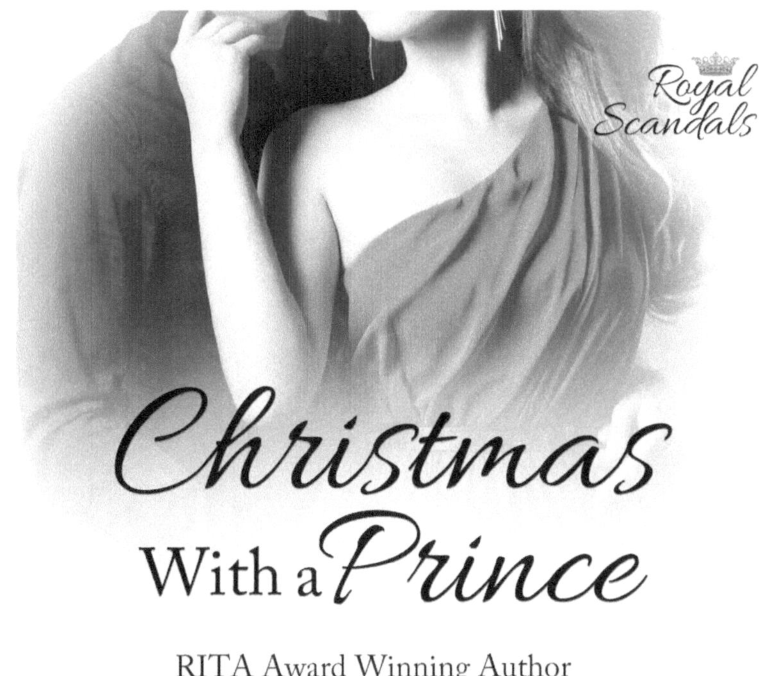

Christmas With a Prince

RITA Award Winning Author

NICOLE BURNHAM

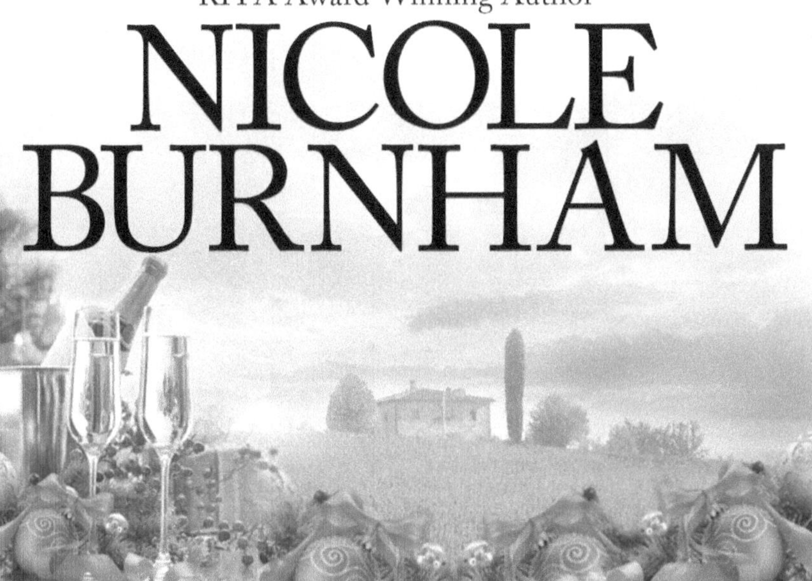

CHAPTER 1

"WELCOME TO HEAVEN. CARE FOR A CABERNET?"

Holly Elliott spun in the direction of the familiar voice. In her hurry to photograph the sunset view from the Famiglia Barrali winery's second floor patio, she'd completely missed her brother's fiancée, Chelsea Davis, sitting in a low-slung wooden chair just outside the door. Two clean glasses, a corkscrew, and a bottle of wine occupied the table beside the petite brunette, who looked at Holly with a smirk on her face.

"I saw you walking up from the bed and breakfast and figured I could persuade you to help me taste test before the rehearsal dinner. But if you'd rather take pictures...."

"Hey, you!" A wide smile lifted Holly's face at Chelsea's invitation. She crossed the patio to hug her future sister-in-law. "I wasn't sure you'd be back from the church. I'm so sorry I missed the rehearsal. But yes, I'd be happy to taste test."

Chelsea laughed, then leaned over the table to uncork the wine. "Planes are late all the time. No big deal. Besides, all you have to do is stand beside me in front of the altar. I can talk you through it before the ceremony."

"Either you're the most calm bride in history or you've already had the wine." Whereas Holly had spent most of the three hours her plane was delayed chastising herself for not taking an earlier flight.

One of Chelsea's shoulders lifted, then fell as she set the cork to the side. "It's a small wedding and Ben planned everything. Makes my life easy."

"If you say so." Holly wasn't sure she'd be so calm at her own wedding. Then again, Chelsea's unflappability was one of many reasons Ben had fallen hard for the vivacious flight attendant.

Unable to resist the pull of the gorgeous scenery, Holly moved to the patio's railing to survey the landscape while Chelsea poured. Nestled in the center of the Mediterranean island of Sarcaccia, the winery truly constituted a slice of heaven. Neatly pruned vineyards climbed the hillsides surrounding the cluster of ancient stone buildings that housed winemaking equipment, storage rooms, event spaces, and a bed and breakfast. Tall, narrow cypress trees lining the entrance to the main building sparkled with white Christmas lights. Throughout the valley, birds ignored the calendar, twittering away under the crisp blue sky as if it were summer rather than the last third of December.

To top it off, the romantic scent of wood smoke permeated the air, likely from the fire pit Holly had noticed alongside the main building when she'd arrived at the winery from Rome less than a half-hour ago. She'd checked into her room, been handed a heavy, antique iron key—given that the B & B had been built in the eighteenth century— left her bags in her room, then hustled so she could take photos before sunset. She couldn't imagine a more charming location for a wedding.

"I can't believe Ben actually works here now," Holly said as she set down her camera on a table near the patio railing. "This is the kind of job he's dreamed of his whole life."

"It's the kind of place I've dreamed of *living* my whole life. Getting married here is a nice bonus." Chelsea came to stand beside Holly and handed her a glass of the winery's prized Cabernet, then pointed over a low hill to their right. "Our house is just over there, a half mile from the village. I'll give you a tour tomorrow if there's time. It's old and it's tiny, and the pipes rattle when we turn on the water, but it's surrounded by vineyards and we can just see the Mediterranean from the top floor. Assuming I ever finish unpacking the boxes so we can get to the windows, that is."

"Make Ben help you. He's perfectly capable of unpacking, you know."

Chelsea arched a dark eyebrow. "You ever meet your brother? He can't be *made* to do anything."

"I figured you're more persuasive than I am where he's concerned."

A wicked glint lit Chelsea's eyes. "Well, there is that."

Holly tucked a wayward strand of hair behind her ear, then raised her glass in a toast. "Here's to having you join the family. Twenty-four hours from now, you'll be an Elliott, you poor thing. Then we can work on Ben together."

Chelsea clinked her glass against Holly's before taking a leisurely sip. She pulled her sweater tighter around her shoulders and said, "Actually, Ben and I plan to work on *you*. Now that you're in Europe, too, we figure it's high time to find you a—"

"Stop right there." Holly waved a hand between them. "No matchmaking. Not that I don't appreciate the thought, but I'm too busy and too far away."

After Ben left their hometown of Boston to accept a position managing the Famiglia Barrali winery's dining operations, Holly decided there was nothing holding her in Boston, either. She'd taken a leap of faith and nabbed a spectacular job with a tour company in Rome. Though she was only two weeks into the job, she knew it was the perfect fit for her. Helping American tourists make the most of their time abroad gave her a sense of satisfaction, and exploring the deep history, rich culture, and eclectic neighborhoods of the city appealed to her personal sense of adventure.

More than that, Rome provided the new start she desperately needed.

Chelsea curled her mouth into a mock pout. "Oh, come on, Holly. Sarcaccia's only an hour away by plane. And you haven't seen Ben's best man yet. When you two are partnered up, believe me, you'll want to be *partnered up.*"

Holly resisted the urge to plant her elbow in Chelsea's ribs. "You're awful. And besides, I thought Ben didn't have a best man with Gabe gone."

In fact, Holly'd counted on Ben's lack of a best man.

"Not Gabe. Prince Stefano. *The* Prince Stefano." Chelsea's voice came out in a squeak. "Can you believe it?"

Holly felt her mouth go slack. The Barralis behind the Famiglia Barrali winery happened to be Sarcaccia's famous royal family. While Holly knew the Barralis kept involved in the winery operations, she never in a million years expected to meet one of them in person, let alone Prince Stefano, who was a darling of the tabloid media thanks to his good looks and the string of catwalk models, actresses, and aristocratic women he'd dated over the years.

If ever a man could make her forget her obsession with Gabriel Maddox, it'd be the larger-than-life Prince Stefano Barrali.

"But how...how did that happen?" Holly asked once she'd recovered enough to speak.

"He was planning to spend a few days here to inspect the property and review the changes Ben's implemented with the menus, and said he'd love to attend our wedding. When Ben mentioned that his best man couldn't make it due to a business commitment, Stefano offered to step in, and...*voila*!" She flipped her hand in the air. "You're now partnered with a prince! And you know the man's a shameless flirt. If I wasn't the bride, I'd be insanely jealous."

Holly made a show of rolling her eyes. She didn't have a mouse's chance in a lion's den with a man like that. Didn't *want* a man like that, even if, as the maid of honor, she'd have plenty of opportunity to enjoy the man's company for the weekend.

"I haven't met him yet, but Ben says Prince Stefano's fantastic," Chelsea continued, her words tumbling over one another. "Smart about the business and a total gentleman, despite his reputation with the press. If Prince Stefano doesn't fit your standards, no one will."

For years, Chelsea, Ben, and nearly all of Holly's friends accused her of holding impossible standards when it came to men, standards that meant she'd either suffered through dates that left her feeling hollow at the end of the night or—more often than not—turned down offers completely. She'd shrugged and gone along with her friends' assessment, figuring it was far safer than telling them the truth: For nearly a decade, she'd been obsessed with her brother's best friend, Gabe Maddox. None of the guys she met had Gabe's charisma or the sharp mind that enabled him to graduate near the top of his law school class. Nor did they possess the subtle attributes that made Gabe so...*Gabe*. The sparkle that lit his face when he told a joke or won a hand of cards. The smooth cadence of his walk. The sweet way he interacted with kids, treating them as if they were his peers. The deep, rolling laugh that emerged from him when he and Ben swapped stories of their college antics. The strong, capable hands and muscle-corded arms that came from hours upon hours of hard, physical work taking care of his mother's home and yard when she was too ill to do so herself.

On the other hand, none of those men held a candle to Gabe when it came to loving and leaving women. Given what he'd seen of his parents' relationship, Gabe made no bones about the fact he wasn't wired for long-term relationships. And that was why, no matter how deep her attraction, Holly would never, ever let anyone know how she truly felt. If Gabe didn't possess the need for a singular, passionate romance, then neither should she. At least not with him.

She savored a mouthful of rich, red wine before telling Chelsea, "I'm honored you think I'm a good match for a man like Prince Stefano. But I'm not looking for...*that*...right now."

"You've got to be kidding me." Chelsea turned her face skyward, as if pleading with the heavens. "Christmas with a prince and she says no."

Familiar male laughter came from behind them. The women turned to see Ben crossing the patio. "I see you two found each other."

"And the Cabernet!" Chelsea raised her glass, then stood on tiptoe to give Ben a quick kiss before Ben turned and pulled Holly into a welcoming hug.

"You look phenomenal," Holly told her older brother once she stepped back from his embrace. Living in Sarcaccia agreed with him, but she suspected Chelsea was the real reason for her brother's cheerful expression and the buoyancy in his step.

"So do you," he said, though after a few polite questions about her flight, his attention quickly went back to Chelsea. "Do you have enough time to get ready for the rehearsal dinner?"

"Plenty," she assured him. "I was just telling Holly about Prince Stefano."

"And I was pretending I didn't overhear you playing Cupid." He waved them toward the doors. "Leave your drinks here and follow me. Prince Stefano's downstairs and I want to introduce you."

"Now?" Chelsea's hand flew to her hair. "I'm in jeans and I've been out in the breeze—"

"You look spectacular. Besides, I thought you wanted the prince to be impressed with my sister?" He winked, then led them through the second floor of the winery and down the stairs to the main room.

Though the building was centuries old, it had been remodeled to let in more light and serve modern entertainment needs. Wide-planked oak floors and stone walls kept the feeling of old Sarcaccia, while long, broad tables provided a place for guests to enjoy wine tastings and savor freshly-made dinners from the kitchen. A massive stone fireplace, its mantel decorated with Christmas greenery and topped with a carved and painted wooden angel, served as the room's focal point. The atmosphere breathed romance and family tradition.

A broad-shouldered man with dark, wavy hair sat at one of the tables, a sheaf of papers spread before him. He looked up as the trio approached, then stood. After warmly greeting Chelsea and wishing her the best on her upcoming wedding, he turned to Holly and extended a hand.

"You must be Ben's sister."

His handshake was as warm and friendly as his voice was seductive. Holly couldn't help but beam. "It's an honor to meet you, Your Highness."

"Please, call me Stefano. And I'm the one who's honored to participate in your family's big event." His eyes crinkled at the corners when he smiled down at her. They were intelligent, unusual eyes—green irises outlined in black, flecked with gold—which, when combined with his smooth olive skin and strong physique, made her suspect women would flock to this man even if he didn't hold a title or come from one of Europe's wealthiest families. "I understand that you're the maid of honor?"

"I am."

"Then we'll have to work together to ensure Ben and Chelsea have a memorable wedding." His hand tightened fractionally around hers. "Perhaps we can come up with something during the rehearsal dinner?"

The question was left hanging as the main door to the winery opened. A gust of cool air blew through the room as a man entered carrying an overnight bag.

"Gabe!" Incredulity filled Ben's voice as he crossed the room in long strides to greet his best friend. "How in the world did you get here?"

"Airplane," Gabe replied, humor lacing his voice. "They have several flights a day connecting through Paris, as it turns out."

Holly froze in place as her brother and Gabe exchanged a back-slapping hug. Despite the fact Gabe sported an uncharacteristic five o'clock shadow, he looked as breathtakingly handsome as ever. Perhaps, if such a thing were possible, he looked better. His perpetually sunkissed hair had been cropped shorter than when she'd last seen him, giving him the appearance of a tough, take-no-prisoners military man.

"I can't believe this. Weren't you supposed to report yesterday?" Ben asked. What he didn't add was, "to Quantico." After two years practicing law in the Manhattan district attorney's office, Gabe decided to follow his dream and apply to become an FBI agent. He'd undergone rigorous physical training, a series of interviews, and had taken a battery of written and psychological tests after submitting his application. Despite clearing every hurdle, he still wasn't sure he'd be accepted. Receiving the notification that he'd been selected for agent training was a cause for celebration. Unfortunately, his scheduled report date at the FBI Academy was the day of Ben's wedding, and missing it meant missing out on his dream.

"Last minute change in the schedule," Gabe said. "I hope it's all right that I decided to surprise you."

"We're thrilled!" Chelsea assured him as she threw her arms around Gabe's neck. "It didn't feel right getting married without you here. There's even an empty room on the third floor of the bed and breakfast with your name on it."

Gabe spun Chelsea around, making her squeal with delight, but as he did so, his rich, golden brown eyes locked with Holly's. A frisson of heat surged through her, igniting her clear to her core. The impact of it caused her to take a half step backward.

A subtle pull made her realize she was still holding Stefano's hand.

She glanced up at the prince and extracted her fingers from his. "Um, sorry. Distracted," she mumbled.

A curious smile curved his lips. "Entirely my pleasure."

Before Holly could respond, the prince moved to introduce himself to Gabe. "And this must be the missing best man. I'm glad you could make it."

"About that," Ben said, "Gabe, I asked Stefano to step in for you—"

"No problem," Gabe said at the same time Stefano shook his head.

"No, please. I'm more than happy to remain a guest and hand the duties back to you." Stefano glanced over his shoulder at Holly and added, "As long as I still get a dance with the maid of honor."

"I'm sure you can twist Holly's arm," Ben replied, his relief at avoiding a potentially awkward situation apparent. "Thanks."

"Speaking of whom" —once more, Gabe's piercing gaze landed on her— "I haven't gotten a hello. Long time, no see, Holly."

Chelsea glanced from Holly to Gabe, a confused frown creasing her forehead. "You saw her in Boston three weeks ago, didn't you? She told me you were there wrapping up the sale of your mother's house."

Gabe nodded. His mother passed away from cancer the previous year. It had taken Gabe and his siblings a while to sort through her belongings, put her home on the market, and find a buyer. "I did. She took me out to all my favorite places. Much as I've liked living in New

York, it's not Boston. I doubt even Sarcaccia can compete with the restaurants in the North End."

He skirted around Chelsea to lean in and kiss Holly's cheek. Holly forced a polite smile to her face as his lips brushed her skin and she caught a breath of his scent. How could a man smell so amazing after spending an entire day on an airplane?

And why, oh why, did it make her want to close her eyes and kiss him full on the mouth, when she knew from experience exactly what a mistake that would be?

She managed a chipper, "Hello, Gabe. Glad you're here."

At the same time, he lingered near her ear long enough to whisper, "We need to talk."

A shuffle of feet nearby indicated the approach of the winery's head chef from the direction of the kitchen, giving Holly an excuse to turn away. The older man, a longtime employee of the winery, asked Chelsea if she wanted to make a last-minute check of the dinner preparations.

"Ben's more likely to have an opinion," she said. "And I need to get to my room to dress for dinner and make sure my parents are ready. Anyone else heading downhill to the B & B?"

Seeing her chance to escape, Holly gestured toward the staircase. "I need to run back to the patio to get my camera. Why don't you and Gabe go ahead? You can show him his room."

"Actually, I'd like to see the view before it gets too dark." Gabe's words were innocuous, but Holly caught the determination in his dark eyes. He wanted her alone, and he wanted her alone now.

Chelsea, on the other hand, didn't notice a thing. "I suppose I can wait for you. Don't take too long, though. My parents are going to take a zillion pictures tonight and I need to look good."

"I'm happy to walk you down," Stefano offered. "I know the path well. Holly and Gabe can follow when they're ready."

At Ben's urging, Chelsea left with Stefano, leaving Holly to head to the porch with Gabe at her heels.

G ABE WATCHED Holly's backside as she climbed the stairs in front of him. He could tell from the rigid set of her shoulders that she was resisting the urge to stomp her way up.

What right did *she* have to be mad? She was the one who oh-so-casually announced she was leaving for Rome after he'd finally told her how he felt about her. She was the one who blew him off as a joke.

And now here he was, twelve-plus hours after boarding a plane in New York, gambling his future on her.

Without looking back at him, she made her way across the large stone patio to a wooden table holding two half-full wineglasses and her camera. "Shoot," she said. "Chelsea and I left our wine up here. I should take all this downstairs. Do you see where she put the bottle?"

As Holly pivoted to scan the patio, he caught her in his arms. Even in the fading light, he could see the shock in her clear blue eyes as his hands spread across her narrow waist. "Gabe, what are you—"

"I'm finishing what we started in Boston."

"There's nothing to finish." Two hands planted on his chest, sending his mind reeling back to the last time she'd touched him. "Even if there were, Prince Stefano and Chelsea are right below us on the path and Ben will be following them down any minute. If they look up here—"

"It's dark and I can be very, very quiet." Never had he wanted a woman so badly he physically ached with it, but he sensed now wasn't the time for that particular approach. "I just want to talk. Without you running away."

A few strands of long, dark brown hair blew across her face as an evening breeze came in from the vineyards. Resisting the urge to swipe them from her cheeks, he released her and stepped back.

She didn't bolt. Instead, she crossed her arms in front of her and regarded him as if he were a schoolchild in need of a lecture. "What do you want to talk about?"

"How about the fact we slept together?" There. He'd dropped the bomb.

She didn't flinch, but her eyes narrowed in warning...and if he wasn't mistaken, in fear. "Shhh."

"No one can hear me."

"*I* can hear you." A long, soft sigh escaped her. "Look, this is inappropriate. We're here for Ben and Chelsea's wedding."

"I'm here for a lot more than the wedding."

"This weekend is about them," she barreled on as if he hadn't spoken. "What happened with us was a fluke. A one-time thing, no strings attached. No need to discuss it."

And you're lying through your beautiful teeth. He could tell from the mix of panic and desire that flitted across her face the moment he crossed the winery's threshold. When they'd locked eyes, it was as if nothing else existed in the room. She'd even seemed to forget she was in the middle of shaking hands with an honest-to-goodness royal. If that glimpse of her emotions hadn't convinced him, it was apparent in the way she looked at him now, taking in the sight of his travel-wrinkled shirt and freshly-shorn hair as if she itched to reach out and smooth the creases in the fabric, then check the texture of his hair with her fingertips, but feared what would follow if she did.

Keeping his voice low and controlled, he said, "We've known each other for what, twenty-plus years? Ever since Ben and I were in preschool together. I know you well enough to know you don't have one-night stands. What happened between us was no fluke."

"And I know you well enough to know one-night stands are your forte," she retorted.

"Wow. Speak your mind, why don't you?"

"I didn't say there was anything wrong with it." One side of her mouth jerked up and she shook her head before he could argue. "But that's neither here nor there. My life is here now, in Europe, and you're starting with the FBI. That's been your dream for as long as I've known you. Hanging out in Boston a few weeks ago was fun. And maybe you needed someone familiar and safe to be around, given that you were saying goodbye to the last of your mother's things and the house where you were raised. I was more than happy to be that comfort for you. I *enjoyed* it. But you and I both know it's ridiculous to pursue—"

"Holly, you couldn't be more—"

"You guys still up here?" Ben's voice came to them from inside the winery, followed by the pounding of his feet on the stairs. A heartbeat later, he emerged onto the patio. "I'm heading down to the B & B to get ready for the dinner. Figured I'd grab Gabe to show him his room."

"Good idea." Holly's bright tone made it sound as if they'd been discussing a topic as fluffy as wedding cake frosting. "Let me take the wineglasses down to the kitchen."

"You want us to wait?" Ben asked, though Gabe already knew what she'd answer.

"Nah. I can see well enough to make it down the path. I'll catch you both at dinner." With that, she swiped the glasses and her camera from the table, then disappeared.

"Heaven up here, isn't it?" Ben asked, looking out toward the western hills where the sun dipped below the horizon, leaving only the deep purple of clouds fading to black.

"Most romantic spot I've seen in a long time, if ever," Gabe agreed. When Ben slid him a sideways glance, eyebrow raised in question at the uncharacteristic statement, Gabe quickly added, "Let's go get you married."

CHAPTER 2

THE CHEF'S tarragon chicken had been roasted to perfection. Squash from the winery's gardens, homemade bread, a delicious tomato and mozzarella salad, and decadent chocolate blackberry soufflé left the entire room in a relaxed, chatty mood as wedding guests savored generous pours of Famiglia Barrali's finest red dessert wine. Ben and Chelsea stood near the fireplace, arms around each other's waists, glasses raised in a final toast to their friends and family as they celebrated their last night as an unmarried couple. Holly held her glass aloft with everyone else, warmed by the happiness that filled the room. Cameras flashed as cheers of *salute!* and *cin cin!* echoed through the room.

Despite the picture-perfect scene, she struggled to remain still. She didn't need to look for confirmation to know Gabe's tawny-lashed gaze was upon her, watching her every move from his seat at the far end of the table. She doubted he'd stare openly—he was too discreet for that—but she could feel his scrutiny. He had the ability to heat her skin with nothing more than a glance or a smile.

She wished she could attribute the intense feeling of warmth to the wine, but she'd consumed very little, knowing she'd need to keep her wits about her.

I'm here for a lot more than the wedding.

Gabe knew exactly what to say and how to say it to entice her. With no other single women present and a twenty-one week training session at Quantico looming, he knew this weekend would be his last hurrah.

She balled her fists under the table. She'd been right to push him away. She'd known what she was doing when she'd let him seduce her in Boston. She'd been well aware he was going away, that it was a one-time deal. It had been *her* last hurrah. And she'd moved on. To Rome. No matter what, she couldn't allow him to corner her again tonight. Because if he slid those strong, sensuous hands around her waist once more, if he locked his dark, expressive eyes onto her face, then leaned in and told her he wanted to *talk*…she suspected the talking would never happen. She'd allow his mouth to do any of the other wondrous things she knew were in Gabe's repertoire.

I'm here for a lot more than the wedding.

"They seem very happy," Stefano murmured beside her.

Holly snapped her attention from thoughts of Gabe to the prince. Though she'd seen Stefano before on television and in newspapers, seeing him in person was an entirely different experience. It wasn't just the finely-tailored suit or the confident smile that came with fame, wealth, and power; his voice enveloped a person with the smoothness of a silk blanket. She suspected he knew exactly what that voice did to women and wielded it as a sexual weapon as easily as Gabe worked his affable grin and wicked glances.

Unfurling her curled fingers, she smiled and placed her napkin beside her empty dessert plate. "They are. They love each other to death and they're living and working in paradise. Your family's winery is unbelievably romantic, like a movie set come to life." She stole a look at her brother, who leaned down to plant a kiss on his bride-to-be, before focusing once more on Stefano. "Thank you for hiring him. This position is the perfect fit for him."

"Wish I could take the credit, but it was the general manager's decision. I heartily agreed with it, though." He handed his empty soufflé dish to a passing member of the waitstaff as he added, "I saw a television interview with Ben when I was visiting Boston last year and was intrigued."

Holly remembered the piece, which aired at the end of the evening news as a local interest story. Ben discussed the renovation of the Beacon Hill hotel where he worked. He'd highlighted the updated menus and wine pairings, showing off the fifth-floor private dining room with its view of Boston Common while noting its availability for everything from high-end business luncheons to romantic, once-in-a-lifetime dinners. He'd taken great pride in modernizing the centuries-old hotel while retaining its colonial charm.

Stefano leaned in closer, resting his arm against the back of Holly's chair. "I meant it when I said I wanted to do something special for them. Perhaps since Gabe's here and he's the best man, you'd rather arrange something with him—"

"Oh, I'm sure he's doing his own thing."

Stefano tipped his head, acknowledging the comment. "In that case, what would you say to decorating Ben and Chelsea's house with me? The manager mentioned that Ben keeps a spare key here in his desk. Since Ben and Chelsea are staying at the B & B tonight, we could head over the hill and put up a Christmas tree for them without anyone being the wiser."

"They don't have one yet?" She found it hard to believe with Christmas less than a week away.

"Not according to what Ben told the winery manager. He's been too busy getting acclimated to the job and unpacking to look for a tree. I made a call a few hours ago to have one delivered along with several boxes of ornaments and accessories from one of the village shops. It should be on their doorstep now, but I'd appreciate your assistance getting it into the house and decorated."

Holly's hand went to Stefano's sleeve. The man truly was a prince, in every sense of the word. "They'll love that. Ben and Chelsea are both crazy about the holidays."

"So you'll help me?"

"Of course!"

Mischief flashed in Stefano's eyes at the knowledge he had a co-

conspirator. Keeping his voice down and moving his head closer to hers, he said, "Things are wrapping up here. How about you say good night to your brother, then meet me by the fire pit in fifteen minutes? I know a shortcut through the vineyard. I'll bring the house key and flashlights."

"Done."

She reached for her glass to take a last sip of wine only to see Gabe and one of Ben's college friends crossing the room toward Ben and Chelsea. Though Gabe's smile made it appear as though his focus was on the couple, his gaze had drifted to Stefano's arm, which remained on the back of her chair.

Instinct for self-preservation drove her to shift closer to the prince. Winking at Stefano over her wineglass, she whispered, "We are going to have so much fun!"

"You know, I think we are." His mouth curved into a playful smile. "But beautiful as it is, don't wear that."

She glanced down at the form-fitting purple dress she'd bought especially for the rehearsal dinner. "I'll find something more appropriate."

"As will I. See you in fifteen."

LOCATED at the edge of the vineyard along a twisting country road connecting two rural Sarcaccian villages, Ben and Chelsea's ivy-covered stone cottage seemed conjured from a fairy tale. Lit by the glow of wrought iron porch lamps on either side of its aged wooden front door, the place was the epitome of old country romance.

Maneuvering the freshly-cut tree through the home's narrow door proved a challenge that threatened to take the romance out of it.

After several grunts and groans, a cut finger—Stefano's—and a face full of spruce needles—Holly's—they managed to wiggle it into Ben and Chelsea's cozy living room. Securing the fragrant evergreen into the tree stand Stefano situated opposite the fireplace proved a far easier task.

"They're going to be so surprised when they see this," Holly said after stepping back to inspect the tree and brush the needles from her clothing. She'd managed a quick change into jeans and a sweater before meeting Stefano at the fire pit, which turned out to be smart. After traipsing through the vineyard and wrestling the tree, she was filthy.

"Only if we get it decorated and make it back to the winery before anyone realizes you're not at the bed and breakfast."

She glanced over at him. She couldn't help the wryness in her tone as she asked, "You don't think anyone will miss you?"

He shook his head as he bent to withdraw a string of colored lights from a large cardboard box. "My family keeps a private room in the winery itself. People will assume I'm there. On the other hand, I suspect your absence will be noticed, if it hasn't been already."

She grabbed a chair and set it beside the tree to use as a makeshift ladder, then gestured for him to hand her the lights. "Let's be quick. I'll string these if you lay out the ornaments. We'll figure out which are the heaviest so they can go on the lower branches."

"Done this before, have you?"

"Every year. Love it." She hooked one end of the light string at the top of the tree, then stretched to loop the lights in a circle. "You haven't?"

"Never," he admitted as he unwrapped the ornaments one by one and laid them out on Ben and Chelsea's coffee table. All of them appeared handcrafted, which Holly knew Chelsea would adore. "We have several trees in the palace each year, but they're professionally decorated. Showpieces, really. I was allowed to put on a few ornaments when I was a child, but now that I'm an adult, there's no real reason for me to do it."

She grinned. "Perhaps you needed this tree as much as Ben and Chelsea?"

"Perhaps," he answered with a laugh. "The older I get, the more I enjoy time away from the palace doing ordinary things. I've found they're not so ordinary." He studied the ornaments, then looked back at Holly, an odd expression on his face. "May I ask you a personal question?"

Holly paused. While the words themselves surprised her coming from Stefano, who didn't strike her as the type to ask anyone personal questions, it was the sudden softness of his voice that put her on alert. "I suppose."

"You have no romantic interest in me whatsoever. So why the flirting back at the winery?"

Holly's grip tightened on the string of lights. She forced herself to resume hanging them along the wide branches, working her way down the tree bit by bit, in an attempt to hide her shock. "That's a rather blunt question. And it assumes a lot."

"That you have no interest in me, you mean?" His quiet, confident tone unnerved her. "Don't worry. Contrary to what the tabloid press might say, women who have the ability to resist my charms actually do exist. Many women. But I think you're the first to out-and-out flirt with me who harbors no hopes of a relationship. Do you?"

The curiosity in his voice made her turn on the chair. He extended a hand to help her down, given that she'd looped the lights low enough that he could take over from floor level. When her feet hit the hardwood, she looked up at him. "No. I admit, I don't. Though I must say, you're perfectly attractive. And kind."

"Well, thank you." He flashed the dimpled grin that made him world famous. "Yet somehow, I don't believe you were flirting with me to bolster my ego."

That brought a smile to her face. She might not be romantically attracted to him, but she liked the man more and more every minute. "No. You appear to have a perfectly healthy ego without me. Plus, you seem to be under the impression I was flirting rather than simply being nice."

He touched his index finger and thumb to his chin, pretending to ponder a serious issue. "Let's see…winking at me, touching my arm, leaning in closer than necessary…I'd say that constitutes flirting."

"Maybe a little." She hadn't contemplated how she'd address the issue with Stefano. She'd assumed he was used to women far more glamorous and sophisticated flirting with him nonstop and wouldn't think a thing of her behavior during dessert.

She really had winked at him, hadn't she? The thought of what she'd done brought a rush of heat to her cheeks.

"It's for Gabriel, isn't it?"

"No!"

Stefano laughed as he took the light string from her hands, knowing from her knee-jerk reaction that his remark hit the target.

"What makes you think that?" she asked.

"Men know when other men have their sights set on a particular woman." He began to wind the lights around the tree near his eye level, moving lower as he went. "From the minute he walked into the winery, his attention was squarely on you. Even if he pretended it wasn't."

Holly bent over the coffee table to study the ornaments, hoping Stefano couldn't see her embarrassed expression. After selecting two lightweight pieces, a camel and a star carved from olive wood, she stepped onto the chair and hung them on upper branches. She climbed back down as Stefano plugged in the lights, illuminating the tree. She'd always been a fan of the all-white-lights look, considering it classy and clean, but the multicolored strands Stefano had ordered gave the entire room a nostalgic air. It was the perfect tree for a traditional couple's first Christmas as husband and wife.

"It's gorgeous," she breathed. "And we haven't even done the ornaments."

"That it is." A broad grin lit Stefano's face as he handed her another ornament, then grabbed two for himself. "Now, about Gabriel…were you hoping to make him jealous? Because I don't think it's necessary."

She selected a spot for the tiny Santa Claus, then eyed the prince. "You realize I'm feeling self-conscious as it is, sneaking through a vineyard in the middle of the night and decorating a Christmas tree with a prince?"

"You forgot handsome. You should've said, 'decorating a Christmas tree with a handsome prince.'"

"What I said earlier about your healthy ego—"

"Yes, yes." His richly accented voice made her smile as she found a spot for a snowflake crafted of sparkling lace. "So, are you trying to make him jealous?"

"No. The opposite, actually." It hadn't been a conscious thought at the time, but deep down, she'd hoped to dissuade him. "He thinks he's interested in me, but he's not."

She managed to sound lighthearted, but saying the words aloud pained her. For too many years, she'd watched Gabriel Maddox from afar. Through grade school, when he'd innocently held hands with girls at the movie theater or in the school hallways, then in high school, whenever he'd stopped by the Elliotts' house with a pretty girl at his side to pick up Ben for a weekend night out. While Ben dated the same girl throughout much of high school, Gabe seemed to find a different one every few weeks. Always one of the popular girls, or the super-talented girls who could play an instrument or sing, or, in one case, a girl nearly his height who'd broken the school's point record for a single basketball game.

Always girls who had more to interest him than Holly did, the two-years-younger sister of his best friend who loved history books and wanted to travel and see the world, but had no particular attribute that made her stand out from the crowd. Always girls who had their pick of guys and never seemed to expect anything more than a few weeks of entertainment during their time with Gabe.

Stefano and Holly continued taking ornaments from the table and hanging them on the tree, occasionally making adjustments to ensure the look was balanced and none of the pieces dragged down tree branches. Neither of them spoke until Stefano handed Holly the richly dressed angel destined for the top of the tree. "You think flirting with me will deter him, rather than make him jealous?"

"Positive."

He absorbed that for a moment, then said, "Whether you think so or not, Gabriel is deeply attracted to you. In my experience, a man in that situation is more likely to be encouraged than discouraged."

"Not Gabe. He may be attracted—and it's lovely of you to say so— but I'm not his type. And even if I were, it's pointless where he's concerned." If he'd really wanted her, he'd have done something about it long ago. Long before he was scheduled to head to the FBI Academy for a five-month stint, followed by an assignment who-knows-where.

"Because you don't live in the same town? Ben mentioned that Gabe's in New York."

"That's a factor, but it's not that. Not really." A deep, hard knot formed in her throat. She couldn't believe she was about to spill her guts to this man—this *prince*—but the caring way in which he spoke to her made her trust him. "Gabe has said on more than one occasion that he thinks love and romance are for suckers."

"Hasn't every man on the planet?" Stefano offered his hand as she climbed the chair to secure the angel. "Common masculine bluster."

"Not for Gabe. I mean, he knows other people believe in happily ever after, but he doesn't. I can't blame him, either. His father was a first-class jerk. Treated Gabe's mother like dirt, had affairs with other women, then finally left her and the kids."

"Sounds rough." Stefano walked around the chair and put his hands on the back to steady it. "Surely he doesn't think he's like his father?"

"No. It's more about his mother. Right up until her death, she believed her husband would come home. She answered the phone whenever he called, watched his house when he traveled, even paid his bills from time to time over her children's objections." She shrugged as she fluffed the angel's lace skirt, using it to hide the end of the light string. "I know that makes it sound like Gabe had an awful childhood, but he didn't. He and his siblings are all happy and loved their upbringing with their mom. But when it comes to romance, Gabe's understandably jaded. He thinks it caused his mother to waste a lot of her life."

"I see." Skepticism laced his expression, though he kept it from his voice.

"Anyway...if Gabe thinks I've moved on, he will, too," she explained as she hopped down. "I've watched him do it a dozen or more times over the years. But I've never, ever seen him act jealous. It's simply not in his psyche."

"He's a rare individual, then." Stefano located an empty spot near the middle of the tree, then picked up the final ornament, a wooden piece depicting elves in Santa's workshop, and slid it over a branch to fill the space. "In which case…I'm happy to help you."

"What do you mean? Are you…are you offering to flirt with me?" The idea struck her as ludicrous now that she said it aloud. Prince Stefano Barrali, flirting with *her*?

His deep, resonant laugh filled the small room. "Or you could flirt with me. Perhaps you'll find that Gabriel isn't the man you believe him to be."

She'd known Gabe more than twenty years. Watched him through high school, through college vacations, then during his visits home from New York. If he was anything other than what she believed, he was an incredible actor.

"I suppose we'll see," she finally said. "Though it might not even be necessary. He'll likely pay attention to someone else tomorrow. Come on, let's pack up the boxes and put them in the storage shed."

"First this," he said, opening a bag she hadn't noticed.

He withdrew a tree skirt depicting a small village decked out for Christmas, which he handed to Holly, then two knit stockings and weighted hooks. While she arranged the embroidered skirt around the tree, he hung the stockings on either end of the mantel. As he finished, he asked her to grab the last item in the bag. Her fingers wrapped around a solid piece of plastic, which she realized was a light timer.

"For someone who's never decorated a tree, you've certainly thought of everything," she marveled.

"I can't take all the credit. The store owner had a number of suggestions. I deferred to her judgment." He attached it to the plug while she gathered the boxes, readying them for storage. When he finished, he stood and surveyed the room "I think we're all set. Back to the winery?"

"Back to the winery." Emotion clogged her throat as she looked at what they'd done. It was a perfect, romantic Christmas scene. Chelsea and Ben would love it. For a moment, Holly felt a pang of jealousy at the intimate holiday the two would share.

Someday. When Gabe is gone and you've moved on.

She couldn't help but give Stefano a watery smile. "Thank you. This was unbelievably generous of you to do."

"Thank you for your help." As they exited and he locked the door to the house, she picked a few needles off the shoulder of his sweater. "For the record, that's not flirting, that's being nice."

"Good, because I prefer nice to flirting. More rare and more valuable." His smile could've sold a thousand newspapers. "But don't tell anyone I said that."

"I won't," she promised.

"And I won't tell anyone that you're in love with Gabriel."

She nearly dropped the empty ornament box to the walkway. "What?"

"You said Gabe isn't really interested in you. But you never once said that you aren't interested in Gabe." He clicked on the flashlight, then headed toward the storage room. "Come on. With any luck, we'll get back through the vineyard without being seen."

CHAPTER 3

"I NOW PRONOUNCE you man and wife. Benjamin, you may kiss your bride."

Cheers, lighthearted applause, and a few celebratory whistles filled the rustic village church as Ben captured Chelsea's tear-streaked face in his hands, then leaned in to give her a gentle, love-filled kiss. Gabe joined in the cheers as Ben pulled Chelsea into a brief embrace, then took his new wife's hand to lead her down the aisle to the back of the church. The organist, located high in the choir loft behind the guests' seats, began to play, and the rich, elegant sound seemed to swell with every heart in the room.

Even Gabe had to admit that it had been a beautiful ceremony.

As he'd been instructed before the service, Gabe moved to the head of the aisle and offered his arm to Holly. The routine action left him inexplicably unsettled. He'd been unable to tear his eyes from her during the ceremony. The ruby dress Chelsea had chosen for Holly was intended to match the joyful spirit of the season, but left Gabe with far more prurient thoughts. The silk glided over Holly's smooth shoulders as if it were liquid, then dipped below her collarbone to a level low enough to entice without being inappropriate for the setting. Glorious red folds swirled around her narrow waist, ending just above her knees to show off her long, lean legs and a pair of sparkly gold heels.

Most captivating of all, however, was Holly's expression as she watched her brother and Chelsea exchange their vows. The couple had opted to write the words themselves, and their promises left the witnesses blinking back tears at points, and in stitches at others. When Ben promised Chelsea that he'd, "always eat the crunchy corner pieces of the lasagna, and leave you the gooey middle," the wistful smile on Holly's face took Gabe's breath away.

It also made him wonder what—or who—went through her mind as she stood alongside the beaming bride.

Holly had a glow about her from the moment she'd entered the village church, and Gabe couldn't help but question how much of that radiance came from the joy of the day and how much came from her nighttime ramble through the vineyard with Sarcaccia's sophisticated Prince Stefano.

After the rehearsal dinner, he'd missed catching Holly as the group departed the winery, so he'd waited for the bed and breakfast to quiet, then knocked on the door Ben had mentioned was Holly's. There'd been no answer. He'd returned to his room assuming she'd either decided to take a bath or had retired early. Less than an hour later, a beam of light hit his window from the direction of the vineyard, then disappeared. Curious, he'd glanced out to see flashlights bobbing through the rows of vines. The late-night wanderers extinguished the lights as they approached the B & B, but there was enough moonlight for him to recognize their faces as they approached the door.

He couldn't see the main door to know if Stefano kissed her goodnight, but a moment later, the prince took the path back to the winery alone, hands in his pockets.

Gabe sat at his window for several minutes afterward, wondering what Holly could've been doing running through the vineyard in the dark. Tempted as he was to knock on her door, to ask what she was doing and to tell her the real story behind his change in schedule, he didn't want her to know he'd seen her.

Thankfully, neither Prince Stefano nor Holly seemed to be paying attention to one another this morning, a thought Gabe held close through the wedding ceremony. When Holly finally settled her hand on Gabe's forearm, her bright smile was all for him. Moisture clung to her top lashes, evidence of the high emotions she struggled to hold in check.

"I have tissue in my pocket if you need it," he said under his breath as they followed the newlyweds along the rose-petal strewn aisle.

Her fingers tightened fractionally on his arm, but she didn't respond. The vestibule was empty save for Ben and Chelsea, who were sharing a more passionate kiss now that they were out of view of those inside the sanctuary. After turning away to give them a moment of privacy, Gabe pulled a small package from his pocket, withdrew a tissue, then put it to the corner of Holly's tear-filled eyes.

"I'm sorry," she whispered, even as she took the tissue from him so she could blot the tears herself.

"Why? They're deliriously happy. It's natural to be happy for them."

Holly let out a long breath, then looked up at him. The sun streaming through the high windows at the front of the church made her blue eyes appear more luminous than ever. "Are you?"

"What kind of question is that? Of course I am."

Lines etched her forehead, as if she were curious about something, but the question never left her lips. Instead, she looked beyond him to where Chelsea's parents were exiting the service, ready to hug their daughter and welcome Ben to the family. A faint smile hitched the edges of Holly's mouth before she exhaled and blinked back a fresh set of tears.

"Oh, Holly" —Gabe couldn't help but curve his arm around her shoulders as realization dawned— "I'm so sorry. You must miss your parents today."

Mrs. Elliott died in a car accident soon after Holly's birth, leaving Ben with only vague memories of her and Holly with none at all. However, their father, who'd raised them alone despite his own challenges with multiple sclerosis, passed away only three years ago, just after the holidays. Gabe imagined his absence today left a hole in both Ben and Holly's hearts.

"I do." She pressed the tissue under her eyes, then wadded it against the bouquet of red and white flowers she carried. "My dad would've loved visiting Sarcaccia, exploring the little towns and vineyards, soaking in the culture. Seeing Ben married and happy. Meeting Chelsea. It's awful to know he's missing it."

"I'm sure he's watching. Your mother, too. And I bet they're proud and happy for you." He gave her a comforting squeeze, then released her.

She nodded her thanks for the reassurance, inhaled sharply, then met his gaze once more. "Do I look okay?" she asked, her voice steadier now. "Mascara messy or anything like that?"

Unable to resist, he ran the pad of his thumb across the soft skin under one of her eyes, then reached to tuck a fallen piece of chestnut hair back into one of the tiny hairpins adorning the side of her head. He'd never seen her with her hair up. Much as he liked it down and natural, this showed off her neck and afforded him a rare glimpse of her upper jawline and the smooth curve of her ear. A small ruby earring drew his attention to the delicate skin he'd kissed only a few weeks before, as they'd made love in her Boston apartment.

Her eyes remained locked on his face as he fixed her hair. Desire filled their depths, followed by a deliberate attempt to mask it. It occurred to him to ask her why; after what they shared, she shouldn't hide from him. Instead, he told her, "Everything's perfect."

"No mascara problems, then?" The words were breathed more than spoken.

"No." He paused with his hand to the side of her head, his gaze on hers. "You look extraordinary."

"Thank you." Their eyes held for a heartbeat longer, then the guests began pouring out of the sanctuary to congratulate the bride and groom and board the bus that would take them back to the winery for the reception.

"I should see if Chelsea needs anything."

He nodded, then reluctantly withdrew his hand, ending the tender moment. Before he could say, "see you for the photos," Prince Stefano approached. With a confidence befitting his position, the dark-haired man walked with his shoulders squared and his gait relaxed. A crisp, charcoal suit in a faint pinstripe seemed cut specifically for him.

Of course, given the wealth and power behind the Barrali name, it probably was.

Stefano nodded at Gabe, then bestowed a warm smile on Holly. "Lovely ceremony. And you looked wonderful up there."

Holly returned the prince's smile, her composure firmly in place. "Thank you."

The man stood a few inches taller than Gabe. While normally Gabe wouldn't care in the least, in the close confines of the vestibule the fact rankled. Worse, the prince's hand went to Holly's bare arm as he asked, "Are you two heading back to the reception now, or staying here with Ben and Chelsea?"

"The photographer needs us for a few pictures, but we'll be there shortly."

"Don't forget you owe me a dance. I'll look for you." His hand moved a few inches higher on Holly's arm, resting there for a split second longer than necessary before he nodded to Gabe and said, "See you there."

Gabe watched as the prince eased through the crowd to congratulate Ben and Chelsea. When he turned back to tell Holly he'd seen the photographer go outside, she was gone.

CHAMPAGNE BUBBLED across Holly's palate as the guests drank to the new couple. Gabe's toast, the perfect blend of humor and sentiment, was followed with an encouraging grin that made it easier for her to stand and give her own toast. She'd been nervous about it for weeks, but now that it was over, she realized it wasn't as difficult as she'd imagined. All she'd had to do was say what was in her heart. Even the flash from the photographer's camera and the knowledge that Gabe's dark brown eyes were locked on her as she spoke hadn't fazed her. Surprisingly, his attention had bolstered her confidence.

She smiled at Chelsea's parents as her father patted her mother's hand, then kissed her temple. Though Gabe was seated on the other side of Ben and Chelsea, further down the long table in the center of the room, Holly noticed his smile, too, as he watched Chelsea's parents. It almost made her think he could believe in love.

Almost.

Sighing, she looked away and took another sip of her champagne. When he'd stood before her in his tuxedo and wiped the tears from her eyes after the wedding, she'd nearly lost her composure. The overwhelming urge to put her hand over his, to cup his palm to her cheek and turn to kiss his strong fingers, had scared her speechless. She'd escaped as soon as she was able, then kept her distance during the photographs in an attempt to regain her equilibrium.

Did he know what he did to her? Physically, he knew, of course. That had been painfully obvious when they were in Boston. However, she suspected he had that effect on every woman he'd ever dated. His perfectly sculpted shoulders and chest, the intelligent—yet mischievous—sparkle that lit his dark brown eyes, and the absolute confidence he had when he kissed a woman ensured that.

But did he realize the emotional pull he had over her?

If so, why was he being so...so...*attentive*? He had to know the appreciative way he eyed her during the ceremony and the tenderness he showed her afterward, particularly when he realized she ached for her father's absence, would only serve to pull her deeper into his thrall.

Beside her, Chelsea and Ben beamed through dinner, alternately laughing with each other and with others who approached the table. Thankfully, the banter kept Holly distracted from thoughts of Gabe. When Ben and Gabe began chatting with a friend from high school who approached their table, Chelsea took the opportunity to lean closer to Holly.

"So far, so good," Chelsea whispered. "No mistakes at the ceremony, the food all turned out perfectly, and the decorations are even prettier than I'd hoped."

"I thought the winery was beautiful before, but this" —Holly swept her hand toward the centerpiece— "is stunning. It's like a Christmas fairy tale."

Chelsea leaned forward to run her polished fingertips over the fragrant greenery lining the center of the table. Interspersed with soft white lights and bright red Christmas ornaments displaying the occasional flecks of gold, the elegant decoration made the winery both festive and romantic.

"You're right. The booze isn't bad, either."

"Chelsea!"

"Oh, come on. I'm having fun. And I'm giddy in love and I want everyone else to feel the same way." She polished off her champagne, then nodded as the bandleader glanced at Chelsea from the adjacent room, which had been set up for music and dancing.

"Time for your first dance?" Holly asked.

"If I can convince Ben to stop jabbering," she said, though the complaint was a teasing one, and spoken in Ben's direction more than in Holly's.

Ben's reached to cover Chelsea's hand with his own even as he finished his conversation. At the bandleader's invitation, guests began making their way to the winery's large back room. Music filled the air. As Chelsea swirled across the floor in Ben's arms and guests oohed and aahed once more over the loveliness of the couple and the exquisite cut of Chelsea's gown, Gabe materialized at Holly's side.

"Nice toast," he said, raising his champagne glass, which, like hers, had just been refilled.

"Same to you," she replied, carefully clinking her glass against his. "You made Chelsea tear up and laugh at the same time."

"As long as her mascara looks good for the photographs, it's all good, right?"

"Right."

They watched in silence as Ben briefly dipped Chelsea, then brushed his lips against her temple as the music reached a crescendo.

A barrage of sensation hit Holly at once: the swell of the music, the romantic sparkle of the wrought iron chandeliers overhead, the awareness of Gabe's large, protective body beside hers. The scent of the B & B's olive soap blending with the heat of Gabe's skin if she allowed herself to inhale deeply.

As the couple twirled toward the opposite side of the dance floor, Gabe said, "We're up next, you know."

She glanced sideways at him. "What do you mean?"

He set his champagne glass on a nearby cocktail table, dropped his iron room key beside it, then looked down at her. "I mean that when Ben and Chelsea are done with their song, the bandleader will invite everyone to join them for the next one. As best man and maid of honor, we're supposed to set the example."

"Oh, of course." How had she forgotten that?

Cheers cascaded through the room as the band held the last note of Ben and Chelsea's song. As Gabe predicted, the bandleader urged the guests to join the bride and groom. Gabe took Holly's glass and small handbag, set them on the cocktail table beside his glass, then extended his hand before Holly, palm up. "Care to dance?"

"Do I have a choice?" She kept a light note in her voice, though her heart beat double time. Having Gabe's arms around her, spinning around a dance floor to the slow, dreamy number, would be both heaven on earth and the ultimate torture.

"You always have a choice with me." His voice was serious, making her look up at him in surprise. "But in this instance, it may be a social faux pas to say no."

She placed her hand in his, and he swung her onto the floor in one smooth motion, as if he'd danced with her a hundred times before. His arm came around the back of her waist and his fingers spread to warm her through her silk dress. She smiled, hoping she looked polite and calm, and placed her hand on his shoulder, only to discover the firm muscle hidden beneath the soft fabric of his tuxedo jacket.

"We're rather good at this." His voice was soft enough only she could hear. His hand tightened at her lower back, pulling her closer as he added, "Though I'm not surprised."

Holly couldn't respond. Her left hand felt too good cradled in Gabe's, the solidity of his shoulder too enticing underneath her right. It was all she could do to keep her fingers from sliding further, exploring the nape of his neck, pulling him closer.

"But I wouldn't describe it as comfortable."

Her head jerked up as he emphasized the last word. "What?"

"On the patio last night." His eyes locked with hers, leaving her unable to divert hers. "You said, 'I was more than happy to be that comfort for you,' as if what happened between us was a favor."

"Gabe." She knew the look on her face was pleading, but she couldn't have this conversation here, even if their voices were low and the people around them were focused on their own dance partners, the music, and the celebration. "That wasn't what I meant."

"Good." His fingers flexed against her lower back. "Because when I took you home after dinner that night, I had no intention of going to your place for comfort. I went for you. And I would *not* call what happened between us comfortable."

"It was uncomfortable?" The wrong thing to say, but it popped out of her mouth before she could consider it.

"No." His mouth moved closer to her ear. "I'd call it mind-blowing. Blissful. Erotic. And maybe even—"

"Gabriel, stop."

She closed her eyes against the mental imagery the word *erotic* brought to mind when coming from his lips, especially when he held her now, so very close. When he'd come to her apartment that night, they'd shared a bottle of Chianti they'd purchased at one of the family-owned shops in Boston's vibrant Italian North End neighborhood. They'd laughed over stories of their childhood. Reminisced about how wonderful Gabe's mother had been and how sad it was to see her house go, but how fortunate it was that a family with small children purchased it.

As the bottle neared the halfway point, they talked about where their futures were headed. Gabe described the FBI Academy and the training program he'd experience. For twenty-one weeks, he'd be completely off the grid, immersed in challenging classroom and physical training at Quantico. Holly'd kept quiet about her job offer in Rome, because when the time came to raise the topic, Gabe was sitting close to her at her kitchen table, as close as they were now. And she'd sensed that he wanted to kiss her.

When he did, it'd blown her world apart.

After years of lusting after him, wondering what it'd be like to have his lips on hers for even a moment, to feel what it'd be like to be on the receiving end of his passion, she'd been unable to resist. He'd cupped her chin in his hand, giving her the chance to withdraw, but she'd stilled. Waited. Slowly, with his gaze meeting hers, he'd leaned in and given her a deliberate, gentle kiss. He pulled back fractionally, gauging her reaction. She didn't move. A ragged breath escaped him, his eyes drifted shut, and she was gone. Their kisses quickly turned passionate, the heat of his touch searing her deep to her soul. She'd been the first to move beyond kisses, pulling his T-shirt from his jeans so she could run her hands along his back, up his spine, exploring the hard muscles that seemed to go forever.

When she pushed his shirt higher and kissed his chest even as he yanked the offending fabric over his head, the sound that escaped him was positively primal.

They never finished the wine.

She told herself not to worry about a broken heart. That if she could only have one night with the man of her dreams before he disappeared, to take it with no regrets.

"Maybe even overdue." The wash of Gabe's breath against her cheek as he breathed the emotion-packed word jerked her back to the present. "Holly, no one makes love like that for comfort. They make love like that—"

"We're at my brother's wedding."

"—because they share strong feelings for each other. And likely have for some time. I'd have said all that to you on the patio last night if Ben hadn't interrupted us. Hell, I'd have said it in Boston if you hadn't popped out of bed in the morning announcing that you hoped I had a wonderful future with the FBI and that you were heading to Rome."

His words made her sound so callous. But what else did he expect? He wasn't one for relationships, let alone the type to start one before he went incommunicado for more than five months. She'd thought she was giving him exactly the relaxed, no-pressure evening he'd wanted, and at the same time giving herself the once-in-a-lifetime experience she'd always craved.

The band segued to another song, but Gabe held her fast, guiding her toward the center of the dance floor, where she'd have no opportunity to politely excuse herself.

"Well, I did say I enjoyed it." At Gabe's hard look, she continued, "Isn't it possible that you wanted me that night because I reminded you of home? We had a fabulous life growing up in Boston. With the hard hours you worked in New York, don't you think you came to me because you wanted a night with no tension, no stress, to just be yourself? Maybe have one last fling to say goodbye to a life that doesn't exist anymore with Ben in Sarcaccia, your mom gone, and your next job sending you off to who-knows-where?"

"No." The single word was quick and decisive.

"There's nothing wrong with that, you know."

"Don't insult me, Holly." An angry muscle twitched beside his mouth. "I knew exactly what I was doing. And why."

At that moment, Ben caught her eye from where he and Chelsea danced behind Gabe. A quizzical look flashed across his face. While she was certain Ben couldn't hear their conversation, he'd obviously discerned something awry from their body language.

Gabe chose that moment to tighten his hold around her waist and pull her closer, forcing her to meet his gaze. "And I know exactly what you're doing with Prince Stefano."

He couldn't have stunned her more if he'd hauled off and smacked her. "What?"

"Flirting. It's the why I can't figure out. Is it because you want him? Because you're curious about what a man with power, charisma, and piles of money might be like? Or is it because you want to make me jealous?" He shrugged, not expecting an answer. "It doesn't matter. Flirt all you want. At the end of the day, you're mine."

"Excuse me?" Now it was her turn to be furious. How dare he?

He stopped dancing, holding her in place. Despite the worry building in her that Ben would notice and say something, she couldn't tear her attention from Gabe's face as he spoke. "I think you've been attracted to me for a long time." The words were smooth and sure, as if he were stating a fact as plain as the color of the Christmas decorations. "I think you may even love me, but you won't admit it to yourself because you're scared."

Tension made her breathing labored, but she fought to keep her tone civil. "You can think whatever you like. Fact of the matter is, I'm in Rome now. You're going to Quantico. So none of it matters. In the meantime, I'd like to enjoy myself at my brother's wedding."

"I imagine you *are* enjoying yourself. But you damned well start better being honest with yourself, or we'll both regret it."

"Pardon me," a distinctive, rich voice with a Sarcaccian accent came from nearby. "May I cut in? I believe I'm owed a dance with the maid of honor."

The knowing look that flashed across Gabe's face before he turned away from her was sheer wickedness. Nodding to Prince Stefano, he said, "Of course, Your Highness. Grab her while you can," then disappeared into the crowd, leaving her momentarily speechless.

Stefano took Holly's hand in his and guided her along the floor, keeping a healthier distance between them than Gabe had. Holly immediately noticed the difference between the two men; where Gabe was intense, Stefano was light. He smiled down at her in an attempt to put her at ease. "You had a rather murderous expression on your face. Thought that might be my cue."

"I hope it wasn't that bad," she replied before adding, "but thank you for paying attention." So maybe Prince Stefano wasn't her type. But he was perceptive and kind, and unbelievably easy on the eyes. She could see why both his countrymen and the European tabloids loved him.

"I sense that your plan isn't working. Gabe seems a rather…confident type."

Confident was a nice word for it. Arrogant would be more accurate. But unwilling to either disparage Gabe or admit that flirting with the prince might've backfired, she said, "His life is in flux right now. Between starting a new job and seeing his best friend get married, he's making a big transition."

"Probably." He waited a few beats before adding, "But as a disinterested bystander, I think you're misreading him. His attraction to you runs deeper than you think."

He spun her past Chelsea's parents, who were laughing as they danced near their daughter. "I don't think you're disinterested. I think you're finding this all highly entertaining."

A dark eyebrow arched in amusement. "Of course I am. So let me rephrase and say that I'm an *unbiased* bystander. And my unbiased opinion, having known you both for roughly a day, is that your plan isn't working. Gabe doesn't seem jealous, but he doesn't seem dissuaded, either."

"Your Highness?"

"Stefano," he corrected.

She anchored her hand more firmly against his shoulder. "It's not often I get to dance with a prince, particularly one so light on his feet. I'd like to savor the moment."

"Ah," he said. "Using flattery to distract. Good tactic. I'll allow it."

Stefano took advantage of the airy tune, spinning her around the dance floor with humor. She had to admit, the handsome royal had a way of distracting her from Gabe. Though when she glanced Gabe sitting at a table near the edge of the floor with a young girl standing in front of him, a goofy grin on her face as she spoke to him, another wave of yearning coursed through her.

No. Don't watch Gabe with children.

The song wound down and the bandleader announced that the next song would be for Chelsea and her father. Stefano surprised Holly by slowing to give her a gentle kiss on the cheek. "Thank you for a lovely dance."

"You know you don't need to flirt with me," she said.

"That was heartfelt." Her cheeks heated at the compliment even as he tucked her hand in the crook of his elbow and escorted her off the dance floor. They paused beside the cocktail table where she and Gabe had been standing as the dancing began. A moment later, he surprised her by asking, "If you're not required here for the next few minutes, could you help me with something?"

"I suppose." Ben asked her to dance with him a few songs after Chelsea and her dad shared their dance, but Holly suspected that'd be a half-hour or more away.

"Run to the B & B with me? I left a gift there for Ben and Chelsea and I could use your help with it."

She didn't bother hiding her skepticism. His voice held an odd note that pinged her internal lie detector. "I thought you were staying in a room here at the winery?"

"I am, but it's something I want to move to their room in the B & B, so I hid it there this morning."

"In addition to decorating their house?" She withdrew her hand from his elbow and turned to face him. "Plus, from what Ben told me, you've also given them free use of the winery this weekend. I know there must've been dozens of requests to book this place over the holidays."

A wry laugh burst from him. "What can I say? I'm having fun. It's not often a winery employee gets married."

She glanced at Ben, but he was surrounded by well-wishers as Chelsea and her father began their dance. "All right. As long as we're quick, I'm happy to help."

If nothing else, it would keep her out of Gabe's eyesight for a while. And him from hers.

CHAPTER 4

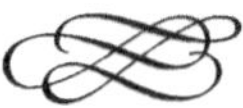

"Mr. Maddox, why aren't you dancing? You look sad."

Gabe tore his attention from Holly—and the blush tingeing her cheeks as she danced with the prince—to see the flower girl standing in front of him. About seven years old, her chestnut-brown hair had been curled at the ends and adorned with a red ribbon for the wedding. Her red dress was the same garnet shade as Holly's, but in a demure, short-sleeved cut appropriate for her age.

"Hi, Abby. I'm taking a break. Why aren't *you* dancing?"

"It's all slow stuff." She plopped into the seat beside him and looked out at the dance floor. "Aunt Chelsea promised that there would be some fun music later, though. Like, after the cake."

"Hopefully the cake will be soon, then."

"I hope so, too. Have you seen it?" She turned to Gabe, her eyes wide with excitement. "It's on a cart in the kitchen because it's too big to carry. It's hee-yuge!"

Her childlike fascination elicited a grin from him. "I'm not surprised. Wedding cakes usually are."

"You think it'll taste good?" Her feet swung as she talked. "My mom says that wedding cake doesn't always taste good, so I shouldn't make faces if it's not like a birthday cake. She says that sometimes it has filling inside that kids don't like. Do you think Aunt Chelsea got filling?"

"No idea." He shifted in the seat to look Abby in the eye. How wonderful was life to have cake as your biggest concern? "But I'll tell you what. If you don't like the cake, your Uncle Ben might be able to score a different dessert for you. He knows everyone in the kitchen. I bet there's gelato hiding back there. There might—*might*—even be some leftover chocolate soufflé from last night."

"Cool! That soufflé was awesome." Her demeanor quickly went from overjoyed to serious, as if remembering that she'd been warned to be polite. "But it's okay if he can't. I mean, I'm sure the cake is going to be really good, even if it has filling."

The song ended as the bandleader announced that the next dance would be for the bride and her father. Abby craned her neck to see around the crowd leaving the dance floor, looking for her aunt.

"Ooh," she said once she spied Chelsea. "Isn't her dress pretty? She looks like a fairy princess."

"She sure does." Though he gave Chelsea an admiring look for Abby's benefit, his attention was drawn by the flash of Holly's red dress as she wove through the dancers, moving with Stefano to the opposite side of the floor. They paused beside the cocktail table where Gabe had left his champagne glass and Holly's prior to dancing, then Stefano kissed Holly on the cheek.

"Do you think when I get married, Aunt Chelsea would let me wear her dress?"

"She might. Though I suspect you'll want one that's made just for you," he replied, keeping Holly in his peripheral vision. Judging from the expression on the prince's face, he and Holly seemed to be having a serious conversation, though Holly's expression was one of skepticism.

Good for you Holly.

The prince was a decent guy, Gabe would grant him that. But that didn't mean Gabe wanted Holly with him tonight. Or any night. He'd meant it when he told Holly she'd be his. He'd come this far; he wanted her for a lifetime or nothing, and he refused to accept the latter.

Holly smiled up at Stefano, then followed him out the side door that opened to the path leading to the bed and breakfast. The closing of the door felt like a punch to his gut. Instinct made him want to follow them, but common sense kept him in his chair.

"Is your real name Gabriel?"

What could Holly and Stefano be doing? "It sure is. Just like I bet yours is Abigail."

"Abigail is stupid. But I like Gabriel."

He pursed his lips, pretending to consider the matter as if it were of utmost importance. "I would argue that Abigail is an intelligent name. Did you know that the second president of the United States was married to a very smart woman named Abigail? She was from Massachusetts, just like you are."

"Really?"

"Really." He grinned as Abby scooted closer to him, wanting to know more. "She lived in an era when few girls went to school, but she could read and write and loved learning from any book she could find. And when her husband, John Adams, was sent to Paris to work, she went along. So she was able to visit Europe and see a whole new culture."

"Like I am, for Aunt Chelsea's wedding?"

"Just like you are." He shrugged. "I think when you get older, you might start to like being named Abigail. It suits you. Though Abby is nice, too."

She continued to swing her feet as she mulled over Gabe's words. "Well, did *you* know that Gabriel is the name of an angel? Like the one on the mantel in the next room?"

"I did," he replied. "See, I knew you were smart."

"It's a good name for Christmas," she said. "Oh, and did you also know that my Uncle Ben's sister is named Holly? That's a Christmas name, too."

Abby's proclamation brought Holly to the forefront of his mind once more. "I've never considered that, but you're right."

"Do you think that's why you got to be in the wedding? Because you both have Christmas names?"

"I don't think that was it. But you're pretty sharp to think of the coincidence."

Guests cheered as the song came to a close and Chelsea hugged her father. Abby and Gabe clapped with everyone else, then Abby leapt off the chair and pointed toward the back of the room, where the kitchen door swung open. "They're bringing out the cake!"

"Looks like it'll be tasty," Gabe assured her as the crowd parted to allow the waiters to bring the cake to the center of the dance floor. "Once Chelsea and Ben cut the first slice, the waitstaff will put pieces out on the tables. You'll have to tell me what you think."

"Okay!" She waved at him and said she'd find him later, then sidled through the grownups so she'd have a better view of the cake-cutting ceremony.

Gabe stood behind a group of women who'd staked out spots alongside the dance floor to watch Ben and Chelsea. Though the newlyweds teased each other, acting as if they planned to smash the cake in each other's faces, the first bites they offered each other were as easy as if they were alone in the room. Ben's pleasure as he popped a small bite of the white cake into Chelsea's mouth was evident to all.

Watching his friend now, Gabe wondered if a groom had ever been as happy. The couple looked at each other as if all was right in the world, as if they knew their place was at each other's side.

He scanned the area around the dance floor, but there was no sign of Holly. Nor did he see the prince. As the waitstaff wheeled the cake back to the kitchen to be sliced, he fought the urge to walk toward the B & B to see where they were.

It wasn't his business. She was a grown woman. She had the right to choose.

But he'd meant it when he'd told her she was his. With every fiber of his being, he knew she loved him. No woman ever looked at him the way Holly did. The way she'd looked at him for *years*.

Only he'd been too stupid to take the chance on a relationship. Too concerned about what Ben would think to ask her on a date. Too concerned about his ability to truly love anyone and have it work, given the idiocy he'd watched take place in his own house.

He exhaled and shoved his hands in his pockets.

When he'd kissed Holly that night in Boston, he knew. First there'd been a faint, testing meeting of their lips. When he'd eased back to make sure he hadn't taken advantage, he'd seen everything in her eyes. She wanted him. Hell, she *loved* him. And he'd been lost. Never in his life had kissing a woman gratified him so deeply as the next meeting of their mouths. He'd cupped her face in his hands, reveling in the soft moan that escaped her as she opened to him, tilting her head to allow him better access. He'd plundered her mouth, allowing himself to delight in the sensation of her tongue flicking to meet his as she snaked her arms around his neck, before he moved to savor the soft skin of her neck, the curve of her jawline, the tendrils of hair at her nape...then slowly unbutton her blouse to slide his hands along her passion-warmed skin.

When she'd risen from the dinner table, taking his hand in hers and silently leading him to her bedroom, he'd hardly been able to breathe, desire burned so powerfully within him.

The night they'd spent in her apartment, wrapped in her sheets, wrapped in each other, convinced him he'd made the right choice. Finally, he'd discovered a woman he wanted to be with and who wanted him. A relationship that could go the distance. A relationship about more than sex, more than companionship. With Holly, he knew he could have everything he never thought possible—a partner, a friend, a lover. A woman whose curiosity about the world, about history, and about culture fired his own imagination.

Best of all, he could trust her.

As he'd drifted off to sleep with Holly lying partially on top of him, trailing sweet kisses over his chest while he ran his hand along the small of her back, then the smooth curve of her rear, he'd smiled in bliss and told her what was in his heart.

"Holly Michelle Elliott?"

"Hmmm?" she'd murmured against his chest, the sound like a balm to his soul.

"I have fallen hard for you."

"Sleep," she'd whispered. And he had, deeply and comfortably.

In the morning, as he'd sprawled in her bed and weighed whether to take a shower, make her breakfast, or indulge in another round of lovemaking, she'd casually announced that she'd accepted a job in Rome and had to hurry to make her appointment at the passport office. Rolling over, he'd caught her around the waist, certain she was kidding.

It quickly became apparent that she was dead serious.

Shock left him unable to respond as she'd eased from the bed and fished through her dresser drawers for clothing. He'd finally, *finally* risked his heart for a woman—kissing her knowing that she expected more from him than the casual relationship he'd had with every other woman in his life, and knowing that failing this woman meant failing his best friend—and she'd already made plans to move on without him. She'd viewed him in the same way he'd viewed every woman he'd ever dated: as a temporary affair.

Though he'd never slept with a woman *before* making his position on their relationship clear, the irony of it hurt.

It'd taken him the last few weeks to decide what to do about it.

Abby went skimming across the dance floor in her stocking feet as the band transitioned to an upbeat pop tune. Fists pumping over her head, she was soon joined by Chelsea and her grandparents. Her exuberance brought a grin to Gabe's face and steeled his spine with fresh resolve.

Deep down, Holly still wanted him. They could have everything Ben and Chelsea had and more. He only needed to convince her she could trust him, just as he'd been ready to trust her.

Assuming she wasn't running off with a royal in the meantime.

Unable to help himself, he glanced at his watch. He turned from the dance floor and crossed the room in long strides. So what if he followed her? He'd already sacrificed everything to be here; he could sacrifice his dignity for a future with Holly. The payoff would be worth it. As he neared the exit, he picked up his pace, suddenly anxious to find her.

"In a hurry?"

Gabe stilled at the sound of Ben's voice coming from behind him. Though the words sounded casual to most who might've heard them, Ben picked up the edge underlying the question. Schooling his features to project a relaxed air, he turned to his friend. "Not really. So how's the groom?"

"The groom is fine. But I haven't seen you move that fast since we were seventeen and you thought your mom was about to catch you sneaking back into the house at two a.m."

"Very funny." Gabe waved off Ben. "I was just heading to the restroom."

"The wrong direction."

Ben's stern countenance brooked no argument. Conceding defeat, Gabe exhaled and closed the gap between them. "What do you want to know?"

"You're following my sister." Ben's voice was quiet enough to keep others from overhearing. "I can assure you, based on what I've learned here at the winery, he's not the guy the media portrays. She's perfectly safe with him."

So Ben noticed she'd left with him, too. "I'm sure she is. I haven't spoken with him at length, but the prince seems like a—"

"Or are you worried that she'll run off with him instead of you?"

The question caught Gabe so off guard he couldn't hide his surprise, not from his best friend. But judging from Ben's astonished expression, the question had been a shot in the dark.

"You're kidding me," Ben whispered. "You? Holly's not your type."

"What's my type, Ben?"

Ben's jaw worked as he considered the question. He glanced toward Chelsea, ensuring she was occupied, then looked back to Gabe. "You and I both know that we're wired differently. And Holly's wired like I am. For the long haul."

"What if I told you I don't have a problem with that?"

Ben's eyes narrowed in skepticism, then, as he studied Gabe's face, they widened in shock. "You're serious."

"Very."

"But you're scheduled to go—"

"Schedules change."

Ben stared at him for a moment, then closed his eyes and massaged the bridge of his nose as he absorbed the meaning of Gabe's statement. "Oh, man…Gabe, this is out of left field. I don't know what to say."

"Say it's all right."

Gabe waited. When Ben opened his eyes, their depths revealed a mixture of disbelief and concern. He inhaled, as if drawing strength from the air. "All right. Go."

The words to erase his friend's worry didn't exist. Instead, Gabe settled for a woefully inadequate, "Thank you."

Silently, Ben nodded and clapped Gabe on the back, then spun on his heel to go in search of his bride.

In time, Gabe hoped he'd put Ben's fears to rest. If he didn't…well, he'd have bigger issues to face. After sidestepping a waiter distributing slices of wedding cake, Gabe slipped out the side door and into the darkness.

He forced a confident, casual air to his walk, going on the assumption that anyone in the B & B would be able to see him approach if they passed by a window. Much as he wanted to fly down the hill, to interrupt whatever Holly might be doing with Prince Stefano at the B & B, Gabe knew his future could ride on Holly's perception of him. Despite the hour, only the two exterior lights and one small lamp in the entry hall were illuminated. A deep sense of foreboding pulled at Gabe's chest; if Holly and Stefano had gone to her room, they'd chosen to remain in the dark.

"This doesn't feel right." Holly's voice floated through the darkness from upstairs, near the rear of the building. From the direction of *his* room, rather than her own.

A male voice, rich and deep, answered. Given the timbre, it had to be Stefano, but Gabe couldn't make out the words. Only that Stefano was attempting to reassure Holly.

Gabe eased along the wall, making his way past the empty break-fast room before climbing the stairs, bypassing the second floor, and making his way to the uppermost floor. Rounding the corner, he saw one heavy oak door closed—the room opposite his—and one cracked open. His. A key protruded from the ancient lock. Frowning, he patted his pocket, then remembered he'd taken it out and left it near his plate on the table, not wanting the heavy key to damage his tuxedo.

"You're sure about this?" Holly's voice sounded muffled, as if she were standing behind the curtains. Or speaking from under the sheets.

"Positive." Stefano's voice was clearer this time.

Gabe put his hand against the cold stone wall. They couldn't be doing what he imagined. Not in his room.

"Ben and Chelsea will wonder where we are." This time, there was no mistaking the *phloof* of a comforter being lifted, then dropped. Nor could he mistake Holly's breathlessness and sense of urgency. "We have to get back."

"They're quite occupied. Besides, I doubt they'll object if we—"

"Wait…is that a suitcase over there?" Holly sounded genuinely surprised. "Whose suitcase would be here? And there are clothes on that chair."

Gabe steeled himself against what might be on the other side of the door and pushed his way through.

"THE SUITCASE on the luggage stand would be mine. As would the clothing on the chair."

If a voice could be encased in ice, surely there was a thick layer around Gabe's as it reverberated against the room's stone walls. He stared down at Holly, taking in the sight of her kneeling beside the bed, clutching the bottom of her red dress in an effort to maintain modesty even as shock sent her scrabbling to her feet.

"This is your room?" Even as she asked the question, she noted the hard set of Gabe's mouth, the angry flush of his skin, and the cold suspicion in his eyes, and knew it to be true.

"Yes. And that's my key in the door."

The heat of embarrassment flashed through her. She spun to face Stefano, who'd been rummaging in the room's oversized armoire, to see him close the doors and calmly turn to face Gabe.

"Mind telling me why you're here?" Gabe directed the question at her.

"We were looking for a gift for Ben and Chelsea. Stefano seems to remember" —she glared at the prince for confirmation— "hiding one in here."

"What, using the key he swiped from where I'd left it with my champagne?" Gabe's head whipped toward the prince. "I don't think so."

"My apologies, Gabriel." Stefano shrugged as if he weren't the least bit sorry, nor the least bit concerned about Gabe's wrath. "I'm obviously not in the proper room."

Before Holly could respond, Stefano slipped past Gabe and closed the door. Gabe lunged for the knob, only to be stopped by the heavy sound of the key being turned and the bolt sliding home.

"What the—" Gabe ground out a four-letter word as he tried the door to no avail. He eyed the lock for a lever that might open the door from the inside, then crouched to peek through the keyhole. Fists formed at his side as he stood, then pounded on the ancient oak hard enough to set Holly back a step. "Your Highness, with all due respect, open the damned door. *Now*."

"Seems these locks do work from the outside. Good to know." Stefano didn't sound remotely bothered by Gabe's threatening tone. "Expect me back in an hour. I'll cover for you at the reception if you're missed."

"What? You're...you're locking us in here?" Dread filled Holly's stomach as understanding took hold. He'd done this on purpose. Dragged her from the room across the hall into this one, then dawdled until Gabe appeared. "There wasn't a gift, was there? Stefano!"

"Consider this my gift to you," came the answer.

"He can't really be doing this," Gabe muttered, though the

pounding of Stefano's feet against the stairs indicated otherwise. "He stole my key. The damned prince stole…my…key!"

Shocked, Holly raced to the window. It took a moment for her to figure out how to twist the lock and release the lever so she could stick her head outside, but once she did, her only reward was a view of Stefano's back as he took the path uphill in rapid strides.

"He really left us here. He's halfway back already." What in the world possessed him?

His belief that you love Gabe, you idiot.

She squeezed her eyes shut for a moment, then closed the window against the cold before turning to flop in the chair. There wasn't a doubt in her mind Stefano would wait the full hour to return.

It might be high treason to threaten the life of a royal, but at the moment, she didn't care. She could kill him.

"You care to explain what the hell is going on?"

Holly started at the fury radiating from Gabe. Over the years, she'd seen nearly every emotion possible from the man: jubilation when he'd caught a game-winning touchdown pass in a high school football game, devastation when his mother passed away, quiet determination when he and Ben stayed up all night cramming for finals. Satisfaction and pride when he'd passed the bar exam, landed his job in New York, or talked about gaining entrance to the FBI Academy. But never once had she seen such anger, let alone laser-focused in her direction.

The intensity of it rattled her.

She curled her fingers around the plush arms of the chair and raised her chin, sensing that—since she'd done nothing wrong—the best defense was a good offense. "I could ask you the same question. What were you thinking, following me here from the reception? What if I were having a wild affair with the guy? Don't you think that would've been awkward?"

"You forget that *I know you*." Gabe advanced until he towered over her. "I know you well enough to know His Royal Highness Prince Fancypants isn't your type. You're apple pie, not cherries flambé."

"Oh, and you're saying you're apple pie?" Farcical, considering the man wore a tuxedo that made him look like he'd stepped straight from the pages of *GQ*. No one stopped and stared at apple pie the way women stared at Gabriel Maddox in a tux.

Large hands planted on either side of her, forcing her back against the clothes he'd left draped over the chair. "What the hell were you doing in my room with him, Holly? And why the hell were you in the vineyard with the guy last night? What are you trying to do to me?"

"Do to you?" The crinkle of dried leaves against her skin distracted her. Reaching over her shoulder, she pulled on the sweater behind her. Sure enough, she'd crushed a leaf clinging the knit. Holding the pieces in the space between them, she turned his anger right back at him. "You followed me last night, too? Are you kidding me?"

"I did not."

"This is from the vineyard!"

"I saw you and Prince Fancypants coming back from right there" —he nodded toward the window behind her— "after your flashlights shone into my room. That leaf must be from this morning, which is when I wore that sweater."

"You were in the vineyard this morning." She didn't bother hiding her disbelief. "Chelsea told everyone at breakfast that you'd walked to the village."

"I did, not that it's any of your business. I got there just when the stores opened and bought a Christmas wreath. When I returned, I asked the chef how to get to Ben and Chelsea's house so I could put it on their front door. He directed me through the vineyard."

She wanted to argue. Wanted to doubt him. But the thin line of his lips and set of his jaw told her it was the truth.

"So tell me, Holly, what's going on with you and Prince Stefano?"

"Nothing. Not that it's any of your business—"

"Holly." Temper flared from under his thick, burnished lashes.

Fine. Better to explain than to continue a pointless argument. "We came here because he told me he needed help retrieving a wedding gift he'd hidden in the B & B and that he planned to move it into their room." She licked her lips before adding, "I should have figured out that he was full of it, but I didn't. As for why we were in the vineyard…would you believe we were decorating Ben and Chelsea's house?"

"No." The response was automatic, but a split second later, as he studied her face, he pulled back from the chair and shocked her yet again with a roaring, self-deprecating bark of a laugh. "You're serious, aren't you?"

"Yes."

He swiped both his hands over his face, then rested them atop his freshly-cropped hair. The motion obliterated all signs of the fury that dominated his physical carriage only a moment before. "Ben mentioned that he and Chelsea hadn't had time to decorate between the wedding planning and the new job. That's what made me think of the wreath. But there was a tree inside, right by the front window—"

"Prince Stefano's idea. Ben apparently keeps a spare house key in his office desk. Stefano had everything delivered last night, then asked me during the rehearsal dinner if I'd help him decorate."

Gabe squinted, considering. "Could Stefano have done it on his own?"

"He must've thought so, since he'd already ordered everything." She shrugged. "Getting the tree through the door might've been a challenge, but I'm sure any of the winery staff would've helped him if I hadn't."

"And did he ask you about me while you were there?" Gabe didn't wait for a response, knowing from her hesitation that Stefano had, indeed, raised the topic. "He's no idiot."

"No, but—"

"He knew when he took you there how we feel about each other. Not sure how he figured it out when even you won't acknowledge it, but he did. And for whatever reason, he's made it his mission to get us to deal with it."

"For the last time, Gabe, there's nothing to *deal* with," she protested.

"Then answer this. Did what happened between us in Boston mean anything to you? If you can honestly say that it didn't, I'll drop it."

CHAPTER 5

SHE CLOSED HER EYES, unwilling to let him see the emotion his softly spoken question unleashed within her, and let out a slow breath. She couldn't lie. "Of course it did."

"Then?"

Then what? She forced herself to meet his gaze, knowing he'd never accept what she had to say if she didn't. "You and I both know that a night in the sack doesn't mean everything."

"It depends on the circumstance. In my case, and in that circumstance, it did mean everything." He sank to the bed, propped his elbows on his knees, and loosened his bow tie. A classically masculine action, yet there was a vulnerability in it she'd never before witnessed in Gabe. "Actually, let me correct that...*you* mean everything. And I said as much when we were in your apartment that night."

"No." How many times had she replayed the night in her head, wanting to hold on to the memory of Gabe's hands caressing her spine, of his warm mouth trailing across her collarbone, of the sweetly intense pressure as he'd moved to her neck and lightly nipped and sucked the delicate spot at the base of her throat?

Surely she'd remember if love or romance were mentioned, because she damned sure remembered everything else.

"We'd nearly drifted off. I told you that I'd fallen for you."

She couldn't stop the gasp that escaped her lips as the moment crystallized in her mind. Gabe's long, languid body kicked back in her bed, the sheets askew. His hands folded behind his head as she sprawled alongside him, utterly spent. She'd been half draped over his torso with her cheek resting on his chest, running her fingers over the light dusting of hair that covered the expanse of muscle there. Every so often, she'd pressed a kiss to his heated skin as she reveled in the afterglow of their lovemaking, savoring the knowledge that he'd been everything she'd fantasized and more.

When the words came from his lips, his eyes were closed and a deeply satisfied, masculine post-sex smile lifted his face. She'd grinned, then teased one of his nipples with her tongue, causing him to flip over and pin her to the bed to stop the torture.

They'd ended up making love again. Slowly, sensuously, before sleeping wrapped in each other's arms. But she hadn't thought.... Frowning, she pushed out of the chair, suddenly needing to move.

"You remember now."

She shook her head, as if she could knock away the ramifications. "You weren't serious."

"Holly, I was. And I am."

Panic and denial clogged her throat. "Maybe you thought so then, in the moment." In the real world, he couldn't love her. As she'd told Stefano, it wasn't in Gabe's psyche.

"The fact you believe that is my fault." A ragged, exasperated sound escaped him. "I admit, I *was* nostalgic that night, being back in Boston. But Holly, my siblings could've closed up Mom's house. I went because I wanted to see you. I'd just found out about the FBI and realized I could lose you forever if I didn't face up to how I felt about you and do something about it."

An involuntary spasm made her jaw shake. She turned toward the door so Gabe wouldn't misinterpret it, but he came up behind her and framed her shoulders with his hands. His voice was low and sure. "I've known for years that you were attracted to me. I saw it in the way you watched me whenever Ben and I were at your house. I saw it whenever I came back from New York to visit my mom. But I took it for granted that you'd always be there."

"That makes me sound unbelievably pathetic—"

"Let me finish." His fingers flexed as he ground out the words. "I knew how you felt, but I also knew you respected yourself too much to act on those feelings. You understood that I wasn't sufficiently mature to love you the way you deserve to be loved."

"It wasn't a question of maturity." Hot tears burned at the back of her eyes as he spoke, but she gritted her teeth and squeezed them back. "Gabe, you had the worst possible example of love in your house. Your mom was a wonderful, wonderful woman. We all adored her. But Ben and I knew how painful it was for you whenever your father called or showed up at the door. We knew how it angered you, and we knew how jaded you were about love and marriage."

A wash of warm breath at the nape of her neck, then the soft touch of Gabe's forehead to the back of her head nearly made her collapse.

"All I need to know" —his fingers came around to her collarbone, smoothing the neckline of her gown before his hands rested on her shoulders once more— "is that you truly love me."

Holly pressed a palm to her forehead in an attempt to stop her racing thoughts. What could she say? She couldn't tell him she didn't; she did. Desperately. But if she uttered those words, if she admitted the truth out loud, she'd expose herself to even worse heartbreak than what she experienced now.

And dammit, with his hands on her, she couldn't think.

He brushed a kiss against the back of her hair, where bobby pins held her updo in place, then whispered, "How about this. Let me tell you why I love you, Holly Elliott."

Instinct made her start to turn, but his powerful grip held her in place. "No. Don't move. I want you to hear what I have to say. Don't turn around unless your answer is yes."

"Yes?" Her breath stilled in her lungs. "Yes to what?"

"To taking a leap of faith."

His thumbs slid to her nape, then drew a path down her spine, first over skin, then over the silky fabric of her gown, until his hands came to rest at the small of her back.

"Gabe—"

"Shhh. I'm about to open a vein here." He shifted so his mouth was inches from her ear. "I love that you can smoke every competitor on *Jeopardy!* when it comes to World History, even though you majored in Accounting because you thought it'd be more practical. I love the way you convinced dozens of summer camp kids that back floating is fun when they were scared to death of the water. And I love that when you walked home from school, you'd pause at old Mrs. Sosher's to pull her weeds so she wouldn't have to get on her knees to do it herself."

Her mouth dropped. She'd only done that when she'd been certain no one was watching because Mrs. Sosher insisted she could take care of her yard despite being in her nineties. And it'd been ten years ago! "How could you know that?"

A quiet laugh escaped him, skittering over her like a caress. "I love that you can't stand onions on cheeseburgers but pile them onto hamburgers. I love that you've read three different biographies of John Adams because you find him fascinating, and that it intrigued me enough that I actually read one myself to find out why. I love that you never want anyone to catch you looking in a mirror because you're afraid they'll think you're vain."

"I do not—"

"I love that you know exactly how many calories are in an Oreo but eat them anyway. I love the little blonde hairs that hide just under here" —his lips pressed to her nape— "but most of all, I love that you never settled for any of the arrogant bastards Ben or I met during grad school, the ones all our friends said would be great for you just because they were as smart as you are. Because they could never love you the way I do. Or for as long as I've loved you, with all your little quirks, even if I was too chickenshit to admit it, even to myself."

The last was said with such intensity and passion, Holly ached to turn and see his expression. But she couldn't, not yet, even if the tears she'd been holding back finally spilled onto her cheeks as he spoke.

"If all that is true," she managed, "why the change? You've always been so *sure*." She swallowed back the lump forming in her throat. She had to know what prompted such an outpouring before she succumbed to the temptation of having his body so close to hers. "So *determined*. Making the football team, getting into law school. Passing the bar. Becoming an FBI agent. But you've also been sure that romance is—and I've heard you say it to Ben more than once—fine for other guys, but not for you."

"And when I said that to Ben, I believed it." His hands remained near the small of her back, though his thumbs shifted higher, pressing against the muscle of her lower back, as if the motion helped him process his thoughts. "But the last time I saw my mother, she made me realize I was wrong."

"Your mom?" The person who'd convinced him through her actions that he couldn't love?

"The day before she died, I was alone with her at the hospital. She made me promise to call my father and let him know. It was the last thing I wanted to do—frankly, I wasn't sure he'd care about my mother's passing, and if he didn't, I didn't want to hear it—but I told her I'd respect her wishes."

"You were a good son."

"No. I wasn't. She told me she knew how much I resented her adoration for my father, but that she regretted nothing. She would marry him all over again, even knowing what he'd do to her. I told her that she shouldn't excuse his behavior. And she flat-out told me that she agreed. His behavior was abominable." He paused, as if knowing he needed to phrase his next words carefully. "What really got me was what she said next. She told me she went into the relationship knowing his strengths and his faults, understanding it was a huge risk. She said, 'I hope you feel that way for someone someday. When you do, you won't regret the risks you take for them. If you're lucky, they'll feel the same for you. But if you don't take the chance, you'll end up heartbroken either way, won't you?' And she pointed out that if she'd never taken the chance with my father, she'd have regretted it the rest of her life."

Unable to help herself, Holly let her hands drift down to cover Gabe's, where they now rested low on her hips. "I can't imagine that was an easy conversation to have in the hospital."

"No. And for a few days, I dismissed it. I was too overwhelmed by her death. But when I got back to New York, I kept turning it over and over in my head." His fingers rose to thread through hers. "When I was admitted to the FBI Academy, it all hit. I knew I couldn't go without seeing you. Without taking the chance."

Holly blew out a breath, thinking back to his phone call. "I was clueless. I never thought…I mean, you've been friends with Ben so long, I just figured you called me because Ben wasn't there and I was available. And that what happened was a fluke on your part."

"I wouldn't gamble my friendship with Ben on a fluke. However, it was worth gambling my friendship with Ben to find out if I could love you for a lifetime. I knew the moment I saw you waiting for me outside the restaurant that I could. When I made love to you, I did it knowing you didn't have one-night stands. I finally felt safe telling you how I felt, even after it took so long to admit it to myself."

"And then I told you I was going to Rome."

"And then you told me you were going to Rome. You'd moved on with your life. And I flew home heartbroken."

"No—"

"And you know what? That's when I finally understood how my mother felt. You were worth the risk."

Holly squeezed her eyes shut. "I'd never treat you the way your father treated your mom."

"I know." Once again, his forehead came to rest on the back of her head. "And that's why I'm here. To give this one more shot. I've said what I needed to say, even if I had to get locked into a room with you to say it. But it's your decision."

A vortex of emotions swirled within her. "We have terrible timing. After all these years…we're thousands of miles apart. And you'll be gone for at least five months."

"If none of that were an issue, what choice would you make right now? Would you pull one of these bobby pins from your hair and use it to try to force the lock?" The light touch of his hands at her hips sent a shiver along her spine. "Or would you take a leap of faith and turn around? I can't promise to never hurt you. But I promise I'll do my best to love you. And to make you as happy as it's in my power to do."

"I can't—"

"If you can't—if you don't want to risk it—know that I understand. And I know that it was my fault."

"No." Slowly, she turned in his arms to face him. The bright sheen of his coppery eyes made her bring her fingers to cup his cheeks. "I can't not love you anymore. Even if you do hurt me. Even if we can't overcome an ocean between us. I'm willing to give it a try."

A mixture of relief and happiness brought a smile to his face. "Well, then" —he extended his arm so his watch was visible under the cuff of his jacket— "we have twenty-eight minutes to get started in private."

The coolness at her back combined with his words to jolt her to awareness. She stared at him, incredulous. "Wait, how'd you…you unzipped my dress! You *knew* I'd turn around!"

"No, I didn't. But I hoped." The crinkles at the corners of his eyes made her skin prickle with desire. "And I took a chance."

"So determined. So *cocky*," she said, knowing her accusation was a tease. As he turned his head in her hands just enough to kiss the inside of her wrist, she added, "I'm glad."

"Holly?" His voice was thick with desire. "I'm crazy in love with you."

"Emphasis on the crazy?"

"What do you think?" he ground out.

He drew her body flush to his, sliding his hands under the fabric at the back of her red dress even as his hot mouth came down on hers. Her response to his unabashed need was instant and powerful. She wound her arms around his broad shoulders and opened to him, allowing him to satisfy his hunger as she did the same. She'd thought the first kiss they'd shared in Boston, tentative and testing, would be her undoing.

She was wrong. It was this kiss. A kiss backed with deep emotion as well as deep need.

Angling his head, he intensified the joining of their mouths, nipping at her lower lip, then groaning as he kissed her fully once more.

Foggy from the power he wielded over her, she leaned back, giving him access to her throat. A soft sigh escaped her as the front of her gown fell away, the fabric sliding between them.

"We'll keep this nice and neat."

She felt the words against her skin as much as heard them while he eased the garment to her waist, then to her hips.

"Step out," he commanded.

"Stefano could come back."

"Not for at least" —he paused, shrugging off the left arm of his tuxedo jacket while he held her gown with his right hand, then glancing at his watch— "twenty-two minutes. Step."

She did as he asked. Within seconds, her dress was draped over the arm of the chair, as was his jacket. He ran a fingertip along the top edge of her bra, a ruby red lace she'd purchased because it matched the dress so perfectly it wouldn't show through the thin, silky fabric. Awe filled his voice. "You are perfection."

Slowly, worshipfully, he pushed one lacy cup aside, lowered his head, and drew a hardened, sensitized nipple into his mouth.

"Gabe—"

Her knees softened at the intimate torture, but he caught her, carrying her to the bed. Rather than easing her to her back, he set her at the edge. With slow movements, he unhooked her bra and explored her breasts with his mouth.

Eyes closed, Holly let a soft moan escape her lips. Her fingers trailed over the crisp cotton of his shirt, outlining the taut muscles of his arms.

"I'm going to do this very, very carefully," he whispered as he eased her panties off, leaving her naked, "so when we return to the reception, every hair on your head will be in place. But I promise, later tonight, when everyone else has gone to bed—"

"Shhh. Surprise me." If she was going to take this leap, she'd take it all the way. "Do whatever you want. But I can tell you that when I do this again" —she slid his bow tie from around his collar, then began working on the front of his shirt, suddenly anxious to indulge herself with the sight of his bare, honed torso— "I'll have trouble being so gentle with the buttons. I can hardly do them now."

She hissed a breath between her teeth as he moved her hands aside, then watched in fascination as he nimbly divested himself of everything but his watch. Curving his hands around her waist, he sat at the bed's edge and pulled her to straddle his magnificent body in one smooth motion. He caressed her back, her hips, then her rear, pulling her tighter against him as he explored her mouth with his. The hard lines of his thighs between hers left her consumed by desire, shaking with the need to have him buried deep inside her.

Sensing her urgency, he slid two fingers between them, finding the moist heat at her core. His breath came in rasps near her ear; she grasped at his shoulders, attempting to gain purchase as tension built within her. "Gabriel, please."

"Come for me," came his hushed command.

"No…no…I want…"

"Eleven minutes."

The exquisite movement of his fingers eased, replaced by an entirely different kind of pressure. He reached up, carefully cradling her head, then pulled her down to kiss him at the same moment he impaled her. The sweet sensation of their joining drove him to groan into her mouth.

The low, primitive sound nearly undid her. Then he began to move, urging her to do the same. She caught her lower lip in her teeth, holding back the whimper that threatened for fear Stefano might return early and hear them from the stairs.

"You," Gabe choked out, "are so beautiful. And I am so lucky."

She couldn't respond; she could only ride the wave as it built and built within her. This was so different than last time they made love, and yet not. Physically, he knew exactly where to trail a kiss, when to urge her onward, when to unleash the desire coiled within himself to make her burn with want, to make her nerve endings sizzle. That hadn't changed. But emotionally…oh, emotionally. Everything had changed. A bond existed she knew could never be severed. This time, there would be no goodbye.

Beneath her, Gabe's powerful muscles shuddered. Head bent, his lips pressed to the crook of her shoulder and neck as he crested, he groaned his release. The male sound sent her over the edge. She squeezed her eyes shut, digging her fingertips into his back and holding on for dear life as wave after wave of sensation shot through her. When she collapsed against him, he held her firm, waiting for her breathing to return to normal.

"Your hair," he rasped, "is immaculate. No one will know a thing."

She smiled against his temple. "Not if we linger."

His arm came off her back. "Thirty seconds to spare."

"Well." She took a few more deep breaths, attempting to regain her equilibrium. "Imagine what we can do overnight."

"I already am."

CHAPTER 6

PEALS of feminine laughter and more than one whoop echoed through the winery as Gabe and Holly made their way through the dining hall toward the rear of the building, where the reception was in full swing. Exactly sixty-five minutes had passed since Gabe left to follow Holly down the hill; they'd looked out the window for Stefano at the hour mark only to notice that the iron key had been quietly shoved under the door so they could open it themselves, from the inside, when they were ready.

"I feel like a kid sneaking into the house," Holly murmured as she squeezed Gabe's hand for reassurance.

"Only if the house sounds like it's hosting a Friday night frat party." He stopped a few steps from their destination and eased her into a private spot, near a display of Santa riding an old wooden sled laden with gifts. "You ready to head back inside?"

"No, but we can't wait." She tilted her head in the direction of the music. "It might not sound like anyone missed us, but I'm sure Chelsea and Ben have noticed. They must wonder what happened."

Gabe grimaced. "About that. Ben knows I followed you to the bed and breakfast."

"You told him?" Ben would kill her. After he killed Gabe...though the fact Gabe wasn't dead already shocked her. "I can't imagine what he thinks—"

"It's all right. Or it will be, once he's convinced that I'm not going to stomp all over your heart."

"Does he know—?"

"Not about Boston. I only told him I was going after you. And that I wanted you for the long haul."

"You actually said that?" She pressed a hand to Gabe's chest, urging him further from the reception room's door. "He believed you? And he was okay with it?"

"I'm not sure 'okay with it' is an apt description, but when he realized I was serious, he told me to go. So once we're inside, perhaps you should reassure him. I want him to be secure with this."

A wave of emotion rose within her. How lucky was she to have this man? How close had she come to pushing him away from her forever? She straightened his bow tie and promised to talk to Ben, then gave Gabe one final kiss before they entered the room hand in hand. Within seconds, she felt at least three sets of eyes upon them, each with a distinct reaction: Chelsea, astonished. Ben, wary. Stefano, amused.

As if on cue, the band segued into a new song, with the bandleader announcing that the groom had selected it for a dance with his sister, Holly, the maid of honor. As the first strains of "Someone To Watch Over Me" floated through the room, it was all Holly could do not to roll her eyes. If ever there was a night Ben shouldn't have to act as her protector, it was on his wedding night.

"This is supposed to be a romantic song," she said before being cut off by Ben's tight smile.

"But the title's appropriate, don't you think?" His steps were light enough anyone watching would think they were sharing a happy, brother-sister moment, but the doubt and concern in his eyes cut her to the quick. "I hope you know what you're doing, because it has train wreck written all over it."

"Ben." She kept her smile in place for the onlookers' sake and her voice was as level as she could for Ben's. "It's not."

"I know you've had a crush on him for years. And no, don't deny it. But you need to understand something about Gabe—"

"He loves me. I'm as familiar with his opinions on that topic as you are, but this is different."

"For the sake of argument, let's say he does." Ben's throat worked as the band skimmed through the song's chorus. "But I need to know…do *you* truly love *him?*"

The accusing tone in which he asked the question was the opposite of the reaction she'd expected. What made him so protective of Gabe? Shouldn't he be worried about her? His sister?

"You'd better," Ben continued. "This better not be simple infatuation. Because after what he's sacrificed…for you to have your hand on the prince's arm at dinner last night…. I know Chelsea was encouraging you to flirt with Prince Stefano, but geez, Holly, what are you thinking?"

Unable to prevent frown lines from puckering her brow, she gazed up at her brother. "What are you talking about?"

"You were flirting with—"

"No. About Gabe. What do you mean, 'after what he's sacrificed'?" Sure, he'd taken a risk by telling her how he felt, but she couldn't imagine he'd shared that with Ben. Gabe never wore his emotions on his sleeve; she certainly couldn't imagine him baring his soul to another male, no matter how close their friendship. And even if he had, it wasn't exactly a sacrifice.

"Quantico. The FBI." Ben's face paled as he looked at her. "He didn't tell you?"

Her feet wouldn't move. A cold knot of dread formed in her stomach.

Ben nudged her to keep dancing.

"He said his schedule changed," she murmured as the impact of Ben's revelation hit her.

"It was his mind that changed. And not because of my wedding."

"Oh, Ben. Please tell me he didn't." He shouldn't have. "He already quit his job in New York. And I'm in *Rome.*"

"I'm well aware."

Dazed, she allowed Ben to guide her around the floor even as it became packed again, thanks to the bandleader urging the wedding guests to join in once more. "I had no idea. I would never ask that of him."

"I know you wouldn't." His voice was quiet, but worried. "But he did it. And I'm afraid you're both going to end up hurt if it doesn't work out."

"It will. I know it will. But that…he shouldn't have done that." Desperately needing to speak to Gabe, she searched him out. Finally, she spotted him on the opposite side of the dance floor, doing the twist with Abby. The sight threatened to shatter her heart. He'd always had a knack for making children smile, mostly because they could sense how much he enjoyed being with them. But how could he enjoy himself, knowing what he'd given up to be here? Being accepted to Quantico was the culmination of a lifetime of work.

She felt Ben roll his eyes, even if she didn't see it. "Go."

She was out of Ben's arms without bothering to ensure that he could partner with Chelsea or one of the other women. After snaking through the dancers to approach Gabe, a blow to her knees made her stumble. Before she could catch herself, she was on the floor, one shoe off, her hands planted on the wood planks.

"I'm sorry!" Abby's face appeared inches from Holly's. "I didn't mean to knock you down!"

"It's okay," she assured the earnest girl, who'd crouched down to assess the damage she'd caused. "How much fun can a dance be if no one falls down?"

Abby's eyes squinched. "Are you hurt?"

"Nope." Only her pride. She pushed off the floor, then spun to find her missing shoe. It appeared in front of her, dangling from Gabe's finger.

"Looking for this?"

"I am. Thank you." So much for appearing dignified as she approached.

"Abby and I got a little carried away, huh, kiddo?"

A giggle erupted from the flower girl, causing her curls to wobble.

"Yeah. Do you want to dance with us?"

"I'd love to."

Much as she wanted Gabe alone, she couldn't shoo Abby. A few seconds later, however, Abby asked Holly if she'd tried the wedding cake yet.

"No. Have you?"

"It's really, really good. But my mom would only let me have one slice. At least until everyone else gets theirs, because that's polite."

"It is," Holly agreed. "But I'll tell you what. There's a slice sitting at my spot. I'm too full to eat it, but I don't want to hurt your Aunt Chelsea's feelings. Think you could eat it for me?"

Abby glanced from Holly to Gabe, then back again. "If I do will you dance with Mr. Maddox?"

"Sure."

The girl's legs couldn't carry her off the floor quickly enough. Nor could Holly confront Gabe quickly enough. The instant she had his attention, she whispered, "You turned down the FBI?"

His arms went to her waist, pulling her into a slow spin despite the fact the band transitioned a lively pop song. "Not turned down. I simply told them that I would be unable to make my report date."

"That's turning them down," she argued. When he'd explained the process to her in Boston, he'd mentioned that recruits weren't given a choice about when to begin their training. They went when they were told. "You shouldn't have."

"It was worth it."

"Call them. Now. They're six hours behind. I know today's your report date, but maybe they'll allow you to come a day late. Maybe there are still flights tonight, if you go through Paris. You can't give—"

"Holly." The dead calm in his voice told her what he was going to say before he uttered the words, "It's too late."

She allowed her forehead to fall against his shoulder. How could he simultaneously devastate her and make her feel so loved? "Gabe, you wanted that more than anything."

"Not more than I want you."

"But...why didn't you tell me?"

"I needed to know you believed in me, and I didn't want my FBI decision to be a factor." He lifted her chin to drop a tender kiss on her lips. "It was the right thing to do. Look how it turned out."

Regret welled inside her, not at what they now shared, but at what he'd lost. "Call them. Please."

"Holly, I'm perfectly happy."

"But I'm not." She stilled in his arms, needing him to see her seriousness. "It's so much a part of who you are. And, frankly, you'd make a fantastic agent. I've waited my whole life for you. I can wait another five months."

Divots appeared between his brows. "You know the FBI doesn't assign agents to Rome."

"We'll cross that bridge when we come to it."

"I doubt they'll take me back."

"Then what will you do? You've left your job in Manhattan."

"Then...I wouldn't ask you to wait." A slow, wicked smile lit his face. "I'd ask you to marry me now instead of asking five months from now. Though I suppose I if I were to go about it the traditional way, I'd ask for Ben's blessing, first."

Warmth spread through her. No matter what, no matter where they lived, they'd be together. The idea of a lifetime with Gabriel Maddox left her dizzy. "Will you call? Right now?"

"Yes. And I'll have a talk with Ben, just to reassure him." He tucked a loose strand of hair behind her ear as the song ended. "In the meantime, perhaps you'd care to talk to our jailor? He just took a seat and no one's with him."

She shot a pointed look toward the handsome prince. "You trust me?"

His responding grin dripped sensuality. "I do."

After extracting a promise from Gabe that he'd make the call before approaching Ben, given the hour back in the States, she crossed the room to slide into the empty seat beside Stefano.

"You're not getting a single bite of my cake." His gaze remained on the delighted crowd as the band launched into a song that had just hit the pop charts. "It's your own fault if you gave yours to Abby."

"I don't want your cake." Waiting until he looked her way, she asked, "How did you know?"

"That Abby ate your cake?" he deadpanned. A beat later, he said, "It was clear from Gabriel's expression the moment he walked into the winery. He looked the way I imagine Odysseus did upon seeing Penelope. You were his destination. And you were rather obvious about your feelings for him, yourself."

She remembered the way she'd stood motionless, her hand in Stefano's, at the sight of Gabe crossing the threshold. "No one else saw what you did. Not when it came to Gabe, at least."

"I'll never say this to anyone else…but I recognized Gabriel's emotion because I experienced it once. Only in my case, I waited until it was too late." He pushed the rest of his cake to the side. "When we went to decorate Ben and Chelsea's house, I hoped to convince you to give the man a chance, but it quickly became apparent that nothing I said would matter. When I saw his key sitting on the cocktail table, I made a spur-of-the-moment decision to give Gabriel the opportunity to convince you himself. If he felt half as strongly as I suspected, I knew it'd be worthwhile."

"I can't say I approve of your methods…but thank you."

"You're quite welcome." His dark head tipped slightly as he shot her a tabloid-worthy grin. "I just wish I hadn't had to use such a flimsy story to lure you over to the B & B."

"And gamble that he'd follow."

"Oh, I knew he would."

The wistfulness in his voice gave her pause. "The woman you mentioned…does she know?"

"She lives a completely different life. I don't even know where she is. I missed my opportunity with her." He picked up his champagne glass and swirled it, halfheartedly watching the bubbles form, then dissipate. "But it's good to know that Christmas miracles are possible."

"Perhaps next Christmas, it'll be your turn."

"Perhaps," he replied, though without conviction. "And perhaps next Christmas, if things go well for you and Gabriel, you'll come back to Sarcaccia. I know a winery that hosts weddings. Very romantic place."

Warmth suffused her cheeks. "That's a big jump."

"I don't know about that." He shot a sidelong glance toward the dance floor. Turning to follow his gaze, she saw Ben clapping Gabe on the back. "But promise me something?"

"Of course."

"If you get married in Sarcaccia, I want to marry you." He laughed aloud at the confusion she knew clouded her expression. "Members of the royal family may officiate at any wedding ceremony on Sarcaccian soil. You only need a license forty-eight hours ahead of time."

Before she could respond, he pushed back from the table. "I believe I owe you an apology," he said as Gabe approached. "But if you're willing to visit next Christmas, I'll make it up to you."

"Next Christmas? I may be working. In fact" —his quick glance at Holly filled her with relief— "it looks like I won't even be able to stay here through Christmas this year with the rest of the wedding party. Though I certainly appreciate the thought."

Stefano flashed a secretive smile in Holly's direction. "In that case, suffice it to say that you are both invited to spend next Christmas in Sarcaccia and I won't take no for an answer."

The winery's head chef caught Stefano's attention, pulling him away. Gabe took the seat beside Holly and grinned. "Care to tell me what that was all about? Prince Fancypants can't let you go?"

"If you're willing to trust me, I'd prefer to keep it to myself for now," she replied, reaching for Gabe's hand. "But I can tell you this much: I've found my prince."

"Charming."

A burst of laughter erupted from her before he leaned forward, closing the gap between them to graze his lips against hers.

"This is Ben and Chelsea's day," she whispered. Much as she wanted Gabe, she feared they'd draw attention from the bride and groom.

"Yes it is." Mischief flashed in his dark eyes as he eased back. "But tonight will be ours. And forever after."

Royal
Scandals

Christmas on the
Royal Yacht

RITA Award Winning Author
NICOLE
BURNHAM

CHAPTER 1

April Dietrich ducked her head against a fresh torrent of icy rain as she hurried along the southernmost dock of Cateri's famous marina. The *Libertà*, the largest of the three yachts owned by the Barrali royal family, was moored at the end, beyond a gauntlet of security. She didn't envy the guards their job today. Christmas might be day after tomorrow, but this morning's weather felt more typical of a bitter December in New York City than one on the Mediterranean island of Sarcaccia.

She used one hand to hold her hood in place as a wind gust forced her to take a staggering step sideways, which drew a laugh from her chilled lips. Despite today's rain, living and working in Sarcaccia beat her old life in New York. She never would've believed it five years ago when Queen Fabrizia approached with a generous employment proposal...then called back two more times to raise her offer. April had loved the business she and her brother Mark took over from their father, which specialized in rehabbing prewar buildings in Manhattan. Still, she'd needed a new start in her personal life and finally took the leap and sold her half of the business to her brother. She never once regretted the decision. Most of her days were occupied with repairs and renovations to Sarcaccia's centuries-old palace, but her weekends and evenings were spent basking in Mediterranean sunshine, enjoying wine, cheese, fresh veggies, and, on occasion, the casual company of some very sexy Sarcaccian men.

The laid-back, relish-each-day attitude she'd developed was the complete opposite of her driven life back in New York.

"You find this amusing?" Marco, the captain of the *Libertà*, eyed her from beneath his own hood. He wore a heavy raincoat over his dress whites and clutched a lidded plastic container to his chest in a futile attempt to keep it dry. April suspected it contained a batch of treats Marco's wife, Sabrina, baked to share with the crew.

"You know, I kind of do." One of the few times she was sent to work outside the palace and the island's perpetual sunshine disappeared on her. "I thought you sailor types were immune to the weather."

Marco made a show of rolling his eyes and muttering in Italian. April knew enough of the language to gather he was cursing the oddities of the feminine mind.

"Did you get breakfast?" he asked once they showed their identification to the drenched guards and proceeded to the end of the dock. "The galley has plenty of food, but you'll have to ask the chef on duty where to find it. Everything's been moved to make space for the New Year's Eve banquet supplies."

"As long as there's coffee, I'm happy," she assured him. "No one needs to go out of their way for me."

Every year, the Barralis invited VIPs from across Europe for a night of dinner and dancing on their yacht. Afterward, the guests had a prime spot from which to watch the fireworks over the capital city of Cateri. While many guests then adjourned to the palace to spend the night, a few stayed on board the *Libertà* or one of the family's two smaller yachts, which was what brought April to the dock today. Marco sent a punch list of minor repairs needed to the *Libertà* before the big event.

"Good, because they're too busy anyway." Marco winked at her before gesturing for April to lead the way up the ramp to the yacht's lower deck. Even in the pouring rain, the vessel took her breath away. Its white hull and silver trim gleamed despite the day's cloud cover. After making her way up the crew stairs to the rear deck, she bypassed the row of lounge chairs and opened one of the sliding glass doors to the salon, the yacht's main gathering area. The clean lines and luxurious silver-blue sofas of the expansive windowed room made her want to collapse with a warm blanket and steaming hot chocolate to watch the raindrops. It was a space meant for self-indulgent lounging.

"The worst are the doors below the television," Marco told her, pointing to the long row of sleek cabinets on the far wall. "The one on the far left won't stay shut. With the others, I suspect it's a matter of tightening and realigning the hinges to keep everything from creaking. The rest of the issues are in the master stateroom, the second guest room on the starboard side, and the galley."

So much for lounging, not that she would anyway. "How 'bout I take a look at what needs fixing in the galley while I grab a cup of coffee? I can see when it's most convenient for me to work in there, given the staff's schedule. I can tackle the rest of the repairs whenever the galley is busy."

"Thanks. I know renovations are more your job description than repairs, so it's appreciated."

"Bet you say that to all the girls."

Marco laughed, indicated he'd be in the pilot house on the top deck, then left her to find the galley. Before making his way up the stairs, he turned and warned April to be kind to the yacht's new head chef.

"You don't think I'm nice?" She put a hand to her chest in a mock affront.

"Of course you are. I'm warning you because he may end up being *your* chef. He's been on board for six months, but he's still warming up to the crew's sense of humor."

She frowned at him as she set down her toolbox and removed her raincoat, taking care not to shake too much water onto the floor. "My chef?"

"The queen hired him with the idea he'd replace Dominic when the old guy retires in the spring."

April had heard the rumor circulating through the housekeeping staff that the palace's longtime head chef planned to move to London to be closer to his children, but she'd hoped it wasn't true. This was the first confirmation she'd heard from someone likely to know the facts. "Dominic's really going?"

"Once the king and queen are certain about their choice of replacement. The New Year's Eve party is his big test, but given how he's performed so far, I'm pretty sure he'll get the job. So be nice to the man or one night, when you're working late at the palace and order food from the kitchen, Rock may poison your panini."

An involuntary jolt shook her as the name left Marco's lips. "His name is Rock?"

"It's not his real name, but apparently he's gone by Rock since childhood. You don't mess with a man named Rock."

No, you don't. She angled a look at the container in his hand. "It'd be easier to be nice if I were sweetened up with, say, a few of Sabrina's cookies."

"They're cannoli, and not on your life," Marco called out over his shoulder as he disappeared. "At least not until after lunch."

So she was right, April thought as she slid her damp raincoat into an empty closet, leaving the door ajar so air could circulate. Sabrina had prepared goodies for the crew. April didn't take much satisfaction in learning her guess was accurate. Hearing the name of the new chef sent her mind careening back to some of the most difficult days in her life.

How many men in the world went by Rock? How many *chefs* went by Rock?

She shook off the thought—the man was an ocean and a lifetime away—grabbed her toolbox, then made her way down the corridor to the galley, which occupied the forward section of the main deck. She'd only glimpsed the galley once before, when the Barrali family hosted a staff appreciation party on board, and relished the opportunity for a better look now that the boat was quiet.

"Wow," she mumbled once she'd made her way through the yacht's formal dining room and pushed through the swinging door. She'd gotten used to seeing how the other half lived, having grown up following her father around his upscale Manhattan job sites, then working for the Barrali family inside one of Europe's most elegant palaces. While flash no longer impressed her, the *Libertà's* galley was April's kind of space: efficiently designed, easy on the eye, and immaculately maintained. The galley was divided into two sections. The section where she now stood was outfitted for family and guest use. To April's left, four large windows offered a view of the sea from the port side of the yacht. In front of her, three white leather barstools on chrome pedestals were anchored to an island of highly polished, beautifully veined Carrara marble. The cook's work area on the far side of the island boasted sleek white cabinets topped with more Carrara marble alongside a six-burner cooktop with a high-powered vent. A tiled backsplash of light green and blue sea glass added to the room's airy feeling and broke up the expanse of white and chrome that dominated the decor. A bowl constructed of twisted chrome held fresh bananas and apples. Alongside it, bottled water was arranged on an elegant wooden tray, ready for whoever needed refreshment.

Yep. She could live in a kitchen like this one. Especially if it came with its own private chef...though in this case, the guy was nowhere to be seen. Odd, given the arrangements necessary for the upcoming New Year's Eve party. And she wouldn't be surprised to learn that one or more of the royal couple's adult children planned to use the yacht in the days between Christmas and New Year's, which meant even more planning and preparation on the part of the crew.

April set her toolbox on the floor and withdrew the punch list Marco provided. After reviewing it, she set the page on the island, then began testing the cabinets, checking to see which were loose or needed new hinges or pulls. It was easy work, fixing cabinets, and reminded her of her teenage years, when she followed her father to his job sites and he'd allowed her to tackle the simple tasks. Once she'd made note of what needed repairs, April bent to pick up her toolbox and make her way to the other section of the galley, at the very forward part of the main deck. It contained the walk-in refriger-ator, commercial ranges, and counter space necessary to service larger events. It was also where she was most likely to find a fresh cup of coffee. If the chef hadn't already made a pot for the crew, well, she'd make one herself and apologize later if she was out of line.

She straightened at the sound of footsteps approaching from the direction of the dining room. A lean, sandy-haired man in a white chef's jacket entered with a stainless steel tray full of phyllo dough balanced expertly on his shoulder. He shifted his load and smiled. "You must be April," he said in a distinctly German accent. "Marco mentioned that you were coming on board to do maintenance."

"Yes." Relief washed through her at the sight of the friendly—and unfamiliar—face. She covered the space between them, then extended her hand toward his free one. "I take it you're Rock?"

He gave her hand a brief shake, then said, "No, I'm Andreas, his assistant. Rock's right behind me."

April turned slightly, then started at the sight of the man in rolled-up shirtsleeves who'd entered soundlessly behind Andreas. He carried a case of champagne and wore what anyone else would consider a full-on scowl, but that April knew was mild consternation. A full-on scowl from this man would give a lion second thoughts about attack-ing. It'd certainly made her back down more than once.

"Ryan Fournier." Miraculously, April's voice sounded unrattled, as if she were greeting an old friend rather than an ex-lover, one she'd left without a backward glance. It had been the safest thing for her psyche to give him a casual farewell, then cease all contact, though over the last five years, she'd given him many, *many* thoughts, most of them X-rated. Rock fit his name. From the formidable chest and biceps he'd honed through hard work to the capable hands his profes-sion required, he was solid through and through. And oh, how those hands had undone her. Once, even, in the back room of his first restaurant. A room not unlike the workspace only a few feet away.

"Well, what do you know. April Dietrich. The only person who's ever called me Ryan to my face and gotten away with it."

She started to respond, then snapped her mouth shut. The only time she'd called him Ryan was when they were alone, either in bed or en route, and usually in a heated rush. The first time she'd done it, she'd been half-naked and he'd been walking her backward toward his bedroom. He'd run a thumb over her lower lip and warned her, "You're only getting away with that because we're about to have mind-blowing sex."

Heat rose within her at the memory and a self-satisfied grin lifted one side of Rock's mouth, making it apparent he knew exactly what memory had gone through her mind.

Rock angled his head and shot a look at his now-curious assistant, Andreas, urging the young German to continue on to the working galley with the tray of pastry. Once Andreas disappeared, Rock set the case of champagne on the marble countertop and plastered a nonchalant smile on his face. His heart thudded against the wall of his chest as he gave April a casual once-over, and it wasn't due to the effort of carrying the heavy load. "I had a feeling you'd show up someday to fix my creaky parts."

"I'm not here to fix your creaky parts. I'm here for routine maintenance."

"I could use that, too." Though from April, it'd be anything but routine. She'd been sexual crack cocaine to him. He'd have done anything, given up anything to spend another night, even another hour, in her bed. But just when he was sure she needed him most, when he'd felt the most connected to her, she'd left him, opting to take a job here in Sarcaccia that she'd turned down twice before. And she'd done it with nothing more than an it's-been-great and a quick kiss goodbye. Her abrupt departure left him reeling.

Hell, seeing her in the flesh left him reeling, despite the fact he'd been told she was coming aboard and mentally steeled himself for a face-to-face. He'd be damned if he'd let her see it, though.

The woman looked even better than when he'd last seen her five years ago, despite the fine mist clinging to her face and the lower part of her pants. Her cheeks were flushed from the chilly weather and her gray-blue eyes were as lively as ever. Her blond hair curled at the ends, just below her shoulders. When he'd last seen her, it'd been cropped around her ears, almost like a boy's, though no one would mistake April's feminine physique for that of a male.

He'd forgotten just how gloriously she filled out a top. The cantaloupe-colored, long-sleeved fitted T-shirt she wore hugged her in all the right places.

"You're awful."

He arched an eyebrow at her. "That's not what you said last time we—"

"Uncle!" She held up a hand and glanced around, as if afraid other crew members would walk in on them. "Uncle. You win."

"Didn't know there was a competition." But he had known that aggressive flirtation would convince April to keep herself at arm's length, which was what he needed for the duration of her time on board.

She leaned one curvaceous hip against the kitchen island. "Can we start over? How about, 'It's good to see you, April. I hope you're doing well.' Will that work?"

"It's good to see you, April. I hope you're doing well."

One side of her mouth cocked into a smile and she glanced at the case of champagne before turning her blue-eyed gaze back to his face. "You're really the chef here?"

"Are you questioning my skills or asking how I ended up in Sarcaccia?"

A dry note edged her voice. "I'd never question your skills."

He ached to make yet another sexual innuendo, but settled for, "I came here the same way you did."

April didn't bother to hide her skepticism as she set her toolbox on the floor. Before she could ask the question he saw in her eyes, Rock explained, "Queen Fabrizia was in New York at my Greenwich Village restaurant a few years ago and asked to meet the chef. We had a nice conversation and she complimented me on the meal. Last spring she and King Carlo were in the States on a diplomatic visit and arranged to have a private dinner. Afterward, they asked if I would consider working for them."

Her eyes widened. "You expect me to believe you gave up two restaurants for what, a boat?"

I didn't give 'em up to follow you, sweetheart. He could tell from her look of doubt it's what she suspected.

"First, this is no ordinary boat." He waved a hand to encompass the slick guest area of the galley.

"I'll grant you that."

"And second, I sold the restaurant at 53rd and Lexington three years ago. I still own the place in Greenwich Village, but I receive at least one unsolicited offer to buy every month." He shrugged. "For now, it's in good hands, so I've given up nothing."

It was the truth. His assistant chef was smart, talented, and knew how Rock expected the restaurant to operate. He was also among those who'd offered to buy the place, should Rock stay in Sarcaccia. And given that the man was from a wealthy Upper East Side family, Rock knew money wasn't an issue.

"I can't imagine you selling either of your restaurants," April said. "They've always been your passion."

"Passions can change." Hers certainly had. "And you know that when Queen Fabrizia puts her mind to something, she usually gets it. Having both her and King Carlo sitting at one of my tables making their best pitch was convincing. They laid out exactly where my career could go, should I perform well on the *Libertà*." He couldn't help but give her a lingering head-to-toe perusal. "I figured it wouldn't hurt to give it a whirl."

"You're hoping to get the palace job?"

"Assuming Dominic doesn't change his mind and stay, you bet." Running the palace kitchen would be a dream come true. He could let go of the financial juggling that went hand-in-hand with the restaurant business to focus on his first love, preparing original, tantalizing meals. He'd have the opportunity to experiment again, creating menus customized to each event. There'd be everything from informal hors d'oeuvres receptions to afternoon garden parties to five-star banquets for heads of state. Should he wish to pursue a more public career, creating cookbooks or even a television show—suggestions from the entrepreneurial King Carlo—employment with the Barrali family would offer him the ideal platform.

While Rock derived a great deal of satisfaction from the restaurants' success, his first thought upon awakening each morning was the bottom line. After years of producing a tightly controlled menu for his customers, ensuring the fare would appeal to the broadest possible market, Rock feared he was losing his creative edge. The endless management tasks exacted a toll, too. If he never had to hire another accountant or stay awake through the wee hours of the morning scouring contracts, he'd be thrilled.

He'd been thinking exactly that while filling out the paperwork to renew his liquor license when the call came from Queen Fabrizia's personal assistant asking if he'd be available to provide a private dinner for the royals. The timing was uncanny.

But then there was April. Knowing she was likely still working for the Barralis kept him from accepting Queen Fabrizia's offer on the spot. If he went to Sarcaccia, would she view him with interest or suspicion? Would being around her affect him as powerfully as when she was in New York? And how much contact would they even have, given that her position required little to no time around the palace kitchen?

In the end, he'd said to hell with the what-ifs and done what was best for him. An offer like Fabrizia's came once in a lifetime, and he intended to make the most of the opportunity.

"If Fabrizia pursued you, it was because she felt you'd be the best person for the job," April said, straightening as she gestured toward the working galley. "I was about to grab coffee and get to work. Do you mind?"

"Be my guest. There's a fresh pot at the drink station just inside the door." He hefted the case of champagne from the counter and led the way through the swinging door to the rear galley, which had become his home away from home the last six months. With his elbow, he pointed to the coffee pot. "Mugs are up top. Put it in the dishwasher when you're done."

Without looking back at April, he headed past Andreas, who was working at one of the stainless steel counters, to the walk-in refrigerator where the champagne would be stored until the New Year's Eve party. He stacked the case on top of the two he'd brought in earlier, then turned back to the galley.

"This is impressive." April already had a cup of steaming black coffee in hand and was studying the working galley. She glanced at the chocolate crusts Andreas was preparing, then allowed her gaze to travel over the room's sparkling surfaces. "You run as tight a ship here as you did in your restaurants."

"Well, we are on a yacht," Andreas said with a grin. Rock didn't miss the look of open flirtation on the blond man's face. Or the laughter that erupted from April.

"True." Her smile faded as she looked past Andreas to Rock. "Marco didn't have any repairs listed for this section of the galley, only in the front section. Was there anything you needed me to look at while I'm here?"

The thought that she could look at him with the same open smile she'd given Andreas zinged through his mind, but he said, "I have everything under control."

She raised her mug to her lips and took a long, slow sip. It was a tactic April had often used to buy time when she needed to compose herself. He wondered what made her feel off-kilter now. But when she lowered her mug, she showed no signs of discomfort. Rather, she moved back to the drink station and topped off her mug.

"I'll get to work, then," she said over her shoulder. "Let me know if I'm in your way. I don't want to inconvenience you."

Before he could respond, she swished out the door, coffee in hand. He managed a good look at her backside before the door blocked his view.

"Do you think any male has called her inconvenient in her entire life?" Andreas asked in a low tone with a glance toward the swinging door.

When Rock didn't respond, Andreas shrugged and muttered, "She's more than welcome to get in my way."

"Andreas? Don't even think about it."

"That's what I figured you'd say." A devilish grin flashed across the younger man's face before he finished with, "Ryan."

CHAPTER 2

A few hours later, April snapped a photograph of the hinges used on the salon cabinets and noted the manufacturer. She'd been able to repair all but one of the doors in the salon without a problem. For the last, she'd need to order a new hinge and have it shipped overnight.

That, of course, meant another trip back to the *Libertà* to install it. And another chance she'd run into Rock. It'd taken every ounce of her fortitude not to let him see how he unnerved her. He was as witty as ever, and even more alluring than she'd remembered. His wavy, dark chestnut hair was slightly shorter than when they'd dated, and the last five years had given his face a worldly wisdom that made him appear even rougher than before. Worse, his intelligent blue eyes, framed by jet-black lashes any woman would kill to have, seemed to see right through her. April sighed as she packed her screwdriver back into her toolbox.

"You're still pouting about the cannoli, aren't you?"

At the sound of Marco's teasing voice, April straightened and flashed him a smile. "Why do you ask? You feeling guilty? Two deckhands and the engineer cut through here about a half hour ago with their mouths full. I bet you sent them this way to torture me."

"Maybe I did, maybe I didn't. Either way, I never feel guilty about anything." The captain leaned against the wall, his eyes twinkling in merriment. "However, if you care for one of Sabrina's cannoli, there are several left in the pilot house. Help yourself. But don't touch any of the controls while you're up there or I'll toss you overboard."

"Aye, aye, cap'n."

Marco rolled his eyes at her mock salute before informing her that two men would be in the salon shortly to set up a Christmas tree and begin decorating the space for the holiday. "Prince Bruno plans to use the salon and dining room to host a few friends for drinks late tomorrow afternoon," he said. "How much longer do you think you'll be in here?"

"All of two minutes," she assured him. "Then I'm going for cannoli before I start work on the guest bedroom."

Once Marco left, April used her phone to look up the information on the hinge, called in the order, then tucked her toolbox into the closet where she'd stashed her raincoat earlier. Though the sky was still overcast, the worst of the rain had stopped, so she opted to take the outside stairs to the top deck. It wasn't often she had the opportunity to look at the marina from this vantage point.

Plus, she figured, she was less likely to run into Rock on the exterior stairs. Until she figured out how she felt about him—and about his presence in Sarcaccia—it'd be better if she kept her distance.

Chicken.

Ignoring her inner voice, April made her way to the rear deck. After pausing to look back toward the mist-shrouded capital city of Cateri, she rounded the boat to the Mediterranean side. Most days, the marina area was packed with traffic, but the weather combined with the time of year to leave the harbor relatively empty.

A bizarre noise from below, a half-screech, half-croak, sent April to the railing. Shielding her eyes against the water vapor blowing off the choppy waves, she leaned out far enough to see two men carrying a twine-wrapped Christmas tree along the deck below hers. They kept their heads bent against the wind as they angled the tree to ensure it fit up the stairs. Though they were yammering back and forth in Italian about the logistics of getting the tree to the salon, it sounded nothing like the noise that had piqued her curiosity.

She'd started toward the pilot house once more when a flash of movement and a whoosh of wings caught her attention. Unsure of what she saw, April glanced over the railing again and was rewarded with the sight of a large heron, the tips of its outstretched wings skimming the waves alongside of the *Libertà*. She'd only seen two herons during her time in Sarcaccia, and neither were here along Cateri's busy waterfront. They preferred the ponds and tall grasses on the far side of the island. The elegant creature made a slow loop over the water, then came back toward the side of the boat. April made her way further down the port side, then palmed the railing and leaned over the edge for a better look. The heron swooped skyward, its long legs trailing behind its body as it headed toward the pilot house. Hearing the sound of footsteps on the nearby stairs, she angled her head to see who approached so she could point out the heron. At that moment, her feet slid on the wet deck and the change in balance sent her hands shooting off the slick metal. Her stomach pitched. She flailed, attempting to catch herself for one dizzying moment, but then her weight shifted forward and her feet slid completely out from under her. With a yelp, April went over the railing, plummeting to the water two decks below.

***

ROCK HAD JUST POPPED a chocolate crust into his mouth and nodded his approval when he heard the startled cry.

Andreas had taken longer than Rock expected preparing the crusts for the miniature chocolate cheesecakes that would be served at both Prince Bruno's get-together and the New Year's Eve party, but the young chef had executed the task flawlessly. This first tray would be filled tonight and chilled for tomorrow's event, while the rest of the crusts would be frozen for next week.

"What was that?" Andreas asked, alarm causing his eyes to widen.

Before the question left his mouth, a large splash came from the port side. The German wiped his hands on a towel and strode toward the window. "Sounds like the guys dropped something overboard. You don't think it was the Christmas decorations?"

"Too big," Rock muttered. He was already pushing out the galley door. With the decks as slippery as they were, given the cool temperatures and the rain, he'd bet his paycheck one of the new deckhands went overboard. Either that, or one of the men hauling the decor had wiped out and sent the entire tree into the Med. It'd explain the yap of surprise Rock heard just before the splash.

Rock exited to the rear deck, his steps quick and sure as he made his way to the port side and looked overboard. Marco approached at a swift clip from the bow, bracing one hand against the side of the yacht to keep his footing.

"Someone went over?" Rock asked.

"I heard the splash as I was coming down the stairs, but didn't see what happened. It's so slick out here today—"

"There!" Rock pointed as a head broke through the water about twenty feet from the side of the yacht. His heart leapt to his throat as he saw long hair and realized it could only be one person. Instinct made him want to leap over the low railing, but common sense drove him to turn and look for the nearest life preserver. Grabbing it from the wall, he unlooped the rope and tossed the ring in April's direction.

"April!" Marco pointed toward the bright orange preserver. "April! Grab the ring and we'll pull you in!"

She turned in the water and pushed the curtain of hair from her face with one hand. She glanced at them and gave a thumbs up…then looked away from the life preserver and disappeared beneath the surface of the water.

"What the hell is she doing?"

"I have no idea." Marco shielded his eyes as the skies opened and sent a fresh sheet of rain pinging across the deck and the surface of the water. "Is she blind to bright orange?"

Rock uttered an oath as he toed out of his shoes. Damned if April was going to drown when he was right there to help.

"Rock, don't—"

He didn't hear the rest. He was already over the railing, jumping feet first. The water bit into his skin as he hit. It was far colder than he'd anticipated and his body tensed against the chill as he descended beneath the waves. Once he slowed, he stretched his arms and pumped his way to the surface. It took only a few seconds to see April, her head appearing then disappearing as waves crested between them. With a few short strokes, he was at her side.

"What are you doing?" Her eyes widened in shock. "Are you crazy?"

"Me? What are you doing?"

"Getting my cold, embarrassed ass to the side of the dock. At least I was until you jumped in." She shot a pointed look in the direction of the dock. "There's a ladder not far from the back of the yacht. It'll take us to the yacht's boarding ramp."

"You guys all right?" Marco called from above.

"We're fine!" April yelled back before frowning at Rock. "Follow me. You can swim, right?"

He glared at her. Her hair was plastered to her head and mascara ran in dark streaks under her eyes. Until this moment, he'd never even realized she wore mascara. Another of his April illusions shattered.

"Well, can you or can't you?" she asked.

Did she think he'd have jumped after her if he couldn't swim? "Of course I can swim."

She rolled her eyes at his snarled response, then started toward the ladder in a breaststroke that kept her head above the water. When they reached the ladder, she grabbed the lowest rung and looked back over her shoulder to make sure he was with her, then started to climb. Just for good measure, he gave her rear end a mighty shove.

"What was that for?" She sprung from his touch, nearly missing the next rung.

"I'm being helpful." Though his voice made it clear he felt anything but charitable toward her at the moment.

"I didn't ask for your help."

"I didn't ask you to go overboard and need my help."

"Unbelievable." She pulled herself up the last step to the dock, then turned to watch him climb, bracing her hands on either side of the ladder. Water dripped from her clothing and hair, hitting him in the face…as if the rain itself wasn't enough. She shook her head at the ridiculousness of their appearance, then swiped a hand over her face, smearing her mascara further. "Look, Rock, I'm sorry I got snotty with you. I just…I can't believe I fell overboard, and I can't believe you jumped."

"Agreed. On both counts."

Rock made it to the top of the ladder just as Marco and one of the deckhands came down the ramp with white towels in their arms. The deckhand gave Rock one of the towels while Marco approached April with the other.

"What happened?" the captain asked as he wrapped a towel around April's shoulders. Given that April was at least two inches taller than Marco, she had to bend for him to do so.

"Dumb accident." She pulled the towel over her head and scrubbed at her hair. "A heron was flying beside the boat. I tried to get a better look before it disappeared and lost my footing."

Marco urged everyone up the ramp so they'd be out of the rain. "I saw it fly by yesterday. Couldn't believe there's one near the marina, let alone this time of year. Didn't want to see it that badly, though. You sure you're all right?"

"Perfectly fine," she assured him. "It was like taking an awkward jump from a high dive, is all. Glad I wasn't another deck up."

"Why didn't you grab the life preserver?" Marco asked, his question echoing what was going through Rock's head.

"No need to be towed in when I could swim to the ladder." She said it with lightness in her voice that belied the snappy tone she'd used with Rock while they were in the water. "I'm sorry if I alarmed you."

"I'm just glad you're all right."

April turned to Rock and said, "And I'm sorry you felt the need to jump in. I should've made it clear that I was safe. You must be freezing."

"No more so than you."

They were on the rear deck now, just outside the sliding glass doors to the salon. April stopped short and used the towel to squeeze water out of her hair as she looked down at her dripping clothes. "If it's all right with you, Marco, I'll come back tomorrow morning to finish repairs to the guest quarters. If the hinge for the salon arrives in time, I'll install it, too. Or if that's inconvenient with Prince Bruno's party, I'll come back later in the week."

"Whichever you prefer is fine by me."

"Thanks." She gave the deckhand her towel with a grateful smile before turning to Marco. "Would you mind bringing me my toolbox and raincoat? I don't want to drip across the salon."

"You're going home like that?" Rock asked. She was soaked to the bone. As upbeat as her tone was with Marco and the deckhand, Rock knew she had to be fighting not to shiver. Hell, he was fighting not to shiver, and he'd always been more cold-hardy than April.

"I'll be fine. It's not a long walk to my apartment."

"I thought you drove to the marina. You walked all the way from home? In this weather?" Marco asked.

"You did, too," she pointed out.

"I live closer than you do."

"My car's here at the marina," Rock said to April, unwilling to think about the fact that after twenty years working for the Barrali family, Marco knew most of the staff well enough to know where they lived, April included. "If you promise not to lean over the railing, we'll take the outside stairs to my quarters. You can get a blanket while I grab my keys, then I'll drive you home."

"You don't need to do that—"

"Andreas has the galley handled, and I need to go to my apartment, anyway. Since we aren't scheduled to go to sea in the near future, I don't have a complete change of clothes on board." He put his hands on her shoulders and spun her toward the stairs. True to his prediction, she felt cold to the touch, despite the fact his own hands were freezing.

"Thanks, Rock. Let me know if you or April need anything else. And if either one of you discovers you're injured, let me know right away. Whether you think so or not, that was quite a drop." Marco turned to April. "In the meantime, I'll leave your coat and tools here by the salon door, out of the rain. Sound good?"

"Thanks, Marco." She shot the captain a mischievous smile. "While you're getting the toolbox, look in the top section. There's a package wrapped in pink with a silver ribbon. It's for Sabrina." At the question in his eyes, she added, "Her favorite lipstick. It's not sold here in Sarcaccia, so I picked up a couple tubes while I was in the States last month. But don't tell her what's in it. Let it be a surprise when she opens it."

Marco's face split into a wide grin. "Just for that, I'll wrap up two cannoli for you."

"I suspect you would've anyway."

Once Marco and the deckhand were out of earshot, April whispered over her shoulder, "I'm really fine. You don't have to do this." She held the railing as they took the stairs toward the lowest deck, but she stopped and turned to face him before opening the door that accessed the hall leading to the crew quarters.

Rock gestured toward the door. "Go."

He was aware of his brusque tone. But dammit, April sometimes needed bossing around. It also helped distract him from the way her melon-colored shirt clung to her curves, displaying the scandalous outline of her lace bra.

She opened her mouth as if to argue, then apparently thought better of it. Once she entered the hallway, he moved to walk behind her, where the view wasn't so distracting. "Third door."

She passed it, then spun to wait for him to open it. *Of course.* Keeping his eyes on his tasks, he entered the small room, fished his keys and wallet from the nightstand, then grabbed a blanket from the built-in drawer underneath his bed. April remained in the hallway.

"Do you need to use the restroom before we go?"

She shook her head. Given the way she was eyeing his room, he suspected she needed to, but didn't want to drip water in the minuscule space. He also suspected that once she peeled off her wet slacks, she wouldn't get them on again. He didn't want to envision how she'd handle that issue.

He shoved the blanket at her. "Let's get you home, then."

CHAPTER 3

April pulled her gaze from Rock's tidy bed to accept the fawn-colored blanket he proffered, careful to keep her fingers from brushing his as she did so. She turned it in her arms, preparing to unfold it, only to be assailed with a scent that had haunted her dreams for years. Masculine, warm, and unique, the plush fabric smelled like *him*. Like being snuggled in Rock's sheets, her head against his chest, listening to his soft laughter over an inside joke as they drifted off to sleep.

It'd been five years, yet that scent brought back memories as vivid as if it'd been last night.

Her jaw tightened and a prickly sensation teased the back of her throat as she fought to control her emotions. In that moment, she knew she'd been naive believing she could step back and make a calm, rational assessment of how she felt about Rock's presence in Sarcaccia.

Where Rock was concerned, she had no reason. One whiff of a blanket—a freaking Culinary Institute of America blanket—and she was a goner.

"Something wrong?" He angled a dark brow at the blanket she'd failed to wrap around herself.

"No, not at all. I thought I'd use it in the car." Grateful she'd managed the quick recovery, she added, "It'll feel better to have it between me and the seat than to sit and create a puddle. I imagine your front seat will be better for it, too."

Back in New York, he'd driven a vintage Mustang, one he'd saved for throughout his teenage years and early twenties. He kept the vehicle as pristine as he kept the kitchens in which he worked. She couldn't imagine that changed. Even his cabin on the yacht—tiny though it may be—was neat as a pin.

They stopped for her tools and jacket before making their way down the ramp, past the guards, and toward the private parking lot used by the royal family and their employees. Rock insisted on carrying her belongings, but was otherwise quiet as they walked. April wasn't sure whether it was uneasiness at being in her presence again or the physical discomfort of having taken a December dive into the Mediterranean. Either way, with each step they took on the long wooden dock, April's tension level ratcheted higher. She clutched the blanket to her stomach, using it to warm her chilled hands.

When Rock pulled a set of car keys from his pocket and hit the button on the remote, she decided to break the silence before they were alone inside his car. "You didn't tell Marco about your room."

He shot a sideways frown at her as he paused beside a black Mercedes and lifted the trunk so he could stash her tools. "Tell him what?"

"The drawer doesn't fit properly under your bed. It took you a few tries to get it to slide in the way it should. May be a humidity issue. And the top of your nightstand looked loose, like it's only partially secured to the wall. Hit a swell in the middle of the night and it's liable to detach and conk you in the head."

"Soaked to the bone and that's what you notice? The proximity of my nightstand to my pillow?"

What she'd actually noticed was that he still used the same old-fashioned, bells-on-top alarm clock he'd had on his nightstand in New York. For all the tech most people kept on their nightstands, Rock appreciated the classics.

"It's part of my job to inspect and maintain royal property." She watched as he set the toolbox in the trunk, which was empty save for a warning triangle and first aid kit. "And not that you couldn't use a good conk in the head from time to time, but I imagine the Barralis wouldn't want their chef out of commission."

"You're the one who went overboard, yet you're saying I need a conk to the head?"

She opened the passenger door to his Mercedes and set the blanket on the seat before shooting him a grin over the roof of the car. Banter was far more comfortable than silence, even when Rock's tone toed the line between flirtatious and insulting. "I was talking about what I noticed in your ship's quarters. That's all."

He slid into the driver's seat and waited for her to buckle before starting out of the marina. "Speaking of quarters, where to?"

She directed him to the road that led to her apartment, then leaned back in the seat. As she'd predicted, the car's interior was immaculate. The rich gray leather seats looked unused. There wasn't a speck of dirt on the floor or dust on the dashboard. Even the cupholders were empty. "Nice car."

"It's not the Mustang, but it'll do." He clicked a button on the dash to start the flow of warm air. "Especially in today's weather."

"Have to admit, I never envisioned you as the Mercedes type."

"I'm not." He switched lanes to allow a delivery truck to thunder past. "The Mustang's in storage in New York. The rental choices here on the island are either tiny European compacts or luxury sedans." He pulled a face. "Given my height, it wasn't much of a choice."

Rain lashed the windows as Rock stopped for a light. The streets were devoid of foot traffic as locals and the few tourists who visited the island for the holidays took shelter from the storm.

"Bet you miss it."

"If I'm hired at the palace, I'd be permitted to store the Mustang in the underground garage. A lot safer than keeping it on the street near the apartment where I am now."

"Oh." She frowned as a thought occurred to her. "I think that's only for employees who opt to live in, though."

"It is, but the head chef's apartment is bigger than what I have now and has a private entrance so I can come and go as I please. It'd be worth considering, especially given the parking situation."

The light changed and he hit the gas, guiding the car uphill toward her apartment, which was located on the edge of Cateri's medieval district. The restaurants, shops, and bars along the street were empty, though the signs in the windows indicated they were open for business.

The idea of having Rock living at the palace, where she could run into him at any time, day or night, sent her heart tripping double-time.

"That a problem?" he asked, as if he could read her mind. "Having me at the palace?"

Maybe. Yes. "Of course not. Why would it be?"

He didn't answer. She pointed out the side street where she lived as a full-body shiver went through her. Now that she was sitting still with a fan blowing warm air and the blanket beneath her rather than wrapped around her hands, she felt colder than ever.

Rock reached in front of her to check the passenger air vents, then maneuvered the car into a tight space on the cobblestone street fronting her apartment. Given the presence of a popular bakery on the building's ground floor, she was surprised he'd found a spot at all. It was the one favor the weather did for her today.

He cut the engine, then turned to face her and asked, "You sure you're all right?"

"Of course. I could've walked, but I appreciate the ride. Thanks." His dark hair was flattened to his head and his shirt clung to his torso, outlining the musculature of his shoulders and chest. She swallowed, yanking her focus back to his eyes.

Big mistake. The same rich blue-green as the Mediterranean in summertime, his irises appeared luminous against the car's dark gray interior. Thunder clapped overhead, and the storm sent another torrent of gray rain streaking down the window behind him, heightening the effect. Surprising her, he reached to touch her cheek, then ran the pad of his thumb along her chin. A deep furrow creased the space between his brows.

"You're like a block of ice. Stay here and warm up a minute now that the heat's going. When the rain breaks, take the blanket with you. I'll get it later."

"Rain won't hurt me." The words came out barely above a whisper. His gentle touch brought back memories of a different period in her life, the joys of their time together…and the guilt of it, too.

"Your lips are blue. You'll never admit it, but cold weather's always done a number on you."

Silence dragged between them. His fingers didn't leave her cheek. In the back of her mind, she registered that the Mercedes' windows had fogged, though she couldn't tear her gaze from his. She couldn't move at all. Then he leaned forward and, ever so softly, grazed her mouth with his. Her entire body tensed, her senses assaulted by the bare brush of his lips, the pressure of his thumb, the dampness of their clothing as it mixed with his unique, comforting scent. Still, she couldn't move.

He lingered a moment, his breath mingling with hers in the stillness of the car, and she allowed her eyes to drift shut. He kissed her again, tenderly, slowly, as if asking for permission…then, as her hand came up to the front of his shirt, he claimed her mouth completely, his tongue finding hers as her lips parted. Where his hand cradled her face, the touch turned from a caress to possession.

It had been far too long since a man kissed her like this. She'd kissed a few since she'd left Rock back in New York, but not even the darkly handsome Sarcaccian men she'd met during evenings spent dancing in the clubs near her apartment could compare. She and Rock had chemistry that could light an entire city.

It was a chemistry that could cause her to combust, to lose herself entirely.

She put a hand against the front of his shoulder at the same time he angled his mouth to deepen their kiss, sending a spiral of lust through her. Dangerous as he was, she didn't want to let go. When she did, it'd have to be for good, and everything in her wanted to savor this moment.

A growl of deep need came from the back of this throat as he nipped her lower lip, then eased back enough to whisper, "Warmer now?"

There wasn't a good answer to his question. A no could be taken as rejection. A yes and he might let her go and send her up to her apartment...and she didn't want to stop. Thankfully, he didn't wait for a response before burying both his hands in her wet, tangled hair and bringing her mouth to his. Desire heated her core, making her forget the chill of her skin. She shifted, wanting to be closer to him despite the gearshift blocking her path, and reached with her right hand to the warm, damp skin of his neck.

Within seconds, she felt sticky, thick fluid. He felt it, too, pulling away at the same time she did. Deep red blotches covered the top of his shirt, just below where she'd touched his neck, and a lighter slash of red went up the front of his shirt.

"Rock—"

"You're bleeding."

"I think you are." What had he done when he'd gone overboard after her? How hadn't she seen it until now?

He clasped her fingers and raised her arm to inspect the underside of her wrist. "No. You. You're cut."

She twisted her wrist for a look and realized he was right. "So I am." Now that she saw the narrow cut, she remembered grabbing for the railing as she pitched forward. She must've caught herself on one of the rail's bolts or on the side of the deck before she plunged into the water.

"That needs bandaging."

No kidding. She shifted to inspect the blanket that covered her seat. Sure enough, deep reddish brown streaks were evident where she'd cradled it. The stains dragged across her lap, too.

"Ugh!" She clamped her hand over the cut. "How did I not notice that?"

"I'd like to say it was my mesmerizing presence, but I suspect rain and the blanket kept the bleeding hidden until we got to the car."

"Where I'm now making a mess." She hoped she hadn't gotten any on the car seats. "I'm so sorry, Rock. I'm sure cold water will—"

"You have bandages in your apartment?"

"Of course." From kissing the man who'd starred in her late-night fantasies to a bloody mess in seconds. "Let me go take care of it. I'll clean your car when I'm done. Least I can do."

"Don't be ridiculous." He pocketed his keys and was out of his seat in one fluid motion. Before she could get her door open, he was around the car, opening it for her. "Hold the blanket against your wrist until we get inside."

Rain splashed the sidewalks and sluiced down his cheekbones as he held the car door. She wasn't going to make him stand there while she argued, so she grabbed the blanket and sprinted the ten steps necessary to reach the entry to her apartment building. He fished her tools from the trunk and then followed, reaching her just as she managed to unlock the door.

She exhaled as they stood in the narrow entry. Worn, carpeted steps led to the upper floors, where the building's apartment units were located. "Thank you. You can leave the tools here. I'll get them once I've bandaged this. And I'll get your blanket back to you next time I'm on the *Libertà*."

"I'll carry them up. And you can keep the blanket as long as you like." He nodded toward the staircase, urging her onward. The hard look in his eyes indicated that any argument from her would be futile.

Fine. So he'd see her apartment. She led the way, tucking the blanket under her arm and wrapping her hand around her bleeding wrist as she went. When she reached the apartment on the third floor, he took her key from her blue fingers and turned it in the lock so she wouldn't have to let go of her wrist. She thanked him, trying not to think of what he would see inside: mismatched, used furniture that she'd picked up at weekend antique markets and repaired herself, a women's health magazine folded open on the coffee table, a small television perched on a stand in the corner. The inexpensive, brightly-colored rug she'd found during a three-day weekend in Malta. Two empty coffee mugs, maybe more, littering the end tables. It was nothing like the swanky, polished *Libertà*, nor was it like the small-but-trendy apartments either of them had in New York. This was a low-key, comfortable place to crash at the end of the day, not much different than the apartment she'd had in college. It wasn't meant for entertaining.

Rock set the toolbox on the edge of the rug, then walked past her, glancing into the kitchen before heading for the arched doorway leading to her bedroom and bathroom. "Bandages in the bathroom, I assume?"

"Kitchen."

He spun back toward the kitchen without entering her bathroom. She sent a quick prayer of thanks heavenward—she was pretty sure she had bras hanging over the shower rod—then followed him into the kitchen.

"Where?" He flicked on the light.

She reached for one of the upper cabinets, but he waved off her attempt and opened it himself. "You keep pressure on that. It's decided to bleed but good."

Angling her gaze toward her wrist, she saw that he was right. Blood now appeared between the fingers of her left hand. "It looks worse than it feels."

He set a box of gauze and roll of first aid tape on the counter before washing his hands at the sink.

"Thank you, Rock, but I can take care of it. It's not that bad."

"I wouldn't be much of a chef if I didn't know how to deal with arm and hand injuries. Cuts, in particular." He grasped her elbow and guided her to the sink, where the light was brightest, then eased her hand away from her wrist for a look. Keeping the injury elevated to minimize blood flow, he gingerly probed the edges of the narrow gash. The lines at the edges of his eyes deepened as he focused on his task, while April concentrated on keeping her breathing even. Not only was Rock touching her, he was standing entirely too close for comfort. His skin radiated warmth as the moisture evaporated from his face and neck.

She wanted him to kiss her again, injury or not. At the same time, she didn't.

Put a lid on your hormones, April. This way there be dragons. It scared her silly how powerfully connected she felt to him. Five years hadn't dimmed their chemistry one iota.

"I don't think you need stitches," he said, leaning in even closer. "It's long, but not deep, and I don't see any foreign material embedded in there. I imagine you caught your arm on the side of the boat as you went over."

He wet a paper towel and blotted the edges of the cut, where the blood had dried, then swiped it lightly over the entire wound before applying pressure once more. Straightening and reaching past her to the cabinet, he retrieved a tube of antibiotic ointment, squeezed a line along the cut, then covered it once more, keeping on the pressure.

"Have you lived here the whole time you've been in Sarcaccia?"

She nodded. He was trying to distract her.

"Bakery downstairs looks good. Bet they do big business with the holiday."

"Armand's. Lines out the door, every time." Bread. Cookies. Cakes. That was what she'd think about. But thoughts of bakers led to thoughts of chefs. And of one chef in particular wearing his whites, which made his eyes appear bluer and his shoulders broader, if such a thing were possible.

April's mind locked on the image of Rock standing in the kitchen of his first restaurant, holding out a spoon, offering her a taste of his cranberry pecan sauce and asking if she thought it'd do well on the menu...then kissing her after she moaned and declared it the most decadent flavor combination she'd ever tasted.

She bit her lip at the memory.

Working quickly, Rock ripped open a gauze packet with his teeth, then swapped the gauze for the paper towel and taped it in place. "That should work. It's not too tight, is it?"

"It's fine. It's what I deserve for leaning over to see a silly heron."

Amusement lit his face as he released her wrist. "All these years handling dangerous tools and climbing ladders, and it's a heron that gets you."

"In front of an audience, no less."

It was impossible not to return his smile, though she wished she could do it with a few feet between them for comfort. Given that her back was to the counter, she had nowhere to move. In as formal a tone as she could muster, she said, "Thank you."

His smile faded and he took a step back. "I'll head to my apartment to clean up, then."

Her gaze went to the blood on the front of his shirt. Though the fabric was still soaking wet, the stains had turned a dark, muddy brown. Propriety made her want to offer to wash it, but that'd mean having him in her apartment, his torso bare. From what she could see where the thin material clung to him, he still had the best abs of any chef on the planet. Hell, he had better abs than most Marines fresh out of boot camp.

Seeing that finely-cut muscle would mean wanting to touch that finely-cut muscle. The last time she'd done that...well, the following morning had been the worst of her life.

"I'm sorry again about your shirt. And your car."

"No problem." His blue-green eyes scanned the kitchen, taking in every detail in a matter of seconds before his focus locked on her again. "And you don't need to clean my car. One thing you learn working in the restaurant business is how to get stains out of everything. A little cold water and dish detergent on a sponge is all it will take, assuming there's even any blood in the car. I suspect most of the mess is on the blanket."

The blanket that smelled so much like him. "I'll wash it and get it back to you."

"No rush."

"I'm planning to finish repairs on the *Libertà* tomorrow. It's not a problem to bring it with me."

"Whatever's easiest."

The air hung heavy between them, as if neither knew what to say or do next. Would he kiss her again before leaving? Or simply go?

A second kiss would have deeper meaning. Second kisses weren't spur of the moment decisions fueled by curiosity. A second kiss was a blatant acknowledgement of one's enjoyment of the first.

"You mentioned my nightstand earlier." His gaze dropped to her lips briefly before he arched one brow and grinned. "Was that your way of offering to make repairs in my cabin?"

"You did ask if I'd come on board to fix your creaky parts." She regretted the words the moment they were out of her mouth. Unlike the way he'd teased her in the yacht's galley, with assertive body language and a tone that kept her at arm's length, hearing the words leave her own lips in the narrow confines of her kitchen felt more intense.

And they'd shared a rather hot kiss since their galley banter.

"It's part of my job, remember?" She managed a light tone. "Routine maintenance. I'm supposed to keep my eyes open for anything that needs doing."

He considered her for a moment. Instead of responding, he moved past her to gather the first aid supplies, then placed them back in her cupboard before heading for the door. He gave her a long look over his shoulder. "See you tomorrow, April."

"See you tomorrow, Ryan."

She pressed a palm to her injured wrist and swore to herself as the door closed behind him.

CHAPTER 4

Rock swiped a hand over his chin as he pulled the Mercedes into the alley behind his apartment. Two simple syllables—his name, spoken in April's sultry voice—affected him as powerfully as her kiss.

And that kiss affected him plenty. He'd wanted to drop the gauze and tape and have his way with her right there in her kitchen, just as he once had in the back room of his first restaurant. Little wonder the first thing that'd popped into his head when she said she was supposed to keep her eyes out for anything that needed doing was to respond, "Right in front of you, sweetheart." It'd taken Herculean effort to keep the comment to himself.

Curses ricocheted through his head as he entered his apartment and stripped off his wet, bloodied shirt. What the hell was he thinking, getting involved with April again?

He'd had no choice but to go overboard after her. He'd have jumped for anyone. But seeing April in the front seat of his rented car with a damp shirt clinging to her curves and wet hair hanging in twists around the goosebump-covered skin of her neck and shoulders drove him to touch her. To breathe in the air surrounding her. Then to kiss her. It was an urge he should've resisted.

Sexual crack cocaine.

Even after five years, she held that fierce grip over him, luring him with nothing more than a thanks-for-the-ride and a sweep of her stormy, gray-blue eyes. He'd been entranced, his body overwhelmed by an intense craving to possess her.

And now, with that one hit, he teetered on the edge of addiction.

Why hadn't any of the women he'd dated during the intervening years affected him the way she did?

But he knew the answer. April was the most dependable, determined, and caring woman he'd ever met. Just as he'd been driven to make his restaurants succeed, to create the best possible experience for his customers, April had been driven to make her father's business succeed. Her passion for the history of Manhattan's prewar buildings inspired their owners to make responsible, sensitive improvements that respected the heritage of their properties while making the spaces livable for modern times. More than once, photographs of April's work graced the pages of *Architectural Digest* as examples of the proper preservation of historic homes. Homeowners felt that the designs fit their personalities and weren't simply connect-the-dots recreations of a bygone era.

He'd deeply admired her work ethic and the way she handled herself with humility as her company's reputation blossomed. Most of all, though, Rock admired the way April treasured her family. Not only did she share her father and brother's zeal for the family business, she valued them as people. Rock had only known April's father briefly, as the man slipped into the final throes of dementia, but knew from the light in April's eyes whenever she spoke of him that she'd loved him fiercely. Then, during the weeks before April decided to leave for Sarcaccia, he witnessed the care she gave to her mother, who was hospitalized with late-stage breast cancer that had spread to her lungs and bones. April sat at her mother's side for hours on end, reading romance novels and comedic nonfiction aloud between checking with doctors to ensure that her mom was in as little pain as possible. April kept her mother's spirits high, ensuring the woman's final days contained as much joy and laughter as possible.

And April had done it despite her own breaking heart.

She was the most resilient woman Rock knew. One evening, as he'd watched April sort through her mother's insurance paperwork after a long day spent at the hospital, a pencil wedged behind her ear and a coffee mug and calculator at her elbow, he'd decided there wasn't another woman on Earth he'd rather marry. He'd made love to her late into the night, hoping to offer April a sliver of the comfort she gave others, and resolved to propose to her once she'd gotten through her family crisis.

Come to think of it, that'd been the week before Christmas, too. As he'd cradled her against his chest afterward, smoothing his hand over her soft hair, they'd heard holiday music echoing up from the apartment below his.

"Damn it all," Rock ground out as he tossed his soggy shirt aside, then made quick work of his pants. He couldn't afford this. Not now. No matter how much he wanted her. No matter how much he'd *once* wanted her. She'd hurt him before and—judging from the mix of apprehension and sexual tension zinging between the two of them this afternoon—she'd do it again. She'd spent the entire time he was bandaging her wrist fighting the attraction she felt for him. He'd heard it in the way she tried to control her breathing when he touched her, saw it in the soft parting of her lips when she looked at him, followed by the determined line of her mouth when she realized that she'd been staring.

If he wanted to get the palace job, the distraction that was April Dietrich would not do.

"Some women are not meant for you, buddy." No matter how perfect. If he said it aloud, maybe he'd convince himself. Despite the heat of their kiss, April didn't want him. Not for the long haul.

As he gathered his sodden clothing and flung it into the apartment's tiny washing machine, another thought occurred to him.

April was completely alone.

She might live in a lively district filled with restaurants, nightclubs, and a vibrant arts scene, but her apartment was a one-bedroom, which meant no roommate. Nor was there a sign of any male presence. In the lightning-fast glimpse he'd had of the bathroom, he'd noticed a single towel on the rack and a slew of women's lingerie hanging over the shower rod. The April he'd once known would've wanted a roommate, as she'd always enjoyed having one in New York. That April also would've chosen to live in the quiet neighborhood nearest the palace, in one of Cateri's medieval buildings, because it was both convenient to work and boasted great architecture.

It was as if she'd decided to surround herself with as many people as possible when she made the move to Sarcaccia, but to keep them at arm's length. The fact there wasn't a man in her life also had to be a conscious choice. After spending a few months living alongside Sarcaccians, Rock had learned a few things about them: they prized family and friendships, they socialized as if it were an Olympic sport, and they relished every opportunity to play matchmaker. Staying single here took effort.

Rock punched the buttons on the washing machine and headed for the shower. There'd been a sea change within April in the time since their relationship ended. Or maybe, just maybe, that change was the reason their relationship ended. And the reason she wasn't in a relationship now.

As the hot water pelted his scalp, he resolved to figure out what changed April and why. One thing he knew for certain: he damned well wasn't going to settle for the status quo, where he could see her, but couldn't have her.

APRIL SLIPPED onto the *Libertà* just before noon. She'd hoped to arrive earlier, but a call from Umberto, the guard who kept watch outside King Carlo and Queen Fabrizia's private palace apartment, had her replacing a split hallway baseboard before she could make it to the yacht.

"I'm sorry to do this to you on Christmas Eve," Umberto had said when April arrived outside the heavily guarded section of the palace.

"I'm sure you have plans, but with so many guests expected for the holidays, I thought it best to let you know right away. The Queen notices these things and assumes her guests will, too."

April hadn't bothered to tell Umberto that she had no plans outside work. Nor had she pointed out that Umberto, too, was at his post on Christmas Eve. Instead, she'd pried off the damaged baseboard and quickly measured and cut a new one, counting the minutes until she could get to the *Libertà*...and then get off the *Libertà*.

April had just finished painting the new baseboard and marking off a protective perimeter when she heard a familiar voice raised in welcome.

"What are you doing here?" April had asked after exchanging greetings with Kelly Chase, the American who'd been hired to redesign and organize Prince Massimo's closet a few months earlier. Kelly had steered April to a hallway bench beside a gigantic Christmas tree decorated with white lights and an angel theme as April said, "Not that I'm not happy to see you, but I thought you were back in Texas."

April and Kelly had gotten to know each other when April installed the custom cabinetry for Massimo's new closet. April admired Kelly's eye for design, while Kelly'd been thrilled with April's expertise when it came to the palace's centuries-old architecture.

"At the moment, I'm going to see Queen Fabrizia. She wants to introduce me to a cousin of hers who's visiting this morning and does a lot of work with small businesses. But long term, I'm looking into the requirements for starting a full-time business here in Sarcaccia. I've been approached by a few of the Barrali family's acquaintances about closet design and think I can make a go of it using the money from the design business I sold back in Texas."

"You're staying here permanently? That's great news."

"I think so, too. I've been meaning to give you a call to see if you'd like to grab dinner one night. After the holidays sound good?"

"I'd love to. Where are you living?" Prince Massimo had given Kelly a palace room while she'd worked on his closet, but starting a new business meant that Kelly must've found a longer-term accommodation. If it was anywhere near April's, April could give her the lay of the land.

Kelly's happy response lit her entire face. "Princess Sophia liked what I did for Massimo and asked me to take a look at her closet. It's a far bigger job than Massimo's was, so for the time being, I'm still here."

April had started to congratulate Kelly on the new gig, but the odd flush creeping across Kelly's face made the real reason for her stay apparent…and it wasn't Princess Sophia.

April's jaw went slack as a smile danced around the edges of Kelly's lips. After she glanced around to ensure they were out of Umberto's hearing, April had whispered, "Something happened between you and Prince Massimo, didn't it?"

"I designed a closet for him and am now working for Sophia." A twinkle brightened her almond-shaped brown eyes. "Nothing more. Officially."

"Then I'll officially keep it to myself," April had promised before squeezing Kelly's hand. Massimo was an enigma, but Kelly had obviously managed to get past the handsome royal's stoic exterior. "I'm thrilled for you."

"Thank you. It's been hard to keep quiet, even though I don't have anyone here in Sarcaccia to tell. I'm just so…so *happy*." Kelly had exhaled before adding, "You know I'm going to need your help on Sophia's closet, right? It's gigantic and she wants a complete overhaul."

"All new cabinetry?"

"You've got it. Custom drawer inserts, moveable shelving, you name it."

"Consider it done." Bright sunshine angling through the palace's windows had reminded her of the time. "I hate to gossip and run, but I'm on the clock. Have a wonderful Christmas, Kelly."

"You, too." As they'd stood, Kelly asked, "Did your family fly in from New York? Or do you have plans with friends tomorrow?"

Usually answers to personal questions like Kelly's rolled right off

April's tongue, but today she'd found herself forcing a chipper response. "Neither. I have the day off and plan to spend it snoozing and eating ice cream in front of a TV movie. The sappier, the better."

Kelly's expression had fallen. "Please tell me you're kidding. Alone on Christmas? That's awful! No family coming in to visit? No church services or Christmas dinner with friends?"

"I'm far from alone, as I happen to count two guys named Ben and Jerry, who spend a great deal of time in my kitchen." She'd shrugged and forced a grin. "However, I plan to ignore them both for some local gelato. I picked up some freshly made pistachio from the gelateria on my block last night and it's stashed in my freezer, waiting for me."

Kelly's hands had gone to her hips. "That's just wrong. If you'd like, I'm sure—"

"No, no, no." She couldn't imagine anything more awkward than intruding on Kelly's Christmas with Prince Massimo. "It's generous of you to suggest it, but I'm more than happy with the plans I have. I never get the opportunity to be lazy. It's a Christmas gift to myself."

Kelly's brow had wrinkled in skepticism. "All right. I'll take your word for it, though I don't understand it. Have a Merry Christmas, April."

"I'll be humming Christmas music while I watch a quality chick flick," she'd promised.

Though in reality, April now hummed along with the *Libertà's* sound system while she knelt to install the hinge that'd arrived that morning, compliments of the yacht's builder. It was amazing what the Barrali name could do when one wanted an order rushed.

As the final strains of 'Winter Wonderland' faded and 'God Rest Ye Merry Gentlemen' began, April rose to test the cabinet door. Prince Bruno's party was scheduled to start in another hour, which meant Rock and Andreas would enter the salon any minute to set up for hors d'oeuvres. She didn't want to be around when they did.

If anything could make her feel lonelier than her quick chat with Umberto or her longer one with Kelly, both of whom seemed to expect she had Christmas plans with loved ones, it was facing Rock while surrounded by festive decorations and listening to holiday music.

She growled as she leveled the door. She hadn't felt lonely since she'd arrived in Sarcaccia. Her apartment was located in a busy area with tons of nightlife, and she'd taken full advantage of it, getting to know the local business owners, the bar owners and their patrons, and even a few regulars at the dance clubs. She didn't know any of them outside their clubs, but it was enough. She had company when she wanted it, and when she didn't…well, maybe she did feel lonely occasionally, but that was the price she'd paid for taking the palace job. She'd chosen this path, and it'd been the right choice. Here in Sarcaccia, she had the opportunity to work on major restoration projects in a centuries-old palace, and kept her skills sharp by handling routine maintenance every so often. She was valued. She couldn't complain about that.

The cabinet door swung noiselessly, fitting precisely in line with the rest of the doors. She gave it a quick swipe with a clean dust rag and gathered her gear. She'd disappear to the crew deck, fix up Rock's room, then head home. And damn if she wouldn't relish that pint of gelato. Maybe she'd stop and pick up a good bottle of Famiglia Barrali Cabernet on the way home for good measure.

"Looks good from this angle," a flirtatious, Sarcaccian-accented male voice came from the direction of the rear deck.

April turned to smile at Prince Bruno as he entered the salon. Though the youngest of the Barrali clan and still a university student, the prince carried himself with all the confidence of his older siblings. On the other hand, he was the most relaxed of the royals when it came to the staff, frequently treating palace employees as he would any of his friends…at least when his parents weren't around.

"Your Highness, you look well. You also have good timing. I just finished, so I'll be out of your way."

"No need to rush off. I don't expect my friends for another hour, and even then, they aren't exactly a prompt group." He strode to the salon's bar and inspected the glassware before lifting a decanter containing clear liquid and tilting it in her direction. "You're welcome to join me for a quick drink. Maybe update me on palace gossip so I know what to expect before I see my parents at dinner tonight."

She couldn't help but grin. "I appreciate the offer, but you know I can't."

"Can't? Or won't?"

"First of all, I'm working. No alcohol until all the tools are away for the day. Second—"

"Oh, c'mon, April—"

Bruno was as wily as his siblings when it came to getting what he wanted. No amount of coercion was beyond him. "Second," she repeated, "I suspect you know all the gossip already."

"I know what my family tells me when I get home from school, which is limited to what they want me to know or what I read in the tabloids. That's not the real dirt."

"And third," she raised her voice slightly, using her ten year age advantage for what little leverage she could, "you know the quickest way for me to get in trouble with your parents is to gossip with you. Besides, what could I possibly know?"

That brought a flicker of amusement to the prince's eyes. "Oh, let's see. How about the story behind Massimo and his closet designer? Or what the staff might be saying about the fact Alessandro has been away for months and no one seems to know where he's traveling?"

"I have no idea—"

"Or about Stefano and his new fiancée? Or the fact my mother seems to worry about me more than ever, despite the fact I got the highest marks in both my Immunology and Neurology clinics last term?"

April leapt on the opportunity to shift the discussion. "You're sticking with your plan to become a doctor?"

"Believe it or not, I am." Prince Bruno couldn't keep the pride from his expression as he selected a glass and poured a healthy serving of liquor from the decanter. "Medicine is far more interesting than politics. Besides, I can't trail along behind my family at state functions forever, particularly once my dear brother Vittorio inherits the throne. Now, on the topic of my family…?" He raised a brow in question as he lifted a second glass in his right hand, using his left to gesture toward one of the salon's soft blue sofas.

She couldn't help but yield to Prince Bruno's affable invitation. "Okay, fine. No drink for me, but in the spirit of Christmas, I'll gift you with a bit of gossip." It would be highly edited gossip, but enough to make the young prince happy.

For the next ten minutes, April answered his questions about his siblings, the staff, and even about renovations planned for the palace, though she was careful to ensure her answers were what she'd say even if Queen Fabrizia were sitting beside her.

"I heard Dominic might be leaving," Bruno said once discussion turned to the palace kitchen. "Is that true?"

"That's the rumor. I imagine he'd like to be closer to his children now that they're working in London." She sighed, trying not to envision Rock in Dominic's place. "If Dominic does go, I'd miss him terribly."

"So would I." Bruno rolled his drink between his palms as a wistful smile lifted the edges of his mouth. "You know, he used to sneak cookies into the nursery for me when I was a kid. Told me it was our little secret and not to tell my siblings."

April grinned. She'd heard the same thing from both Prince Massimo and Prince Stefano. She imagined Dominic had done it for all the Barrali children, making each of them feel special.

"If Dominic's really going, I assume my mother is already on the hunt for a replacement," Bruno said. "I saw Sophia when I arrived this morning and she said it might be the new chef here on the *Libertà*. Rock, isn't that his name? I spoke with him on the phone when I was planning this afternoon's get-together. What's the scoop on him?"

"That's probably a question to ask your mother at dinner tonight." As if on cue, voices rose from the direction of the dining room and galley. One in particular sent April's pulse skittering. She rose from the sofa and gave Bruno what she hoped was an optimistic smile. "Of course, you could always give her your opinion after your party. It sounds as if the chef is heading this way."

Bruno flicked his wrist to free his watch from his shirt sleeve. "Right on schedule with the appetizers. I like him already. I imagine the bartender will arrive at any moment, as well."

He stood and, as Umberto and Kelly had before, wished April a Merry Christmas and asked if she had plans. She managed a generic answer about anticipating a perfect day, then grabbed her toolbox and Rock's blanket. She barely made it out of the salon before she heard Rock's resonant voice behind her, introducing himself to Prince Bruno and asking if all was to his satisfaction.

Against her will, tears sprung to her eyes. How, after five years, could simply hearing Rock's voice make her so emotional?

It had to be the Christmas decorations, like the gorgeous tree that occupied one end of the salon and had her breathing in the scent of pine needles the entire time she'd worked on the hinge. Or the music she continued to hear over the sound system as she made her way down the outside stairs toward the crew quarters.

The fact every single person she ran into today wanted to wish her a Merry Christmas and ask how she planned to spend her holiday.

She slammed through the empty crew hall until she reached Rock's quarters. After knocking—though she knew no one was there —she entered and made a beeline for his nightstand. She tightened the bolts anchoring it to the wall, closing her mind to the scent of the crisp sheets, the ticking of his old-fashioned alarm clock, and the image of Rock lying prone in the bed, his torso bare as he snoozed with one arm tucked behind his head.

How he slept comfortably like that, she never knew.

She pushed on the top of the nightstand, ensuring it was tight to the wall, then moved to the opposite side of his bed to fix the built-in drawer.

Stop thinking, April. If she didn't, before long she'd let herself trip down memory lane, imagining how she'd teased him about his model-perfect sleeping posture, saying it was a wonder his arm and hand hadn't gone numb. How he'd merely grinned in response before showing her exactly how much feeling he had in those fingertips.

She opened the drawer to see two neatly stacked white chef's coats, each with the royal family's coat of arms discreetly embroidered on one side of the chest above Rock's name. Beside them were two folded pairs of black chef's slacks. The man was perfect in every way, even in the manner he organized his clothing.

Forcing herself to sing along with 'Jingle Bell Rock' as a distraction, she set the uniforms on top of the bed and removed the drawer, locating an errant drawer guide and repairing it before replacing the entire unit. Once she ensured that it slid freely, she returned the uniforms to their previous spot and placed the borrowed blanket beside them.

"Done." She closed the drawer and used the bed to pull herself to standing. The effort left wrinkles in the pristine linens. Out of habit she smoothed everything back into place, then realized what she was doing and yanked her hands away.

Rock's bed. Rock's room.

A bell tolled, then the sultry tones of Aaron Neville singing 'Please Come Home for Christmas' flowed through the speakers. It was as if the sound wanted to wrap itself around her, give her a hug, and remind her of the togetherness that went hand-in-hand with the season.

"Oh, for crying out loud," she muttered. The music was nothing more than a random track on Marco's holiday playlist, but could the selection be any worse? It was her all-time favorite Christmas song, and it had been her mother's, too. A wave of remorse hit April as powerfully as if she'd lost her mother a week ago, rather than five years ago. Tears clouded her vision. She squeezed her eyes shut and pressed her fingers to her lids. The universe was conspiring against her today.

She took a deep breath, then grabbed her sunglasses from the top drawer of her toolbox and pushed them up the bridge of her nose before making her way to the ramp. In stark contrast to yesterday's freak rainstorm, late afternoon sunshine glimmered off the waves and the freshly hosed-down dock while the brisk scent of the Mediterranean enveloped her. Behind April, in the yacht's salon, the party sounded as if it was in full swing. Aaron Neville's resonant voice faded, replaced by the opening notes of 'You're a Mean One, Mr. Grinch.' She left the yacht with the sound of male laughter and boisterous singing in her ears.

Uplifting and celebratory though the atmosphere might be, April refused to look back.

CHAPTER 5

APRIL STARED at her apartment ceiling. She wouldn't bet her life savings on it, but the corners of the room appeared to be moving. She squinted, then tilted her head for a better look. Yes, yes they were. It was as if the entire room transformed into a spinning top and she'd become its wobbly center.

"Should be more fun than this," she murmured to the walls. "Like a merry-go-round."

It'd been years since she'd treated herself to more than one glass of wine, and tonight she'd had two. It was official: she'd become a lightweight. Wrenching herself into a seated position on the sofa, she grumbled at the half-empty wine bottle she'd left on the coffee table beside the remote control. After arriving home from the *Libertà*, she'd skipped the gelato and gone straight for the wine. She couldn't remember eating dinner before she'd curled up on the sofa for a nap, yet she had the odd sensation of having eaten.

Then she remembered. When she arrived home, she'd run into her landlord Armand, the baker downstairs. He'd handed her a traditional Sarcaccian Christmas loaf as a gift and encouraged her to share it with her family. The rich, nutty concoction was like pecan pie on steroids. Three or four bites constituted sugar overkill. A full slice could put a woman in the hospital. Crabby from her afternoon on the yacht, April had indulged in a slice and a half. Without a plate.

Cupping her hand in front of her mouth, she blew out a breath then nearly gagged. Sarcaccian Christmas loaf and wine didn't make a good combination, particularly when followed by a nap on the sofa.

She made her way to the bathroom and brushed her teeth, which was enough to chase away her dizziness, and if the mirror was to be believed, she looked perfectly normal. A quick check of the bathroom's wall clock indicated it was nearly seven p.m. Maybe one of the convenience stores nearby was still open. It was a long shot, given the holiday, but it'd do her good to walk downstairs and investigate. At worst, they'd be closed and she'd walk home. At best, she'd get a veggie sandwich and a bottle of water to balance out the sugar in her system. Then she could find something on television besides Christmas Eve services or a Christmas-themed movie.

Mission set, she dropped her toothbrush back into its cup.

Never had she suffered this odd, stomach-dropping sensation of loneliness, even during the holidays. Sure, she'd missed her parents after they passed away, and she missed her brother whenever palace staff members talked about their own families, but never had she felt as wretched—and as guilty—as she did today. And never had she thrown herself a pity party like she had this afternoon.

"It's Rock. That's all," she said to herself as she smoothed her hair into place, then went in search of her handbag. After five years of living independently, of making herself invaluable to the royal family, seeing Rock again brought up every horrid thought she'd ever had about herself. At the same time, it made her realize that she missed him terribly. It wasn't his kiss alone, though that had turned her inside out. It was his devil-may-care smile, the one that hid a huge, protective heart. It made her wish he were here now, despite the fact he threatened her carefully constructed new life.

April wrapped the Christmas loaf and shoved it to the recesses of her fridge, slamming the door on the loaf and the rotten day. "Time to pull yourself up by the bootstraps, Dietrich. Pity party's over."

She grabbed her handbag, shoved her feet into a pair of sneakers without untying them, then opened the door…and started when she saw a man on the landing, a man so broad he filled the entire space. He sported chef's slacks, but his usual chef's jacket was gone, leaving only the fitted black T-shirt he liked to wear underneath. He held a large paper bag that, judging from the mouthwatering smell filling the stairwell, contained leftovers from Prince Bruno's Christmas Eve party.

"Rock. What are you doing here?" It came out in a breathless rush brought on by the fearful leap her heart took in the split second before she realized who was in front of her. "How'd you get in?"

"The baker downstairs was locking up for the evening and let me into the stairwell when I introduced myself."

Impossible. She crossed her arms over her chest. "He'd never let a stranger into the building."

A roguish grin slid across Rock's face. "I showed him what was in the bag. His approval came pretty fast when I told him I made it myself."

Now that she believed. Of all the people she knew, it was Armand who'd appreciate Rock's culinary skills and would view him as a kindred spirit. "That's evil."

"That's effective," he corrected. "Nothing wrong with using the tools in my arsenal to get what I want."

"Which is?"

He held up the paper bag in his hand. "To ensure you're fed on Christmas Eve."

"You brought food…for me?" She blinked, caught off guard. She couldn't imagine what might've brought Rock to her doorstep on Christmas Eve, but a spontaneous offering of food wouldn't have been her first guess. Maybe back when they were dating, but now? She frowned at him. "What makes you think I'm not being fed already?"

"Let's call it a hunch." He cocked his head and glanced behind her. "I don't smell anything cooking. Do you have other plans?"

"It's Christmas Eve. Doesn't everyone have plans?"

His gaze slid over her casual clothes and sneakers. It was obvious she wasn't going to church services or any sort of gathering.

Busted. "Fine. If you must know, I was going to see if I could scrounge a convenience store sandwich."

"They're closed, and this is better." He raised the bag.

She allowed her purse to slide from her shoulder as she stepped back into her apartment and waved him inside. They both knew she'd lost the battle of wills, but she couldn't help shooting him a look that said, *Evil.*

His returning smirk said, *Effective.*

He blew by her, leaving a trail of garlic, warm bread, and the scent she thought of as his in his wake, and entered the kitchen. After setting the paper bag on the counter, he withdrew several plastic containers. Satisfaction radiated from him as he looked them over, folded the paper bag, and tucked it under his arm. Striding to the door, he surprised her again by wishing her a good night.

"Good night? You're not staying?"

He shrugged as he grabbed the handle. "I ate already."

"Oh." Her disappointment over his departure so shocked her that she allowed it to show in her voice. In a lame attempt to cover, she added, "I'm sure I'll enjoy it. Thank you."

He had the door open and one foot in the hall when he turned to face her. The edges of his eyes crinkled into a smile. "Let me guess. No plans for tomorrow, either?"

"I have plans." Watching TV. Reading. Sleeping. Actively choosing not to pout.

"Television?"

"You suck."

His eyebrows shot up and a sparkle lit his sharp blue eyes. "Well, if you were to ask nicely, I just might—"

"I'm not." He crossed his arms as he waited for her to answer his sexual innuendo with one of her own, but she went the safer route and said, "But in answer to your question, I freely admit that I'm planning on a television binge. I never get the chance. What about you?"

"Work."

"On Christmas?" A squeak of surprise edged her voice. The Barralis made it a point to give the staff the day off each year. Only those essential for security ever worked on Christmas, and they were paid handsomely for the sacrifice of family time. "Even Dominic isn't working tomorrow."

"My choice. Beats a TV marathon." She was about to make a smart remark when he added, "Join me on the yacht. You can be my assistant."

She paused, truly befuddled. As if showing up on her doorstep with dinner or kissing her yesterday wasn't enough to make her head spin. Before she could ask what he meant by "assistant," he said, "Ten a.m. Wear comfortable clothes and shoes. And don't be late."

He was gone before she could say no, his steps echoing as he thumped down the stairwell. She waited for the door on the ground floor to open, but before it did, she heard him call up, "There's nothing on TV tomorrow and you know it, so don't be a chicken."

ROCK GLANCED at the Roman numerals on the large black and white clock mounted at one end of the yacht's working galley. Quarter past ten. It wasn't like April to be late. To her, being on time meant arriving at least five minutes early.

It had to be because he'd told her *not* to be late. Stubborn woman.

He placed a large cucumber on the cutting board, sliced off the ends, then diced it. Another glance at the clock. Quarter past ten and thirty seconds.

After using a knife to scrape the cubes into a stainless steel bowl, he set a second clean cucumber on the board. Anyone watching him would think it was a routine day, but the churning in his gut said otherwise. Inviting April to the royal yacht on Christmas with the promise of kitchen work—then calling her a chicken on top of it—had been a risk. Knowing April, she'd likely stayed at her apartment out of spite.

"Don't call me a chicken again."

Adrenaline shot through Rock at the unexpected sound. He'd forgotten how silently April moved. The sumptuous carpets of the salon and dining room and the well-oiled hinges on the door connecting the family galley to the main galley worked in her favor. It was a miracle he hadn't jumped out of his skin…which had likely been her intent, just to get back at him. Without turning around, he sliced the ends off the second cucumber and began dicing. Matching her firm tone, he replied, "You're late. Nevertheless, I'll refrain from calling you a chicken if you'd be so kind as to slice those tomatoes. Rounds, not wedges."

Despite the thudding of his heart, he kept a steady pace with his knife while he waited for her response. She took a few steps closer, then filched a piece of cucumber and popped it in her mouth as she inspected the contents of the countertops. While she was distracted, he stole a sideways look at her. As he'd instructed, she'd dressed comfortably, wearing a pair of curve-hugging jeans and a relaxed black T-shirt, one old and worn enough that it'd faded to ash. Her hair was loosely pinned at her nape and she wore no makeup, yet she glowed with health.

Five years of island living had made her even sexier than she'd been back in New York. Instinct made him want to unpin that hair and have his way with her, right here in the galley. See how her pink-tinged cheeks and lips felt beneath his own. Explore her smooth skin, investigate every nook and cranny of her sumptuous body. But he'd called her here to play for all the marbles, not for a single afternoon of delight, and to do that he needed to tread lightly and stick to his plan.

"You're actually working on Christmas? And you expect me to help?"

"Yes and yes. I'm giving the New Year's Eve menu a trial run before the big event and Andreas isn't here to assist." Rock dared another sidelong glance. "Nor is he here to sample the finished product. Would you be willing to do that, too?"

From the moment he'd left her apartment after their kiss, he'd thought of little else besides how to win April back. How to win her trust. He knew no better way to April's heart than with food and caring. He'd given her a taste of the food last night when he'd stopped by…then left instead of sharing the meal, hoping to tempt her into the caring part of the equation today.

He wasn't lying when he told her he planned to use every tool in his arsenal to get what he wanted. More than anything, he wanted April to believe that he'd cherish her, respect her, and protect her… and that it was all right for her to allow him to do it.

"The food better be good." She crossed the galley to pull a clean apron from one of the hooks at the far end. "I'm giving up a *Star Trek: Voyager* marathon to do this."

"*Star Trek* on Christmas? Space battles don't strike me as keeping with the holiday spirit."

"Nothing more heartwarming than watching Captain Janeway fight to return her crew to their loved ones after Voyager is stranded a zillion light years from home." She gestured to the ingredients spread across the countertops before she began halving the tomatoes. "This looks pretty light for a New Year's Eve celebration. I expected massive hunks of meat or fish. Was this Queen Fabrizia's request?"

He shook his head. While Fabrizia was known for her health-conscious lifestyle, she'd left the menu to Rock's discretion, urging him to be creative. He imagined she wanted to see how well he could tailor a meal to an occasion before making her final hiring decision. "Everyone will have had a week of heavy food by the time they arrive. Christmas dinners, desserts, and that horrifying Sarcaccian Christmas loaf—Armand mentioned he'd given you one, so you're aware of how sweet and dense that stuff is—"

"Well aware."

The amusement in her tone made him grin. Slowly but surely, she was starting to relax. "My point is that people usually crave lighter meals by New Year's Eve. The choices I've made should pair well with the wine and champagne and add to the atmosphere created by the fireworks and the moonlight over the Mediterranean. I'm going for refreshing. New year, new beginnings." He slid the rest of the cucumbers from the cutting board into the bowl. "Right now we're making a crab, cucumber, and tomato bruschetta as an appetizer. We'll use a hint of lemon for flavor, but that's it. Very simple."

April shot him a quick look as she continued slicing the tomatoes. "Nothing you make is simple. I've seen you use ingredients I've never even heard of to create dishes I couldn't make in a million years."

She meant it as a compliment, which warmed him. "On occasion, maybe. But in this case, going overboard with strong flavors would ruin the emotions I want the food to evoke. And given the nature of the party, I decided it's best to avoid garlic, onion, or anything that can give guests bad breath." He walked behind her to retrieve the crab from the walk-in refrigerator, pausing long enough to lean in and whisper, "Lots of kissing at midnight, you know."

Her breath hitched, letting him know his comment had its intended effect. What he hadn't counted on was her effect on him. The hint of her shampoo, the glimpse of the bare skin on her neck where she'd tucked her hair out of the way for cooking, the stray blonde wisp that curled down to the top of her faded T-shirt...everything he caught in that quick moment as he uttered the words "kissing at midnight" made him crave her, so much so the chill of the refrigerator didn't chase it away.

"That's why you'll be offered the job, you know," she said when he returned.

"Kissing at midnight?"

April gave an exaggerated eye roll. "It's because you think of those details when planning an event. It's not simply about the food, but about the greater experience."

"I'm trained to make magic in the kitchen. It's no different than the way you make magic in closets or bedrooms."

"More sexual innuendo, Mr. Fournier? How gauche."

"Not at all. But on the topic of bedrooms—"

"We weren't."

"Thank you for fixing the nightstand and drawer in my crew quarters. I thought I heard you talking to Prince Bruno yesterday, but by the time I came out to the salon you were gone. Didn't realize you'd left to fix my creaky parts."

"We're back to that?" She shook her head as she lined up another tomato and slid the knife through its thin skin.

"*That* was a genuine thank you."

"In that case, you're genuinely welcome."

He smiled to himself at their truce as he ran the crab, lemon, and a tablespoon of dressing he'd prepared earlier through a food processor, finishing just as April completed the tomatoes. He showed her where to find the bruschetta, then demonstrated how to squeeze the crab mixture from a pastry bag and assemble the appetizers.

Skepticism laced her gray-blue eyes as she studied the arrangement of cucumber, tomato, and crab atop the miniature toast pieces. "You trust me to get this right?"

A note in her voice made him realize her self-doubt went beyond the appetizers. He put a hand on her lower back for a heartbeat and smiled. "It's construction. You're more the expert in that area than I am."

Uncertainty clouded her gaze, but she gamely filled the pastry bag with the crab mixture and got to work.

"So what else is on the menu?"

"For appetizers, grilled prawns with tzatziki dip and some fruit skewers."

She glanced at him through her lashes. "No way am I grilling prawns."

"I'll do that in a minute. Hot appetizers are last. I'm making the dip now, then you and I can work together on the skewers."

"All right. Then what?"

"Then we eat. Once we're happy with the appetizers, we move on to dinner and dessert."

One of April's tomatoes fell off a bruschetta and hit the floor, which drew a groan from her. "You should've called Andreas."

"His parents are visiting from Germany. Besides, you're the more attractive dining companion."

"I don't know. He's a good-looking guy."

"Trust me on that assessment."

She shrugged, saying nothing. They worked side by side for the next hour. With each passing minute, Rock felt April growing more comfortable in his presence. Once she mastered the bruschetta, he showed her the best way to prepare the skewers. He didn't miss her secret look of pride when she crafted a perfect line of honeydew, watermelon, feta, and mint, then drizzled it with honey in a design identical to his sample piece. When it was finally time to eat, they ditched their aprons and carried two plates filled with appetizers to the coffee table in the salon. Christmas decorations from Bruno's party lent the room a festive air, and the ornament-laden tree in the corner gave off the scent of freshly-cut pine. April trailed her fingertips over the soft needles while Rock went to the bar to retrieve a bottle of the wine he'd selected for the party.

"I know you're normally a red wine girl, but I think you'll like this," Rock said as he located a corkscrew behind the bar and opened the bottle of white. "It's a blend that's light and crisp. Tell me what you think of it with the appetizers."

She turned away from the tree and arched a brow. "Wine before noon?"

"Five minutes to noon. But for purposes of our taste testing, we'll pretend it's dinnertime on New Year's Eve instead of Christmas morning." He filled her glass, then his, before crossing the room to deposit the wine on the coffee table. With a click of a remote control, they were surrounded by the sound of lively, romantic guitar music playing a traditional Sarcaccian rhythm.

April took a seat on one of the room's plush, silver-blue sofas. "This is perfect. I'm burned out on 'Jingle Bells' anyway."

He took the cushion beside hers and raised his glass. "To new beginnings."

April clinked her glass against his. "New beginnings."

CHAPTER 6

April sank into the sofa cushions in a state of bliss. How could she forget Rock's amazing taste in wines? The liquid was so magical as it danced across her tongue she could almost forget the gravity of his chosen toast. She had no illusions that it had little to do with the date on the calendar and everything to do with the two of them.

"The question is whether the Barrali family's guests will like it. Remember, these are people who can afford any wine on the planet. And, like you, most will be red wine aficionados, so the bar is set high."

"It's exactly the way you described it. Light, crisp, refreshing…but it's not at all boring. There's a decadent note to it that makes me feel spoiled. I don't see how they wouldn't like it."

"Good. Now let's see how it tastes with the food." Rock's voice flowed over April like a warm breeze after a cold snap, draining the tension from every muscle in her body. Or maybe it was the second huge gulp of wine she'd taken. Whatever the cause, she refused to question it.

"The appetizers will be passed on trays," he explained. "Take whatever appeals to you first, since that's what the guests will do, but try them all. Let me know what you think of each of them. Any flavors that are too harsh, anything that doesn't sit well with the wine, whatever comes to mind as you sample. This is the day to make any tweaks."

"You expect me to work instead of kicking back and enjoying?"

"If we've done this right, you can do both."

She grinned and reached for one of the prawns Rock had grilled while she'd finished assembling the fruit skewers. "I suppose it beats staying home and eating Christmas loaf."

When she'd finally jumped in her car to drive to the dock this morning, she wasn't sure she'd made the right decision. He'd baited her by calling her a chicken, and she refused to be baited. But curiosity had gotten the better of her. What compelled him to work on Christmas Day? Why had he gone out of his way to bring her food to entice her to join him? It had to be personal rather than professional, especially given the fire of the kiss they'd shared and the intensity of those moments in her kitchen while he'd bandaged her wrist afterward.

Yet from the moment she'd arrived on board, he'd been serious about the cooking.

It wasn't at all what she'd expected of the morning—not that she knew what to expect—but she had to admit, making the appetizers had been fun. It had given her the opportunity to pour herself into an unfamiliar task. She'd also had the chance to study him when his back was turned. Rather than his usual chef's uniform, today he wore jeans, casual loafers, and a light blue T-shirt that emphasized the strong muscles of his back and shoulders. An apron protected his clothing, but didn't look at all feminine on him. If anything, it made him appear sexier than his white jacket did and lent the galley a relaxed atmosphere.

As she'd worked on the skewers, she'd decided that perhaps—perhaps—she'd grown enough during her years in Sarcaccia to trust herself around Rock. If he took the job, it might not upend her life the way she'd assumed it would when she'd first seen him carrying the case of champagne into the galley.

She swirled the prawn in the tzatziki dip and took a bite while Rock sampled one of the fruit skewers. The distinct flavor of the grilled seafood burst across her tongue, then was mellowed by the tzatziki.

"This is like the best sex ever." The words popped out of her mouth before she could engage her brain.

"In that case, I'm glad to share it with you." Laughter made his eyes crinkle as he watched her eat. "Why don't you tell me what you really think?"

She shook her head. She didn't want to talk. She wanted to indulge. The leftovers Rock brought her from last night's party were divine. This, on the other hand, was possibly the most delicious bite of food she'd ever had the pleasure of introducing to her taste buds. She finished the giant prawn in another two bites, sighing as she chewed.

"Pairs well with the wine?"

"Mmmm…"

"Can you tell the tzatziki is missing the usual garlic?"

"Didn't notice."

"Think it can be eaten by a woman in a cocktail dress without too much mess?"

"They won't care about their clothing once they've tasted this. But yes."

After she finished the prawn—then another—he held out a fruit skewer and encouraged her to take a bite. In the back of her mind, she was aware of the fact Rock was feeding her and they were alone on a sumptuous yacht with romantic music playing, but none of that bothered her. He cupped a hand under her chin in case she spilled, but she didn't.

Her eyes widened as the sweetness of the watermelon and drizzled honey blended with the tang of the mint and richness of the feta. "That's delicious."

"You made it, not me."

"Your recipe."

He shrugged. "Maybe I'll fire Andreas and hire you."

They moved on to the bruschetta. As with the other appetizers, the flavors melded beautifully without being overpowering.

"I'd say that was a successful test," Rock said as they polished off a few more samples. "Want a refill of your wine?"

April looked down and was shocked to see her glass was empty. "I shouldn't."

"But—?"

"Go ahead." As she watched him pour, his hands strong and sure, she said, "I'm amazed those were so easy to make. At least you made it feel that way."

"Food is as complex or simple as you want it to be. There are a lot of chefs who focus on details—like one particular ingredient—rather than looking at the whole. I'm a big picture guy." He topped off his glass, returned the bottle to the coffee table, then stretched his arm along the sofa behind her, angling his body so his knees brushed hers. "It's not much different than the way you design cabinetry. It's not about that singular beveled edge, but the entire presentation. The feeling one has when they walk into the room and are awed by its beauty, then fall in love with the functionality of the pieces. That's how I make my decisions. What's best for the long term."

The seriousness in his tone made her realize he was talking about more than the appetizers. "That's why you accepted Fabrizia's job offer on the yacht? You were thinking about the long term?"

He swirled his wine, studying the pattern along the inside of his glass before taking a long, thoughtful sip. "You know how much I loved the restaurants, but in the years since you left New York, I've lost the fire in my belly."

She gestured toward the few remaining appetizers on the table. "All evidence to the contrary."

The smile lifting the edges of his mouth was wistful. "It wasn't the food so much as the business. When Fabrizia came along, I found her offer intriguing. It got my creative juices flowing again. I woke up each morning imagining new dishes I could prepare. This job gives me the chance to experiment in a way the restaurant business doesn't allow. It reminds me of the passion I had for cooking when I began."

Abruptly, he stood and began clearing the coffee table. "Let's get the main meal going. Feel free to bring the wine."

He balanced the appetizer trays and plates on his arm as she followed with the wine glasses and bottle. With the ease of a man who'd carried challenging loads through narrow spaces for years, he used his hip to open the swinging door to the galley, then unloaded the dishes from his arm to the dishwasher. He asked her to retrieve a cornflower blue covered casserole dish from the walk-in refrigerator, then met her back at the counter where they'd made the appetizers.

"So why'd you leave?"

She paused, chilled casserole in hand, befuddled by his question. "Leave?"

"New York. Me." He took the heavy dish from her and set it on the counter, then moved to preheat the wall oven. "I know an offer from Queen Fabrizia is hard to refuse, but you turned it down more than once before you said yes. The timing left me to believe you had another reason besides the challenge of the work...and that your reason may have had to do with me."

The words flowed from his lips so easily, yet she sensed the enormity of the question that hung between them. This singular moment was the reason he'd asked her to the yacht.

Her throat threatened to close as she forced her answer. "It wasn't you, it was me. *All* me."

"Classic, but I'm not buying it." He took the cover off the blue dish to reveal marinating chicken. Instantly, the distinct scents of lemon, fennel, and thyme permeated the kitchen.

"I needed a fresh start—one where I wasn't working with my brother—and Fabrizia's offer provided that. So don't-buy-it all you want. It wasn't you. It was me."

Divots appeared between his brows. "You left because of Mark?"

"You knew it wasn't all rainbows and unicorns working with him."

"He's a strong personality, I'll give you that, but it was your father's company. You took a lot of pride in it. And you loved your career."

"In many ways, it was my ideal." Her mind flashed back to the job she'd wrapped just before her mother died, a carriage house that had undergone slapdash upgrades in the seventies and needed a top to bottom restoration. "I was able to work on some of Manhattan's most beautiful residences. To see them returned to their intended glory and know I was responsible gave me enormous satisfaction."

She exhaled, hating to reveal the truth, but she knew Rock wouldn't let it drop until she did. "Unfortunately, being Mark's partner left me feeling less-than. I had a great deal of creative freedom on the construction front, but at the end of the day, clients went to Mark with their issues. They saw him as the brains. They didn't seem to grasp that I was the one with the design ideas and who had the architectural expertise to make the business work. Because he was the one signing the contracts and managing the money—and frankly, because he was male—they assumed the company belonged to him and I was his flunky construction person. Worse, Mark started acting that way, taking the design questions that should've been directed to me. When he didn't know the answers, he'd say, 'I'll look into it' or 'Let me double-check that for you,' then he'd phone and ask me for the answers."

"Let me guess. He didn't give you the credit when he responded, either." Rock handed April a bowl of green beans to wash while he gathered ingredients she recognized for his signature cranberry pecan sauce. "You didn't call him on it?"

"When the clients didn't believe in me, it made it hard to believe in myself. I knew I was in trouble when I quit standing up to him. And frankly, I loved him. Still love him. He's my brother. I hated the conflict between us. I knew if I stayed, that one day it would come to a head."

"So you left." The creases on his forehead didn't ease.

"Fabrizia saw one of my projects while visiting New York and came straight to me. She wanted to hire *me*. Not Mark. She saw my talent when no one else did. So I sold Mark my half of the company. Of course, he had to hire another construction guy—two, in fact—to do my job. And they didn't do it as well. But it kept the family peace."

Rock's silence unnerved her. She stopped washing beans and turned to look at him. His usual sharp gaze had gone soft. "What?"

His lips thinned. A heartbeat later, he said, "I did."

"You did what?"

"I believed in you. I saw your talent. I still do."

She turned back to the green beans, squeezing her eyes shut for a moment as his words slammed through her. He'd cared for her all this time. It was in his expression, in the sincere timbre of his voice. She knew it as surely as she knew her own name. And as surely as she knew she'd made the right decision for herself by leaving, even though she'd hurt him. Apparently more than she'd realized.

Forcing herself to finish the green beans, she transferred them to a colander. "Thank you."

He squeezed fresh lemon over the chicken and slid the pan into the oven, then came to stand behind her. His large hands framed her shoulders and his warm breath teased the skin at the back of her neck.

"Rock—"

"I wish you'd told me."

"I wasn't trying to hide it from you. It's just…I needed to deal with it on my own." She swallowed hard, driving back the lump in her throat at the same time she tried to ignore the comforting pressure of his thumbs against the muscles of her upper back. "But that was all a long time ago. Now I'm in a great job, working for a family I adore. I couldn't ask for anything better."

"Yet you're still dealing with confidence issues." He spun her to face him. His eyes searched hers. "Aren't you?"

It took everything in her to hold his gaze. "Rock, I'm fine. I don't need your help. I don't need anyone."

To her surprise, he grinned. "I didn't say you needed my help. I said you have confidence issues. Otherwise, you wouldn't have been so worried about how to stack cucumber and tomato on a silly piece of toast."

He released her and strode to the stove to start his cranberry pecan sauce. The very thought of it made her mouth water, which she was beginning to suspect was intentional. Did he remember the first time she'd sampled it, at his original restaurant? Or kissing her after she'd taken a taste from the spoon he'd proffered?

Then, of course, he'd made her groan aloud for an entirely different reason, one she needed to keep firmly out of her mind.

She grit her teeth. *Firmly* wasn't a word she should think of, either.

"And who needs 'no one'?" he asked over his shoulder, yanking her to the present.

"Let me rephrase. We all need people. But I'm not needy."

His whisk went double-time. "I never said you were."

"You didn't have to say it."

"Meaning?"

"Meaning you've always *treated* me that way. As if I'm in need of help. I'm not."

He frowned at her, then turned back to his sauce. "April, no one would ever accuse you of being a helpless female. You're, what, nearly six feet tall? I once watched you install a curved staircase railing you designed yourself. I've seen you fix a rooftop dormer without an ounce of fear at being five stories above a Manhattan street. And—as you like to point out to people—while you might not look like a typical carpenter, you do know a bandsaw from a jigsaw and you know how to use them. You're as mentally tough as any man and tougher than most of them physically, too, though I suspect it makes me a traitor to my gender to say it."

He set the sauce to simmer, then closed the space between them. His hand went to the countertop beside her, essentially trapping her. He was so close she could smell the hint of white wine on his breath, could see the tiny creases at the corners of his eyes and the beginnings of dark stubble on his cheeks.

"What's this all about?" His voice was so low and serious, it was as if he were speaking to her in a crowded room and didn't want anyone else to hear. "It's not the fact I went overboard after you, is it? It's not even about Mark."

No. "Ryan—Rock—this is a button you don't want to push." The words came out sounding breathless rather than definite, and she'd been aiming for definite. But how could she when he stood so close, rattling her last nerve? Geez, she'd even called him Ryan.

"I'm pushing."

The music on the speakers switched from romantic Sarcaccian guitar to Johnny Mathis's whiskey-smooth version of 'Have Yourself a Merry Little Christmas' at the same time Rock said, "What's the harm in telling me?"

It was the shove that sent her over the edge.

"Fine. You've always been too nice to me. Too ready to swoop in and be my Superman. While that sounds like I'm criticizing you, I'm not. It's truly my issue. I've been too ready to accept that help when I shouldn't."

"I can't for the life of me remember an occasion that would make you think—"

"Rock, *please.*" She couldn't go down this road. As it was, the Christmas music was making her tear up, and she refused to allow her emotional dam to breach with Rock as a witness. And he was standing so freaking *close.* What had happened to pulling herself up by her bootstraps? "People call you Rock for a reason. It fits you. Maybe everyone here in Sarcaccia thinks it's because you're built like" —she waved a hand in the narrow space between them— "I don't know, a mixed martial arts fighter or an Olympic decathlete. But I know otherwise. It's because you're everyone's support system. It's how you built a successful restaurant from scratch by the time you were twenty-eight, then opened a second location in less than two years. You keep everyone and everything around you organized. You give them confidence and keep them on an even keel. Even when you wear a scowl on your face that could turn water to ice, like you are right now."

He didn't back off one bit. "Isn't supporting people and keeping them organized a good thing?"

"Of course it is. But I've learned that I'm better alone. When I lean on someone else—even someone who's as wonderful as you are, despite the fact you can be bossy as all get-out when you think it's for my own good—I forget that I have responsibilities. I let people down and that" —oh damn, she couldn't stop the waterworks now— "and that's very hard on me. I won't put myself in that position again."

İT WAS the cracking of her voice that got him more than the tears. The pads of his thumbs went to the soft skin below her eyes, blotting away the moisture at the same time she squeezed her lids shut in frustration.

Did she have any idea how strong and beautiful she was?

"Who do you think you let down?"

"My family. Myself. And apparently you."

"You didn't let me down. Left me confused, but not down." He allowed his forehead to fall against hers. "You didn't let down your family, either. You said it yourself. You did what you felt was necessary to keep the peace…not that it should've been necessary. Mark's a big boy. You're not responsible for him."

He felt rather than saw her jaw working as she gathered herself. "This is all water under the bridge. I shouldn't—"

"Because it's not only about Mark, is it?" The realization smacked him even as he'd told her she wasn't responsible for him. But the only other people in her family were her father, who'd died years before, and her mother, who'd died only days before April accepted Fabrizia's offer. The woman for whom April had done everything in those last days. "You did everything you could possibly do for your parents."

"Thank you for saying that, but—" She tensed, then turned to the side.

"But—?"

"Your phone is ringing."

"I don't care."

"Look at the screen."

Irritated, he glanced past her to where his phone rested on the countertop. The private number displayed was one he recognized instantly, though it was one he'd only seen a handful of times before. It was the last thing he'd expected on Christmas Day.

He snagged it from the counter and answered, "Your Highness?" at the same time April slipped from his grasp.

"Good day, Rock," Queen Fabrizia's rich voice came over the line. "I understand you're on the yacht."

The security guards registered all the comings and goings on the dock, but he had no idea that Queen Fabrizia made that information her business. "I decided to give the New Year's Eve menu a test run. If it's a problem, I can clear out immediately."

"Not at all. But I do hope you have some holiday time planned?"

"Of course, Your Highness." He asked a polite question about her Christmas, though his attention remained on April, who gave his sauce a quick whisk before checking the chicken through the oven's glass door.

"You've done an excellent job on the *Libertà*. Prince Bruno said the get-together he hosted yesterday went well."

"Thank you. I'm glad he enjoyed it."

April motioned toward the green beans before lifting the pot he planned to use to steam them and raising a brow. He nodded, wondering where Queen Fabrizia was taking the conversation. The fact she'd taken time from her Christmas festivities to call him meant it was important.

"I spoke with Dominic yesterday. I wish for the news to remain quiet, but he will officially retire this spring. I'd like to offer you his position."

April had her back to him, but he knew she could hear every word on his side of the conversation. He eased out of the galley and into the dining room as the enormity of Queen Fabrizia's words settled. "I'm honored. It's a challenge and a responsibility any chef would consider the pinnacle of his career. However, I'll admit that I'm surprised you interrupted your holiday to make the offer."

"I don't want you feeling pressured to prove yourself at the New Year's Eve party. In fact, I had all the information necessary to offer you the position the very first time we met in your restaurant, but was waiting for Dominic to make his decision official."

"I'm flattered."

"And I was impressed. Not only was the dinner that night first rate and the service and cleanliness exactly what I expect, you capped off the evening by serving that wonderful dessert."

Now she'd truly thrown him for a loop. "The turtle cheesecake?"

"Yes, the one with the chocolate crust. Absolutely delightful. Anyone who can create that masterpiece is worth the pursuit."

He couldn't keep the surprise from his voice. "You do recall that when you complimented it, I mentioned that it's not my own recipe?"

"You did, which demonstrates both your good judgment and your honesty, two qualities I seek in all potential palace employees." Her voice carried a smile. "Take your time and think about it, even if you believe you know your answer already. Let me know after the New Year's party."

"Thank you. I will." He was about to hang up when he added, "Your Highness? I have to know...did you know that I intend to serve the turtle cheesecake at the New Year's Eve party?" Even if Bruno had told his mother about enjoying it during his own party, Rock hadn't told the prince he planned to serve it again on New Year's. In fact, he'd never before served the same dessert at events so closely timed.

"My dear Mr. Fournier, I make it my business to know everything that happens under my roof. That includes on my yachts. Have a good afternoon and wish April a Merry Christmas for me."

CHAPTER 7

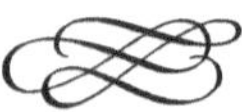

Rock pushed through the galley door just as April set the steaming basket over the boiling water.

"Queen Fabrizia?"

"Yes." He set the phone on one of the stainless steel countertops and came to stand beside April. "She knows we're both on the yacht."

April gave a one-shouldered shrug. "I learned long ago that the woman knows everything. It's a wonder she's only queen of this island and doesn't run the entire world. I assume that's not why she called, though. It's Christmas Day."

"She offered me Dominic's job. He's retiring this spring." At April's intake of breath, he said, "But none of that leaves this room. She gave me until New Year's to give her an answer."

April turned off the burner under the cranberry pecan sauce to allow it to settle. Amazing how she remembered the timing.

"I haven't decided what answer to give her yet."

That got April's attention. She raised her face to his. "After everything you just told me, why in the world wouldn't you take it?"

"You."

She started to speak, then closed her eyes and exhaled. "Don't—"

"Don't let you factor into the decision? That's not for you to weigh.

Just like you didn't allow me to weigh in when you left." He clicked off the oven and cracked the door. He didn't need to check the chicken to know it was done. "Grab the dinnerware."

While April stood watching in silence, he plated the chicken and green beans, drizzled on the cranberry pecan sauce, then moved to the cooker he'd left near the back of the stove to add a mound of red pepper and green chile-infused quinoa to each dish. He balanced the plates on one arm, scooped up silverware and two clean wine glasses in the other hand, then led the way to the salon. As before, he set the food on the coffee table before withdrawing a bottle of wine from the bar and opening it.

"Another course, another bottle?"

"Similar to the last one, but slightly richer on the tongue. The guests will have champagne at midnight, so I don't want anything heavy."

"I don't know that more wine is wise."

"Taste what you need and dump the rest."

The meal was one he'd made before, so he knew it'd play well, both with April and at the party. And though his personal standards dictated he do his best, now that the job was his, the pressure to create a perfect menu vaporized.

"You have to take the job," April said between bites. "This is too amazing not to share."

"I need to know that you won't leave." Her fork wobbled before she speared a green bean. "I need to know why you think you let your family down. If it wasn't Mark, then it must've been your mother. That's what I was about to say before the phone rang."

Rock set his plate on the table, then took April's dish and set it aside, too.

"Excuse me, I was eating that."

"I'll make you another." He took her hands in his. Her chin lifted in defiance, but he saw fear and hurt in her gaze. "I don't know what could make you think you let her down, but you didn't. Her last days were good because of you. You think I didn't know how much of your heart went into those final weeks she spent in the hospital? Reading to her, making her laugh, ensuring she had whatever was necessary to keep her as comfortable as possible? No parent could ask for more. Short of curing cancer, there wasn't anything you could do, April."

"I could've been there when she died."

"I know you wanted to be there." He let go of one hand and reached for her cheek, cradling it, but her expression didn't change. "No one could've predicted she'd pass away when she did. You'd been there all day, you were going back in the morning—"

"She was *alone*."

That's when it struck him. "And you were with me."

THE HORRIFIED EXPRESSION on Rock's face as he realized what had happened threatened to rip her heart out of her chest.

She'd been in love with him. She'd known it then. She knew it now. But it hadn't mattered when faced with the horrific guilt that'd wracked her when she returned to the hospital the next morning. The one night—the *one* night—she needed to be with her mother the most, she'd turned to Rock for comfort. And oh, how she'd been comforted. Orgasm after orgasm comforted, wrap her legs around his waist so tight she threatened to break him comforted, talk dirty and scream in mind-numbing pleasure comforted.

"I'm sorry, Rock." She squeezed back tears as she pulled away from his touch. She'd made a huge mistake coming here, knowing how Rock affected her. And once again, he wanted to comfort her, yet she'd responded by doing the most hurtful thing in the world to him…letting him know her last night with him ended up causing more pain than she could bear. "You're so reliable. You're such a good man, such a strong man. You're everything I could possibly want. But that night" —she held up a hand as he reached for her— "I was so needy. So selfish. I did the worst thing I could possibly do."

"Make love to me?"

"No! I was unreliable." She pushed off the sofa and stalked to the windows. The bright midday sunshine and glittering blue water did nothing to dissipate the dark cloud of guilt that filled her soul. "I was screwing my brains out while my mom was struggling to breathe. Rock, she died!"

Thank God no one else was on the yacht, because she'd yelled the last two words.

"But not *because* of you."

"I—" She choked. Her hands went to her head and she forked her fingers through her hair. Her voice steadier, she said, "No. Not because of me. But I don't think I could have felt worse if I'd killed her with my own hands."

They'd been the darkest days of April's life. A veritable witches' brew of emotions had boiled within her as she'd endured the memorial service and funeral. Facing the reality that her mother was gone at the very moment April was finally old enough to be a friend as well as a daughter. Knowing that she should've been holding her mother's hand, doing everything possible to make her final hours easier. Wishing the hospital paperwork would disappear so she could stop reading details of tests and medications that no longer mattered and worrying about leaving matters undone. Finding little comfort from Mark, who'd leaned on his wife for support through his own misery. Craving privacy so she could mourn. Forcing herself to be strong as well-wishers visited with tears in their eyes, each with more wonderful stories to tell about April's mother than the last, stories that made April miss her mother all the more. Stories that made her feel more and more guilty for letting down such a wonderful woman.

"Everything was going wrong with Mark. You lost your mother after a long, emotional battle." Rock crossed the salon to stand behind her as he spoke, but refrained from touching her, allowing his voice to show his concern. "Every time we saw each other in those days leading up to the funeral, while you were planning the service and dealing with the hospital, you looked hollow inside. Bereft. I thought it was grief, but now I understand that it was grief and so much more."

He moved a step closer, stopping when his large, warm body was only inches from hers. "Fabrizia offered you a golden opportunity to start over."

"After the funeral, I had to make a choice. A former client wanted Mark and me for a new project, and I had to either leave or be locked in for another six months...but I couldn't bring myself to...and then there was you. Rock, I'm so sorry. I didn't mean to hurt you. I didn't realize that I had. Not really."

"I know that." One gentle hand went to her lower back. A cloud drifted across the sun, changing the light so she could see his reflection in the window. His eyes drifted closed, as if he were in pain. When he opened them, she saw him inhale and steady himself. "I wish you could have told me what you were going through. I loved you."

She'd known how she felt about him. They'd spent the most amazing, happy hours together when they weren't working—they'd worked such long hours, both of them—and the sex had been beyond measure. But in all their time as a couple, through brunch dates, walks in Central Park, even the occasional getaway to upstate New York in his Mustang, he'd never said the words to her. She'd believed she was more invested emotionally than he was, and that what mattered most to him was their intense physical relationship.

His reflected gaze went beyond her, out the salon's windows, to some far point on the horizon. "I understand why you kept it to yourself. But—" She saw him shake his head, then look down at her before he spun her to face him.

"But what?"

"Fabrizia didn't bring you here to do penance," he ground out. "She didn't bring you here to live alone, to spend your Christmas watching television reruns and eating that godforsaken Sarcaccian loaf while everyone around you celebrates the holiday with their families. You didn't do anything wrong. Punishing yourself won't bring your mother back. It won't do anything but make me ache for you."

His hips moved against hers as one capable hand cupped her face, holding her in place. "Tell me you didn't feel something deeper than lust when I kissed you in the car. Tell me it wasn't the same magic we had in New York. Or better."

Her gaze dropped from his eyes to his sinful lips. She could kiss him so easily. He was right in so many ways. His body against hers, the piercing intelligence in his gaze, the depth of her feelings for him. Making love to Rock would be pure ecstasy. Mind-numbing, all-encompassing.

"Tell me you didn't feel it," he demanded.

She couldn't deny it. He'd seen it in her heated face, in the way he made her breath quicken. In the way he pulled her attention to him every time he entered a room. In the energy that connected them each and every time their gazes met.

"You know I did." Her words were whispered, her eyes still locked on his lush, captivating mouth. "But if I kiss you again now, what would stop me from falling so hard I forget everything else? I may be alone, but I'm not lonely. People rely on me here, and not it's because of Mark or because my father's name is on the door of my business. It's because I do my job and I do it well. I'm reliable. I don't want to lose that."

"You won't."

Emotion clogged her throat. This Christmas was the first time she'd so deeply craved family. The intimacy and connection that Kelly had with Massimo. That Marco had with Sabrina. That Fabrizia and Carlo and their entire family shared. She knew it was because of Rock. She could've spent Christmas with any number of Sarcaccian men over the years—sexy, intelligent, worldly, witty—but never had. None of them held a candle to Ryan Fournier. He was all she ever wanted.

But did she dare?

"You don't have to prove yourself to anyone." His thumb traced her cheekbone as he brought his mouth ever so slightly closer to hers. "You've already done it simply by being you. You bring lipstick from the States for Marco's wife because you know she can't get her favorite here. You see that my nightstand needs to be tightened and do it without being asked. You offer to clean my car because you bleed in it, for crying out loud."

"It's my job to fix—"

"Your job isn't the reason Marco brings you cannoli and it certainly isn't why Armand wants to make sure you're well-fed." His tone grew rougher as he drove his point home. "You're valued for who you are. *You.* Your generosity. The vivaciousness that infects everyone around you. The work ethic that makes me want to be better at my job. Hell, you flat-out make me want to be a better human being. You make me love you. Being in love doesn't mean being needy. What I hope is that it makes you my partner."

The words so stunned her she couldn't respond. More than the words, it was the tender look in his eyes. The sincerity in his voice. The way he stroked her cheeks, her neck, her shoulders…then lowered his mouth to her temple. The masculine scent of him enveloped her, giving her the overwhelming sensation of arriving home. Of being understood, and being seen as an equal by the most perfect man in the world.

"Rock." It came out as both endearment and a plea.

"Say my name."

"Ryan."

Every muscle in her body went taut in that moment, waiting for the touch of his lips to hers. She knew he felt it, too, but he dragged his mouth to the other side of her temple, slowly playing his warm lips against her skin and hair. Tasting, exploring. Torturing her. "Say it again."

Her eyes drifted shut. "Ryan, please."

Then his lips met hers, sweet and tender and full of promise. A soft sigh escaped her as the tension drained from her body, gratified that he was kissing her at last. His palms went down her arms to her waist, then he pulled her against him at the same time she wound her arms around his neck. They fit together so perfectly, his hips to hers, his hands to the curve at her lower back. Five years of yearning welled in her as his tongue grazed the seam of her lips, urging her to open to him. One kiss blended into another, then another, as if they needed to make up for each moment they'd lost. A thrill shot through her as his hardness pressed against her abdomen. As strongly as he affected her, she'd affected him.

He yanked his mouth from hers with a deep, guttural groan. Her fingertips went to the hem of his shirt, instinct driving her to discard the annoying fabric that kept her from feeling his heated skin against hers.

Partners. She loved the sound of that. Of knowing she was making him as crazy as he made her.

A wicked laugh erupted from him. "Let's finish dinner."

She flinched, caught off guard, then regarded him only to see a mischievous smile lifting the corners of his glistening mouth.

He had to be kidding.

The thought must've been written on her face, because his grin didn't falter as he guided her to the sofa. "We've waited five years to be together again. If you can trust me, and trust yourself, we'll have all the time in the world. I'd rather we take this slowly, given what happened last time. I don't want you to experience an ounce of guilt or regret. Besides, the chicken is getting cold and I brought you here to work."

He'd just said he loved her, then kissed her senseless, and he wanted to stop to eat? What man on planet Earth did that? "That's evil."

"No. Effective. Remember, I'm all about the big picture." He took a seat and raised his fork, a lone green bean speared on the tines. "You do like my food, don't you?"

"Yes, but—"

"Sit. Tell me what you think about the chicken. Be honest about the quinoa. Rave about the cranberry pecan sauce on the green beans, because I remember exactly how much you liked that sauce the first time you tried it. Then we'll have dessert."

Her rear end hit the sofa with a thump as he added, "I promise, the wait will be worth it."

"It better be." Because the sexual energy sizzling through her right now was messing with her senses. "Frankly, I'm not sure I can give a rational evaluation of your cooking right now."

"Try."

So she did. Every bite was delicious, but none of it could compete with the sensation of having Rock hold her, working his magic with his mouth and tongue. With his unbelievably sexy hands. Of knowing what she could do to *him*.

Gradually, his descriptions of the food and wine distracted her, taking the edge off. When she mentioned the spices in the quinoa and asked if he could take it up a notch, he nodded, agreeing with her assessment and noting that it'd taken a while for her to come to that conclusion.

"I was distracted," she pointed out.

"Funny how we can't judge things when our emotions are in overdrive."

He lifted his last bite of chicken to her mouth. Though it had cooled, it remained delicious. The Barrali family's guests would love it. "Your point?"

"You were with your mother when it counted," he said, setting the fork to the side of his plate. "But knowing she was dying, that she was frequently in pain, was emotionally overwhelming for you. Even if you didn't show it, I knew it. She did, too."

After long swig of his wine, he regarded her over the rim of his glass. "Have you ever considered that your mother died that particular night because it was easier for her to let go when you were out of the room? Knowing you were with me and distracted for the evening, maybe finding relief from the situation, gave her a sense of ease?"

"It's possible." More than possible. She'd never considered the idea before, but it resonated. It was just like her mother to find peace in knowing those around her were cared for. "It's also possible you're rationalizing."

"It's no different than what you did by coming to Sarcaccia, choosing to live alone, and mentally punishing yourself for a sin you never committed. Even if that wasn't what you thought you were doing, it's what happened. At least with my rationalization, two people have a shot at a happily ever after."

He took her hands in his and squeezed. "Look April, whether I'm right or not, your mother would've wanted you to have love in your life. I need you to believe that in your heart. I need you to believe it for your own peace of mind, and I need you to believe it for me."

CHAPTER 8

"For you?"

Rock's fingertips circled the back of her knuckles, which did dastardly things to her thoughts.

"Before I make love to you." His fingers stilled, then his hands tightened around hers. "Not today, necessarily, but—"

"Today would be perfect."

A muscle twitched in his jaw. "I meant it when I said that I ache for you, April, but I don't want anything more than that kiss if you're not ready. It's not worth it to risk—"

"Today would be perfect." She knew in the depths of her soul that this was what she was meant to do this Christmas. To start again with Ryan Fournier. To find peace. To find love. "I've never stopped loving you. I just…I didn't realize that you loved me. That you see me for who I am, that you understand me, that you still love me. That I could make you even a fraction as happy as you make me."

"You have no idea."

She slid closer to him on the sofa. "You have the patience of a saint."

"I'm no saint." He lowered his chin, directing a look at the front of her shirt. "You know I could see the outline of your bra after you fell into the water? A very thin lace bra."

"And you looked."

"Looked? Hell, it was all I could do not to touch. It made me remember exactly where to put my hands to make you beg for more, and I was imagining every caress, every suck, every tease. Believe me, they were not the thoughts of a saint."

"So do it." She swallowed hard, watching as desire darkened his eyes. "Make love to me. Let me make love to you. Think of how it can be when it's so much more than sex. When we're brave enough to acknowledge what we really feel instead of teasing each other about creaky parts."

"April, dear God."

"I'm in love with you, Ryan Fournier. Crazy, silly, stupid love. Maybe I don't have to prove myself to anyone, but I *want* to prove myself to you. I want you to know you'll never, ever be hurt again. Not by me, not if I can help it. I want you inside me because it's where you belong. My partner. My teammate. My lover. I don't want to wait."

He was on her before she could say another word, his weight pinning her to the sofa, his mouth ravishing her throat, her chin, the curve of her ear. Her head fell back, and when he moved to kiss her, her lips were already parted, already panting, waiting for him.

Her lover. Her perfect fit.

She arched into him as he kneaded her breast, kissed him with every ounce of pent-up passion. As fiery as her X-rated fantasies had been, this was better. It was about so much more than the physical experience. It was a bonding of two souls.

A masculine grunt escaped him, then he pushed off the sofa, drawing her with him. "Not here. My room."

Even in the fog of want, she knew he was right. They couldn't make love in the Barrali family's salon, on their luxe furniture. Not only would it be disrespectful, a security guard could walk through at any moment. While they'd likely hear him coming and could cover up quickly, this was their time. Private, personal, intimate. Not to be disturbed.

It took only seconds for them to scamper down the interior stairs to his cabin and close the door. The scents of pine needles and lemon chicken were replaced by another, earthier scent. She inhaled deeply as he flipped the lock, then framed her hips with his hands, joining their bodies once more.

"I love your sheets," she whispered as the back of her knees hit the bed and she tumbled backward onto the narrow mattress. He moved over her, his gaze hooded, and she rose to bury her face in his neck. "They smell like you. Completely addictive."

His hands slid under her dark T-shirt to bracket her rib cage. Breath quickening in her ear, he whispered, "You smelling my sheets while you were in here working, ma'am?"

"It was hard to resist."

"So unprofessional." He eased her shirt over her head, then pushed to one elbow and unclasped her bra with a single deft movement. "But as long as we're confessing deep, dark secrets, I've always thought of you as my sexual crack cocaine. Completely addictive. Impossible to resist. Part of my blood and my veins."

"Um…isn't cocaine a bad thing?"

He drew one hand down the center of her breasts, then lower, making worshipful circles across her abdomen as he drank in the visual of her lying bared to him. "You, my dear, are not. You're the best possible addiction. Remember everything I said about how you make me want to be a better human being? Or shall I repeat it?"

"I suspect I remember it all." She'd remember it for the rest of her life.

"That's why making love to you is so mind-blowing I never want to stop. Not because of the parts" —he traced his way back to one nipple, rolling it in his fingers before teasing it with his tongue— "though they're rather lovely parts. Because of the whole. Because of you. And I'll never, ever have enough."

He attended to her nipple, allowing her to bury her hands in his soft, dark hair. When he moved to the other, he whisked off her jeans. "You are so beautiful," he murmured against her skin, but the words were lost on her as he divested her of her panties and his tongue found her center. Her reaction was so fierce, she nearly bucked off the bed.

"Ryan." She was so ready for him she hurt with it.

"Don't move."

With a moan, April let go of his hair and gripped the sides of the bed. She felt him smile against her in victory before he forced her thighs wider and made love to her with his teeth and tongue. The world swirled around her, the force within her building to a crescendo.

"I can't."

"You were made for this. For me."

The words vibrated against her sensitized skin. She felt the heat of his mouth, the scrape of stubble, and she was lost, her climax sending wave after wave of pleasure pulsing through her, arching her against him. Then he was beside her, kissing her neck, cupping her breast, smiling against her skin as she collapsed bonelessly into the sheets.

Her arms wrapped around him without conscious thought, her hands drifting along the soft skin and firm muscles of his back. He was so warm, so right. So naked.

"Your jeans are gone," she whispered.

"All that time in the kitchen has made me very good with my hands."

"All of you is very good."

"Hmmm." She heard the slide of the nightstand drawer. "Tell me, when you fixed my nightstand and familiarized yourself with my sheets, did you also investigate the contents of the drawer?"

"I did not. Should I have?"

He withdrew a condom and tore it from the package. "These have been in here a while, but they're in better shape than the nightstand itself."

"Thank God."

"I love you, April."

It was the last thought in her head before he entered her, filling her slowly and completely. They made love deliberately, silently worshipping each other's bodies, holding each other's gazes and moving together until they each found their release.

Long minutes later, when they'd caught their breath, he eased to his side, spooning her in front of him. "That made me feel like a virgin," he whispered into her hair.

"I know exactly what you mean." It was as if the past were erased. As if they were together for the first time, the slate clean and the future bright. She lifted his hand to press a kiss to his knuckles. "Here's to new beginnings."

HOURS LATER, when the sun was low across the water and they'd napped, Rock pushed himself to a seated position on the narrow bed. "We forgot something rather important here."

"I can't imagine what." April rolled to her side, reveling in the feeling of being naked alongside Rock. "I feel unbelievably satisfied."

"Dessert." He gave her a gentle swat on the rear. "Come on. I told you I was going to make the wait worth your while."

"Now?" Tiny as the bed might be, she didn't want to leave. "You know how much I love dessert, but I can think of other things more worth my while."

"A little sugar for fuel and you'll have that, too."

That brought a catlike grin to her face. He retrieved her clothing from the floor and handed it to her before slipping into his boxers and jeans. After ensuring no one had boarded the yacht and they were still alone, they padded barefoot to the kitchen, with Rock pausing only long enough to grab the dirty dinner plates from the salon. He turned on a single light over the stovetop, which afforded them just enough illumination to keep from bumping into anything, then set the used plates in the sink.

"What are we making?" she whispered, the semidarkness making her feel like a teenager sneaking around behind her parents' backs. "Whatever it is, I hope it's quick."

"It's already made. Stay here and I'll get it."

She loaded the dishwasher while he disappeared into the walk-in refrigerator. A moment later, he emerged with a long, covered tray. "I served these at Prince Bruno's party and they were the most popular item on the menu. I'm doing them again at New Year's because they're a favorite of Queen Fabrizia."

"You had party leftovers you didn't bring to my apartment yesterday?"

"A guy's gotta keep a few secret weapons in his arsenal." He set the tray on the counter and pulled off the cover. "What do you think?"

"That those are too beautiful to eat." The long row of chocolate-encased, bite-sized cheesecakes made her jaw drop. She leaned closer to study them in the dim light. Just as the scent of chocolate and caramel hit her brain, the texture of the topping brought tears to her eyes. "These aren't, are they?"

"They are. It's your mom's turtle cheesecake, but made on a smaller scale."

April's hand went to her mouth. "She gave you her recipe? When?"

"Just before she checked into the hospital the last time." Rock's arms went to her waist and he cradled her body to his. With his lips to her neck, he said, "She told me you and Mark weren't much for the kitchen, but she had me promise to keep the recipe alive. And to save it for your children."

April's eyes closed. What a wonderful, thoughtful thing for her mother to do. And how telling that she'd given her prized cheesecake recipe to Rock and he'd treated it like the treasure it was.

She turned in his arms. "If you made these for Bruno's party…that party was the day after I first boarded the yacht to do the repair work. How did you know that I'd—"

"I didn't. I served Fabrizia a slice of your mother's cheesecake when she visited my restaurant in New York years ago. She mentioned it recently and I thought she'd appreciate having this version at the party." A flicker of realization clouded his eyes, then he shook his head. "She planned this. That wily, wily woman."

"Queen Fabrizia?"

"I told her the very first time she tasted the dessert and complimented me on the recipe that it wasn't mine, that it was a gift from the late mother of an ex-girlfriend. I bet she knew exactly whose mother I meant."

April huffed out a breath and laughed. "When I turned down her job offer for the second time, she asked why. I told her that I loved my job and had a family and boyfriend in New York I wasn't ready to leave behind."

"She would've checked into all of that."

Of course she would've. "When she made that third offer shortly after my mother passed away, I don't think she expected me to take it. She knew I was dating you."

"She never asked about me, though, did she? When you accepted the job?"

April shook her head.

"Tell me something. When's the last time you did repair work on the *Libertà?*"

"Never. I assume Marco has dealt with the manufacturer." At Rock's raised brow, she said, "You think she had Marco send me a last-minute punch list to get me onto the yacht because she knew I'd run into you."

"I'm sure she did. Probably told Marco not to bother the manufacturer over the holidays when you could easily do the work. You know how Sarcaccians love to play matchmaker—"

"It's their national sport."

"And we haven't been disturbed all day, aside from a call from Queen Fabrizia herself."

"Offering you the job and asking you to give her an answer after New Year's."

"She knew you were on board."

April's fingers went to Rock's waist and she angled her head to study his expression. He didn't seem the least bit bothered by the fact they'd been manipulated by the Barrali matriarch. "What will you tell her?"

The warmth in his blue-green eyes thrilled her before he voiced his answer. "That she's given me the best Christmas gift a man could ever want. And that I'm in Sarcaccia to stay."

The kiss he gave her left no doubt in April's mind. This was where she belonged. With Rock—her Ryan—for Christmas, and for all the Christmases to come.

RITA Award Winning Author

NICOLE BURNHAM

CHAPTER 1

BREAKING into a royal palace wasn't an easy task, even for the most skilled thief. When that palace teemed with holiday guests, many of whom were VIPs, tightened security protocols made the challenge even more daunting.

Sara Angeletti was not a skilled thief. Fortunately, she had other key factors working in her favor: familiarity with the building's layout, inside information on the royal family's surveillance system, and a dreary, moonless night. Best of all, tonight's mission was for a purpose near and dear to her heart.

The black umbrella clutched in Sara's gloved hand shielded her from the cold drizzle as she made her way along Via Floriana, the city boulevard that bordered the rear of the palace complex. It also shielded her face from the security cameras and passersby, for despite the late hour, Sara wasn't the only pedestrian on the wide sidewalk of Sarcaccia's capital city of Cateri this Friday night. A smattering of businesspeople and civil servants strode past her purposefully, their heads down and shoulders hunched as they attempted to escape the rain before it soaked through their clothing. The rest were holiday shoppers, their arms loaded with bags as they hurried toward one of the neighborhood's bustling restaurants or dashed for the shelter of the nearby bus stop awning to await a ride home. The few pedestrians who dared raise their eyes were interested only in the glitter of the Christmas lights strung over the street or the route numbers displayed on the front of the approaching busses.

Even for this time of year, it was rare weather for the Mediterranean island, given its sun-drenched location only a ferry ride from Naples, Italy. Sara couldn't have planned it better.

Two buses lumbered to a stop, one behind the other, sparking a frenzy of activity as people queued to board. A few passengers used their arms or elbows to wipe condensation from the windows in an attempt to read the street name over the bus stop and get their bearings. Sara took advantage of the distraction to cover the last few steps to her destination: a spot along the low stone wall she knew was difficult to see on the palace security feed. She checked to ensure no one was paying attention to her, then folded her umbrella and slipped it between the wrought iron rails of the fence that topped the wall. She took care to keep her head down and face aimed away from the cameras as she waited to confirm that the motion detectors had been disabled.

Nothing.

After another quick glance to confirm she wasn't being watched, she stepped onto the stone, grabbed the fence's top rail, and propelled herself up and over to land in the narrow space between the wall and a row of tall, neatly-trimmed evergreens. From the time Sara stepped onto the stone wall until she landed on the softly packed earth, only four seconds had elapsed. She'd timed herself often enough while practicing on a similar fence near her apartment to know.

In one smooth move, she dropped to her belly, grabbed the umbrella, then wriggled under the evergreens. Low, sharp branches scratched her back, but she'd worn a form-fitting jacket and tucked her shoulder-length dark hair into a tight cap to prevent snags. She couldn't risk making a racket by disentangling herself from the bushes while she could still be seen by those on the street.

A few seconds later, she emerged into the royal family's private garden. She rose to her feet, brushed the damp dirt from the front of her jacket, and allowed herself a moment to catch her breath and savor her success. Sarcaccians were fiercely loyal and protective of the royal family. They wouldn't have stood idly by if they'd spotted her scaling the fence. If the cameras had caught her movement, the sidewalk on the other side of the evergreens would've been instantly illuminated. Yet all remained dark and still, and the only sounds coming from the opposite side of the evergreens were typical city noises. The honking of taxis, the low hum of car engines, and occasional voices from the bus stop.

Sara waited for the thrumming of her heart to slow before she bent to hide the umbrella under the evergreens. She took care to note exactly where she left it. Unlike the palace's famed formal gardens, which boasted wide gravel walkways, crisp hedges, and smartly-labeled flowerbeds, this enclosed, private space was a riot of blooms during the spring and summer months. No paths existed save the seemingly random patches of moss and grass that allowed one to walk amongst the flowers and take cuttings of whatever appealed. With the onset of winter, most of the perennials were trimmed down for the season and the fountain in the garden's center emptied of water and silent. She gauged the distance from the fountain to her current position. With no lights or paths to guide her, it'd be easy to lose the umbrella, and she needed it on her exit to avoid being identified on camera.

Though if everything went according to plan, the security staff would never know she'd been here, and they'd never have cause to review the video footage. That was crucial; even if she'd successfully obscured her face, the footage would make it obvious she'd had inside help. All would be for naught if it were traced to the king himself.

Sara shook out her hands, fortifying herself for what lay ahead. Now that she was inside the grounds she faced her toughest challenge: getting into the building without being stopped. She traversed the garden, which was encircled by the high evergreen hedge she'd wriggled under, doing her best to keep to the driest areas to minimize footprints. Only a handful of the palace staff knew of this garden's existence; even fewer visited, which meant any footprints would be easy to spot. Sara herself had only entered the space once, accompanied by Princess Sophia, and that'd been over eight years ago. It'd been during the last week of summer. Sophia had been about to depart for her fall semester in France, and the flowers were still beautiful.

Sara was fired the week before Christmas.

She reached the far side of the enclosure and searched for the narrow break in the evergreens, one barely wide enough for a body to squeeze through. At the same moment she spied the opening, she heard the sound of feet against gravel on the other side, then a sweet, feminine laugh followed by a much deeper one. *Shoot.* She'd anticipated guests would be tempted to sneak out of the charity ball to explore the palace grounds, but hoped tonight's drizzle would deter them. No woman in her right mind would want to ruin a gown worthy of being worn to a formal function at the Sarcaccian royal palace, let alone do so this early in the course of the night's festivities.

The sex better be worth it, sweetie.

Sara pulled back to wait for the couple to pass. When the steps slowed, her pulse leaped.

"I don't see a gate."

"It's along here somewhere," a rich male voice responded. The sound of the wrought iron fence being rattled came to Sara's ears. She pressed herself more firmly into the evergreens at the garden's perimeter. "Got it. The latch is on the back of the gate so it can't be seen. You have to know it's here to find it."

"It's sized for someone the width of a twig! How am I going to get through that in my dress?" Despite her protest, the woman sounded more amused than concerned.

"I'd be happy to help you remove it."

Sara cringed. *Oh, please, no.*

"Little chilly for that."

"I know dozens of ways to keep you warm." Low, sexually-charged laughter carried through the damp air.

Sara closed her eyes and tried to still her breath at the sound of the gate scraping open. Why in the world had she agreed to this?

Because you're a good person, Angeletti.

"Wait until we're back indoors and you can warm me all you want. In the meantime" —Sara heard a muffled grunt— "there. Made it."

A heartbeat later, two figures—no, three—shimmied through the narrow opening in the evergreens. The couple had a dog with them.

The woman took three or four steps into the garden, then paused. "Oh, Massimo, I had no idea this was here!"

"Surprise."

Sara's throat clenched. If anyone could sniff out the fact the garden was already occupied, it'd be royal newlywed Prince Massimo, a tough former soldier, and his well-trained Sarcaccian Shepherd, Gaspare. As if to prove it, the dog swung his head toward Sara, sniffed the air, then trotted over and poked her hip with his wet nose.

Merda.

CHAPTER 2

Sara buried her gloved hand in the damp fur between the dog's ears, willing Gaspare to stay silent. Not twenty feet away, Prince Massimo's Texas-born wife, Kelly, lifted the edges of what appeared to be a gorgeous floor-length gown peeking out from under her raincoat, then took a few tentative steps toward the center of the garden.

"Why haven't you brought me here before?"

"It's my parents' favorite spot. I don't come here that often." In the darkness, Sara saw Massimo move to wrap his arm around Kelly's waist. "When we started walking this direction and Gaspare ran ahead, I realized you'd never seen it."

"I can't see much of it now."

"Then let's explore. The rain's letting up and I'd much rather stay here than spend another hour inside a crowded ballroom."

Kelly and Prince Massimo moved further into the garden, with Massimo describing what grew where during the summer months. Gaspare nudged Sara harder, encouraging her to crouch down to pet him. She did, taking care not to bump into the hedge behind her.

"Missed me, didn't you, big boy?" she breathed into Gaspare's ear, hoping her tone would soothe him. When she'd worked in the palace, she'd become attached to the new puppy and watched his training with interest. She'd heard that while Massimo served in Africa, Gaspare had moved into Princess Sophia's palace apartment. Sara wished she could've been around for that; she'd have enjoyed spending more time with the dog.

Gaspare nuzzled against her, then turned and pushed his rear end into her hip with such force he nearly knocked her over. Sara rolled her eyes. How could she have forgotten? Getting a rump massage was Gaspare's goal in life. If she scratched his backside, he'd moan. But if she didn't, he'd push even harder and possibly whine. Either way, Massimo would quickly realize that he and his wife weren't alone in the garden.

"Gaspare, come."

Gaspare cocked his head in his owner's direction, then looked up at Sara. To her horror, the dog let out a low grumble of protest.

"Sounds like he found a rabbit," Sara heard Kelly say.

"Gaspare, leave it. Come."

"Go," Sara whispered, giving Gaspare a soft swat on his hindquarters. The dog stared at her for a beat longer than he should, given his training, then rubbed his body across her legs before darting through the flowerbed toward the garden's center, where Massimo and Kelly now stood near the fountain. Taking advantage of the noise, Sara ducked through the gap in the evergreens and slipped out the open gate, emerging into the palace's massive formal gardens. Moving quickly, she crossed a gravel pathway, leaped a row of boxwood hedges, then crouched behind them. She waited and listened, but no sound came from behind her.

On a long exhale, she turned to survey the palace, where the party was in full swing. The building appeared glorious at night, being a smaller version of its contemporary, Versailles. Light from dozens of crystal chandeliers glowed through the row of windows that lined the central section of the palace and the faint swell of orchestra music carried on the night air, mixing with the low buzz of hundreds of animated voices. Outside the doors that led revelers to the garden, sentries stood watch. From this distance, it took effort to pick out their forms. They wore suits so they blended in with the crowd, but

Sara knew who—what—they were. Each of them would be armed, given the dignitaries in attendance tonight, and each would have an earpiece connecting him—or her—to Umberto Niro, the head of the Barrali family's security operations.

Sara's gut seized at the very thought of the man and she put a hand to her stomach. In order to succeed tonight, it was imperative she block him from her brain.

Resolved, she crept along the boxwood toward the far wing, where the lights remained dim. The third floor housed King Carlo and Queen Fabrizia's private apartment. Motion sensors and cameras ensured no one could enter through the tall, rectangular windows. The sounds of the party faded as Sara rounded the end of the stone structure and looked up. The curtains in the king and queen's apartment were open, save for the fourth window from the end. There, the curtains were closed.

Her signal to continue.

Even so, Sara remained in place, watching the shadows for movement and listening for the slightest indication of a human presence. With Prince Massimo and his wife wandering the gardens, the guards might not be in their usual positions. Once Sara was certain she was alone, she stood and walked along the gravel path as if she were a guest out for a stroll in the fresh air. A guard with good vision might see that she wore narrow black pants rather than a gown, but if so, she counted on the fact the kitchen staff working the event wore similar pants. It wouldn't be out of the question to see one of them outdoors, taking a break now that dinner had ended.

Then again, Plan A was not to get caught.

She made her way to the service door, grateful no one was taking a cigarette break, then punched the six-digit code into the keypad with her gloved fingers and pressed her thumb against the small screen at the bottom. Three seconds seemed like three minutes as she waited for the light on the screen to turn green. The door clicked. She was in.

The windowless service passage was gloomy and silent as the grave. The rainy weather heightened the feeling, lending the narrow space the smell of damp earth. During the palace's construction centuries before, this hallway and others like it were designed to allow staff to travel throughout the building without being seen in the public or residential areas. Foodstuffs, linens, packages, and cleaning supplies all moved invisibly through the network of service passages. Tonight, with events focused in the palace's massive ballroom, the bulk of the staff would be found in the hallways of the central wing. Sara placed her hand on the wall, using it to guide herself toward the stairs. At the top of the stairwell, she used the same six-digit code, the same thumbprint. Heard the click of the lock as it disengaged. This time, she waited before going through the door.

God help her if Umberto was on the other side, manning his typical evening post along the main staircase. He was the last line of defense against anyone who dared attempt to access King Carlo and Queen Fabrizia's private apartment while the royals were in residence. Tonight, she counted on him being in the midst of the action.

Hearing nothing, she cracked the door and peered into the wide, opulent hallway. Darkened chandeliers hung overhead; the only light came from the windows on the opposite side of the hallway. Nothing moved, no sounds could be heard.

She entered and closed the door behind her so it blended seamlessly with the moldings, then peeled the thumbprint sticker off her glove and stuffed it in the front pocket of her jacket. To her right, a broad marble staircase led to the rest of the palace. Her destination was on the left: the double doors to the king and queen's rooms. She approached, turned the lever, and entered, taking care to close the door soundlessly. The living room was large and comfortable, with plush Persian rugs topping the hardwood floors. A magnificent fireplace dominated the space, and a grouping of sofas and high-backed chairs surrounded a spacious coffee table in the center. A single lamp perched on a glass-topped end table near one of the sofas cast the room in a soft light.

Resisting the temptation to gape at the furnishings, Sara skirted the seating area and made a beeline to the rooms that lay behind the fireplace. It wasn't long before she was in the bedroom. There was no mistaking it for anything other than what it was: the sanctuary of a royal couple worth billions. Sara could fit her entire apartment in the room…twice. The ceilings were easily double the height, and these had been painted in the eighteenth century to resemble the Mediterranean sky at sunset. Gilt laced the moldings along the edges, its gleam apparent even in the semidarkness.

Sara passed by the door to the luxurious master bath and entered the queen's personal closet. As large as a studio apartment in the city, it was professionally designed, boasting floor to ceiling shelves and hang rods crafted of elegant rosewood. A Flokati rug occupied the center of the space and was topped with a comfortable ottoman. Two pairs of shoes lay on the hardwood floor nearby, apparently castoffs as the queen readied for tonight's event.

Sidestepping the shoes, she went to the antique bombe chest situated at the rear of the closet and counted down to the third drawer. Her breath hitched as she surveyed the contents. Everything was as the king described. Dozens of rings, most worth more than Sara earned in a year at her gelateria, rested on a plush velvet tray custom-fit to the drawer and designed to showcase each piece's beauty. She reached to the back of the drawer to free the tray, then placed it on top of the chest. After unzipping her jacket, she unfolded a black bag she'd carried against her ribs, then set it on the floor before reaching into the drawer once more. She felt along the wood until her fingers found the tiny strip of silk. She pulled, revealing the drawer's hidden compartment. Inside, she found the item she'd been sent to retrieve, a gold box roughly the size of two decks of cards. She withdrew a thin layer of bubble wrap from her black bag, wrapped it around the gold box, set it in the bag, then zipped it all inside her jacket. Finally, she shut the hidden compartment, returned the tray of rings to its proper position, and closed the drawer.

Perfetto. Now all she had to do was get out.

"Stop."

Sara flinched at the deep, familiar voice as much as at the sound of a gun being cocked. Though the last time she'd heard the man utter that particular word, it'd been preceded by a *don't* and followed by more intimate sounds.

How had she not heard him approach? How had she not *felt* him approach? Because suddenly, she felt the man's presence as powerfully as if she were wrapped in his arms.

Slowly, Sara raised her hands to her sides and turned. Starting with the dark wingtips the man wore on his feet, she drew her gaze from his precisely tailored tuxedo pants to his lean waist, then forced herself to linger a moment before examining the broad chest and athletic shoulders encased in a white dress shirt and tuxedo jacket. Finally, she lifted her chin to meet the green-eyed gaze and menacing scowl of a man with a rock-hard jaw, sculpted cheekbones, and military haircut. A man whose scowl was far more intimidating than his gun.

Umberto Niro. Her ex.

CHAPTER 3

Umberto stood stock-still, hard-pressed to believe the scene unfolding before him, let alone the *who*. He kept his weapon steady. "Sara Angeletti."

It'd been eight years since he'd seen her in the flesh. Eight years since she'd been fired for theft while on the job and had the audacity to give *him* a lecture on trust on her way out the door.

And damn if he hadn't compared every woman he'd dated since then to her, despite the fact Sara was all wrong for him. That much was evident in the way she was dressed right now, like a cat burglar on the prowl with black pants that hugged the curve of her hips, a close-fitting black jacket that zipped from her waist to her throat, and a black knit cap that covered her hair. She even sported black gloves and black shoes. The only spot of color anywhere was the flash of her eyes, as sharp and clear as the sparkling blue topaz in one of the queen's favorite rings.

A ring that might be in Sara's jacket at this moment.

"Well, if it isn't James Bond, here to investigate. And you actually remember the name of the girl. That's not in the usual script." She kept her hands in the air and jerked her chin to indicate his gun. "I see that you're appropriately armed. License to kill?"

Her bravado didn't fool him for a moment, though he grudgingly admired it. "Nice hat. Explain yourself."

He didn't miss the twitch of her fingers as she started to reach for the black cap, then stopped herself. "As you can see, I'm standing in Queen Fabrizia's closet."

"You were in her jewelry drawers. You were holding her rings."

He could see in her gaze that she was thinking back through her movements, wondering how much he'd seen. "I didn't take a single piece of Her Highness's jewelry. The tray is in the drawer, safe and sound. See for yourself."

A note in her voice made him believe her, which went against all logic. He shot her a black look. "There will be a full accounting. For now, you're coming with me."

"No."

He scoffed at that. "As you pointed out, I'm the one with a gun. Before we go, care to hand over whatever you stuffed inside your jacket?"

"You're not touching anything that's inside this jacket, Umberto. You forfeited that opportunity."

The past eight years made her gutsier, and not only in her language. In all the history of the palace, no one had broken into any of its private residences…a fact of which Sara was well aware. He covered the space between them in two long steps and grabbed her forearm, wrenching it to her back as he maneuvered behind her. "Then I'm touching the outside of the jacket. Move it."

"Hey!" She pressed against him, proving she was as physically strong as when she'd headed Princess Sophia's security detail. He was stronger, and the position of her arm gave him the advantage.

"Dig in your heels and I'll carry you out of here."

"You try and—"

"I'll have half a dozen men here in under twenty seconds if you don't come willingly," he hissed, his mouth close to her ear. He kept his eyes forward, away from the lean column of her neck. "Give it up, Sara. Right. Now."

He could almost hear the four-letter words rattling around in her brain, though the one she finally chose to utter was, "Fine."

She stopped struggling, but Umberto didn't let down his guard. He glanced around the closet to confirm that everything was in order, holstered his weapon, then urged Sara forward.

"We're heading to the dungeon, I suppose."

"My office."

"As I said."

Umberto hustled her out of the apartment and down the stairs. She didn't fight him, but she didn't move at the pace he set, either. Given the angle at which he held her arm, the resistance had to cause her pain. He gritted his teeth. Even in the dark of the queen's closet, he'd seen that Sara was as beautiful as ever, dark cap or no. But the years had made her even more stubborn.

A woman in a sleek white pantsuit stood on the ground floor with her back to the stairs. At the sound of Umberto's footsteps, she turned her head in surprise.

"Have someone take your station," he told Olga Vestergaard, his second-in-command. He pulled a pair of reading glasses from the front of his tuxedo jacket. "Ensure these are delivered to Queen Fabrizia, then come to my office."

Olga, who was every bit as tall, blond, and lethally fit as her name implied, eyed Sara long enough to note Umberto's unbreakable hold, then nodded. "I'll be there momentarily."

"Is the way clear?"

"Should be, but I'll make sure."

"Good." Olga hadn't worked at the palace when Sara left, but many on the staff had. If Umberto crossed paths with any other employees, Sara was bound to be recognized. He didn't want to hear any questions or spark gossip until he had answers. *All* the answers.

Umberto moved on as Olga pressed her earpiece to call for assistance. He steered Sara through a series of unoccupied rooms, keeping her arm firmly behind her back, then turned into the spacious hallway that connected the Barrali family's private wing to the larger, public areas. His office door was in the center of the hallway.

"Don't try anything," he ground out as he used one hand to operate the keypad.

"I was about to say the same to you."

Once inside, he released her and slammed the door. "Sit."

Surprisingly, she did as he asked, dropping into the cold, government-issue office chair beside his desk. There was determination in her gaze as she lifted her wide, innocent blue eyes to his. No wonder she'd fit in as a college student when she'd been twenty-six to Princess Sophia's twenty. At thirty-four, she still looked like she was only a year or two out of high school.

"Take off that ridiculous hat."

He was treated to an eye roll, but again, she did as he asked. Thick, dark hair fell to graze her shoulders. It wasn't quite as long as before. The change surprised him. Then again, neither of them was as young as before. Or as naive.

Umberto put one hand to his hip, allowing his fingers to hover just over his holstered gun. If he hadn't volunteered to retrieve the queen's reading glasses from the apartment and heard the faint sounds coming from the direction of the closet, Sara might not have been caught. That thought unsettled him. "Now, I'll ask again. Explain yourself."

"I can assure you I wasn't doing anything illegal—"

"Breaking and entering. Theft. Assault if I'd given you the chance."

"—but you're going to have to trust me."

The last two words hung in the air. He knew they were both thinking back to the same moment, when she'd walked out of King Carlo's office all those years ago, head held high, and informed Umberto that she'd been fired. He'd told her that given what she did, she should've expected it. Shoplifting in one of Paris's most posh department stores, with Princess Sophia right there? How could the king do anything else, especially since Sara had given the French police a full confession?

Sara had looked him square in the eye and said, *I'm sleeping with a man who doesn't even know me. How, after all this time, can you not trust me?*

She'd looked away, huffed out a breath, and walked out of his life with his heart in her hand.

At least until tonight, when he'd captured her with that same hand in the proverbial cookie jar.

"I didn't get this job by trusting people," he said at last. "In fact, I have this job because I *don't* trust people. It keeps the royal family alive and our country stable."

"Very noble of you." She leaned back in the hard metal chair and crossed her arms as if the office were hers. "I heard you got the promotion about a year after I left."

"I heard that you're running your own business. Successfully, too. Which raises the question...?" He waved a hand in the general direction of King Carlo and Queen Fabrizia's apartment.

To call her business successful was an understatement. After her dismissal, Sara had somehow scraped together the capital to open a gelato shop less than two kilometers from the palace, in the heart of Cateri's medieval town center. It was an instant hit with locals—a tough standard in gourmand-minded Sarcaccia—and started drawing tourists soon afterward. By Angeletti Gelato's third year in business, the shop appeared in *Fodor's* and Rick Steves' guidebooks, and it wasn't unusual to see a line snaking down the street on a hot afternoon. Last year, she'd expanded to a second location on Cateri's waterfront, and in recent months, she'd added ordering capabilities to her website, offering overnight shipments throughout Europe, the United States, and Canada.

He could only imagine the markup on that endeavor. It seemed tourists who'd discovered Angeletti Gelato were willing to pay top dollar for a taste of Sarcaccia after they returned home.

"You heard, or did you visit the shop? Or...perhaps you discovered it because you've been spying on me? Which raises the question...?"

There was a lilt to her voice that made him frown. "What question?"

"Why you'd care enough about what I've been doing to spy on me."

"At this moment, I care very much what you've been doing. Otherwise, you wouldn't be sitting in that chair. You can be charged with a federal crime. You were in the private quarters of the head of state."

Sara straightened at the same time Umberto heard the sound of the keypad being operated on the other side of the door. Olga entered, then looked from Sara to Umberto. "Max has the stairs. Who's our guest?"

"A former employee. Caught her upstairs."

Olga's eyes narrowed. "Her access wasn't rescinded?"

"Long ago." Umberto turned to glare at Sara. "Tell me exactly how you got in."

Sara didn't move. Her blue eyes hardened to steel.

Without shifting his attention, he instructed Olga, "Go in the control room and double-check the motion sensors and security lighting around that entire wing. Lock down the video feed for the staircase and upper hallway for the past twenty-four hours, then get me the keypad logs for all points of entry into that area for the same period."

Olga strode past Sara to enter the massive room behind Umberto's spartan office. It housed the brains of the palace—video feeds, alarm control panels, entry and exit logs—and was staffed by at least three people at all times. One of them should've seen something.

"She's very pretty," Sara noted once Olga left the office. "One of your hires since the big promotion, I assume."

"Jealous?"

"Don't flatter yourself."

Umberto gave her a long, slow smile, one fully intended to knock her off her game. Sara might act invincible, but everyone had a crack in their armor. "Olga's gay. And taken."

"Good for her."

"She's extremely good at her job." He moved a few steps closer, then leaned across Sara, willing her to flinch as he grabbed his desk chair and wheeled it around her. He stopped it directly in front of her, then took a seat and leaned forward. He kept his voice low, so no one in the back room could hear, even if they opened the door. "I'm also very good at my job."

"I'm well aware." He caught a hint of trepidation in her gaze, though she covered it quickly. "She's Danish? Not too many Danes in Sarcaccia."

"Danish father, Russian mother." Sara's attempt to change the subject wouldn't work. "Tell me why you were in the queen's closet and how you got there. I'll discover the how soon enough, but if you tell me everything up front, there's a chance it'll go easier on you."

"You've watched too many late-night American cop shows, Umberto."

He kept quiet. Waited for her to capitulate. Unfortunately, he discovered that staring down Sara Angeletti was the toughest thing he'd done in a long time. Over the past eight years, he'd spent too many nights falling asleep with the vision of her in his head to keep those same thoughts from entering his mind now, especially when she sat so close he could see the details his imagination missed. The soft spread of her jet-black eyelashes. The smooth texture of her pale skin and high color in her cheeks. The contrast between those blue, blue eyes and her ebony hair. The light pink of her bare mouth. The tiny crease down the center of her lower lip. The scent of rain on her clothing.

His fantasies of her were mere shadows when compared to the living, breathing Sara before him.

He leaned even closer and forced himself to imagine he was eye to eye with a thug in the streets rather than the sexy, intelligent woman now in his office. Sara was excellent at reading people, and he refused to allow her to see that he still found her blindingly attractive.

"You're trying to intimidate me," she finally said. "But the truth is, my presence in this building intimidates you. I find that very…interesting."

CHAPTER 4

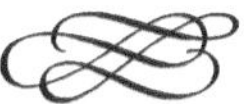

He stunned her by laughing. Loud, booming, and so like the Umberto she'd known away from the palace, before he'd turned into a first class jerk. The Umberto he'd been during their off hours, when they'd hiked in the hills outside Cateri, spent long Saturdays snorkeling at the southern end of the island, or when they'd lounged in bed, making love and talking. Those rare, precious times when he'd put aside his workaholic tendencies so they could savor each other's company.

"Intimidated by you? What gave you that idea?" he asked.

It took a concentrated effort to keep her tone firm. "Tonight's charity ball is to raise money for those orphaned due to unrest in the Middle East. You have the Turkish President in the building. The Italian Prime Minister. The King and Queen of Jordan. Leaders of charitable organizations from across southern Europe who are hoping to prevent a generation from growing up without education or opportunity and creating a burden on the entire region." She couldn't help but shoot him a wicked grin. "The very last thing you want tonight is for it to come out that your security isn't all it's cracked up to be. That for the first time in centuries, someone made it inside the most impregnable rooms in the entire palace complex."

The superior grin didn't leave his face. "That someone is now in my office.'"

"Calling the police could cause world leaders to question your methods. If my entry became public knowledge, it could hurt Queen Fabrizia's charity in the short term and cause problems for state visits in the long term."

She sounded supremely confident. She didn't feel it. She hoped he couldn't tell.

The door behind Sara opened, but she kept her attention riveted on Umberto, refusing to turn at the sound of Olga's voice. "Motion sensors and lighting check out for all wings. However, there's a one-minute gap where the motion detectors along the Via Floriana fence were disconnected. Looks like they were tripped, then re-engaged."

"How long ago?"

"Just over half an hour." Sara could feel Olga's scowl, even if she couldn't see it. "It wasn't done from the control room. Mobile device, most likely, by someone with current security passwords."

Umberto's gaze darkened. "Pull up the feed from the street for ten minutes on either side of the one-minute gap and send it to my computer. What about the logs for the doors?"

"All entries were by sanctioned personnel. Nothing out of the ordinary."

"Send those, too. I'll give them a second look. Then change the security passwords."

"That's being done now."

He thanked her, then Sara heard the door to control room bang shut. Umberto pegged her with an aggressive glare. She knew in that instant that he wasn't going to let her go. If he didn't get a satisfactory explanation, he'd bring in the police, even if it hurt his career. She'd gotten too close to the royal family.

Her heart jackhammered in her chest, the thumping so strong she felt its beat all the way up in her throat. This wasn't at all how tonight was supposed to go.

"You had help from inside the palace. Who?"

"No one on your staff helped me."

He scoffed with the certainty of a man who knew she couldn't have gotten in otherwise. "You don't want anyone to get fired for this."

"No one should, because—again—no one on your staff helped me."

He opened his mouth—no doubt to make another smart remark—when his gaze darted to the front of her pants. Before she could move, he caught her knee in one hand. She tried to pull back, but it was as if her knee were caught in a steel vise. With his other hand, he pinched the fabric, then held two long, chocolate-colored hairs in front of her face.

"You don't own a dog."

Gaspare. She knew that beast would get her into trouble. She forced an exasperated sigh. "I know Queen Fabrizia has quite the spy network, but I can't imagine its purpose is to investigate the dog-walking habits of her former employees."

He stared at her for several beats. "Gaspare. You ran into Gaspare in the garden. Prince Massimo and his wife left the ball less than an hour ago to walk outside. They would've gone to their apartment to get Gaspare first."

When she didn't respond, he released her knee. His green eyes shot daggers at her, but she could tell he now realized there was more to tonight than was apparent on the surface.

"There's no way Prince Massimo assisted you in a theft from his own parents' apartment."

"Look, Umberto, you and I both know how tight security is in the building, especially on a night like tonight. If I got into the palace, there's a reason."

"Yet you won't share it with the head of security." His hand came down on the desktop with such force she flinched. She gritted her teeth, instantly mad at herself for showing fear. It'd only make Umberto more determined.

"I wasn't here to commit a theft," she said evenly. Well, maybe technically it was theft, since she was now in possession of an invaluable item that wasn't hers. "Believe me, I'm well aware of what constitutes theft after that episode with Princess Sophia."

"That *episode* cost you your job and your reputation."

"It cost me you."

The words escaped before she could catch herself, but what shocked her more than her slip of the tongue was the momentary expression on Umberto's face. A flash of pain, as if she'd been the one who'd hurt him, rather than the other way around. Worse, she found herself desperately wanting to believe in his hurt. Practically, because it'd give her a vulnerability to work with, a sliver of hope that he might relent and set her free. Emotionally, because there was consolation in knowing she wasn't the only one whose heart had been broken. What she hated was that the emotional side of it was far stronger than the practical side.

"Ancient history," he said, though it was so quiet she barely heard it, as if he needed to convince himself rather than her.

Well, if he could put practicality before emotion, so could she. She had to get out of here, and the sooner the better. "Umberto, I understand that it's your job to get to the bottom of this. You know I couldn't have done this alone. All I can tell you is that no one on your staff helped me. No one in housekeeping or the kitchen or grounds crew helped me. Think about who that leaves—"

"Not Prince Massimo."

His tone challenged her to reveal a name, but she couldn't. She pressed her palms to her knees. "If you discover anything missing, you know where I live. You know where I work."

"It's not that simple. I have to report this."

She flailed for a way to save herself, then latched onto the fact he hadn't specifically mentioned reporting her to the police, as he had before...which meant he planned to report her to the king and queen first.

She allowed herself a brief grimace, one she knew Umberto would note, then covered it with a shake of her head. "The queen will never feel safe if she knows anyone entered her apartment, let alone opened her drawers to see her personal belongings." She'd heard from former coworkers that the queen adored Umberto and that he knew her better than anyone aside from her family. If it was true, he'd recognize the truth of Sara's statement. "Tell the king. Not Queen Fabrizia."

A furrow appeared across Umberto's brow. "You want me to tell King Carlo that a former employee was caught in his wife's closet."

"I don't *want* you to tell him anything. But your position demands it, and I respect your need to do so."

Skepticism laced his features. All she could do was hope she'd given him enough to keep from going to either the police or the queen. Finally, Umberto said, "You didn't show that respect for your own position while you were here."

She pressed her lips together and counted to three. He had no idea how much respect she had for her job. For the Barrali family. The high price she'd paid for that dedication to duty. "Ancient history."

He swiped a hand over his jaw, then rose, towering over her. "Stand up."

She was hardly out of the chair before he said, "Hands out to the sides."

"You're searching me?"

"Before I let you go, yes."

Astonishment and relief at his decision to set her free so overwhelmed her that she raised her arms without argument. Only when his hands went to her waist, then slowly ran down the outside of her legs, did Sara's survival instincts kick in.

If he found the box, it'd ruin everything.

She looked down at the top of Umberto's head as his hands went around her ankles in a tight loop, checked her for hidden items, then smoothed over the tops of her shoes. He began to rise, drawing his hands up the inside of her legs.

"Missed me that much? Even for you, this is fast."

"Quiet." He continued up her thighs, but stopped short of her crotch before he circled her and ran one hand along the back of her waistband, then spread both hands across her back and worked his way to her shoulders.

"If Olga were to come in now, what would she think?" Sara rolled her shoulders for emphasis. Flirtation was the only tool left in her rather pathetic arsenal. Anything to keep him from finding what was hidden just beneath her bra line.

He ignored her. Instead, he sandwiched her left arm between his hands and felt all the way from her armpit to her fingertips, then repeated the action on her right.

"Can I drop my arms now?"

"You know the drill."

He lifted her hair, felt along the back of her neck. She squeezed her eyes shut for a brief moment, fighting her reaction to his touch. When he'd kissed her there, it'd driven her mad. He'd known it, too. As he finished, she managed to smile and deliver a flippant, "I was wearing a hat. You know nothing's there."

He rounded to face her, then spanned her throat with his fingers to check inside the front of her collar. He didn't so much as pause when she uttered an, "Oooh, baby." He ducked, skirting the outside of her breasts with a hand on each side of her, paused briefly near her side pockets, then moved his palms over her stomach to finish back at her waist again. He didn't check the area beneath her breasts.

She swallowed hard, trying not to let triumph show on her face as he stepped back. "Satisfied?"

"Hardly." She could see the cold assessment in his gaze, the knowledge that she had *something*. The realization that, had she been anyone else, he'd have spent more time searching the area around and under her breasts. The inner debate on whether he should do it now. Then his gaze shuttered. "I'm going to escort you to the side gate. From there, you will go directly home. There will be a full investigation. In the meantime, don't leave Cateri."

"No plans to. As you pointed out, I have a rather successful business to run."

He called out, "Olga, I'll be back in five," then to Sara, he said, "Come with me."

He held her elbow as they exited to the hallway, but thankfully opted not to twist it behind her back as if she were made of rubber. Instead of taking her the way they'd come, he turned toward the front of the complex, winding through a series of dim rooms, illuminated only by lamps in corners or subtle lights mounted to the ancient baseboards.

"If we're going to the side gate, why not take the service hallways?" It'd be a lot faster.

"Just walk."

Finally, they emerged into a hallway that ran along the outside of the palace's large ballroom. Though Sara saw no one, the orchestra sounded so clear here that she could pick out the individual instruments.

"Why aren't you calling the police?"

"I still might. I'll make that decision after I determine how and why you're here."

At the end of the hallway, Umberto turned her away from the ballroom and guided her down the staircase that led to the east gate. At the bottom, he released her elbow to push through a fire door to a gravel courtyard. The rain was negligible now; only a light mist appeared in the haze of the outdoor lights. Several vehicles were parked alongside the building. When she'd worked here, this space was used only for quick loading and unloading when there were events in the ballroom.

"VIP parking for a few of tonight's guests," he said, anticipating her question.

"I see." Upon closer inspection, she noted that the cars all had tinted windows. A driver stood behind one, smoking a cigarette. Windows were cracked on a few others, indicating a driver likely sat in the front, waiting for his passengers to call. A gate wide enough for automobiles to pass through stood at the far side of the courtyard, manned on either side by an armed guard. An adjacent stone gatehouse no doubt housed more men. Security cameras mounted to both the gatehouse and the building swept the entire area.

Umberto signaled ahead to one of the guards as he accompanied her to the tall, locking turnstile beside the gatehouse. "You're free to go…for now. Stay local."

She nodded her assent, then covered the last few paces to the turnstile on her own. She could feel him watching her, could sense his doubt over letting her go. She started to go through, then paused and turned to face him. "Umberto? I'm not a thief."

He stood stock still, feet rooted to the ground, one hand in the pocket of his tuxedo pants as he squinted at her. Even in the gloom, he appeared debonair enough to join the party. Only with a longer glance did one realize he possessed the dark air of a man who was exceedingly dangerous. At last, he said, "Go."

The rain started to pick up as she stared at him. Finally, she spun and pushed through the turnstile. When she turned to walk along the outside of the fence toward home, he was already striding away.

He didn't look back.

CHAPTER 5

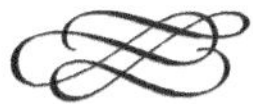

IT COST ME YOU.

Umberto dropped into his desk chair, opened his laptop computer, then curled and uncurled his fists while he waited for the machine to boot.

Sara hadn't planned to say that. Unlike every other word that left her lips tonight, it wasn't calculated to sway his sympathies or to flatter. She hadn't said it as a distraction. In fact, the words seemed to have thrown her for a loop, as if she'd truly had her heart broken and had buried that information deep inside herself, never intending it to be revealed.

Ludicrous. He was the one who'd been betrayed.

He could still picture himself pacing outside the king's office as he'd waited for Sara to emerge all those years ago. She'd been on assignment in Paris as the head of Princess Sophia's security detail and he hadn't seen her in two weeks. He'd stayed after his own shift, anxious to determine if the palace rumors were true, that Sara had come back early because the French press was about to break the story that one of the princess's bodyguards had been caught stealing.

Sara had emerged wearing a conservative navy blue suit and heels, her hair pulled back into a bun and her pearl earrings visible. He knew instantly that the matter was serious. He'd been so used to seeing her in the clothes she wore while with the princess—youthful, trendy outfits that enabled her to blend in with the French college crowd—that the suit shocked him to silence. Before he could recover, Sara stated in a matter-of-fact tone that she'd been caught stealing at Printemps while accompanying Sophia and several of the princess's college friends on a shopping trip, had given a full confession to the French police, and had just been fired. Her words were as bland as if she were delivering the weather report or saying, "I'm heading home, see you tomorrow," rather than confirming the juiciest piece of gossip to circulate through the palace in years.

No one, but no one, broke the rules when they worked for the Barralis. Not because they feared retribution, but because they held the family in such high regard. The king and queen were wonderful employers and truly decent people, the type you'd want for next-door neighbors or as close friends. Reeling from the news and the fact Sara didn't show a drop of sadness or remorse over her firing, Umberto had told her, "Given your actions, you must've expected it."

That's when Sara's emotions surfaced, erupting like a plume of fire from a long-dormant volcano. She'd flung trust in his face and walked out of his life after nearly a year together. After he thought he knew her.

Here she was again. Caught. Once again, he'd been shocked to his core. Back then it'd been all over the newspapers that an employee of the royal household had been caught shoplifting. Hell, when she'd opened her gelato shop several months later, the first people through the door had been reporters, eager to see what had become of Sara Angeletti, palace thief.

He brushed a hand over the top of his head. It was his job *not* to be shocked. He prided himself on his ability to read people and situations so he could anticipate behavior.

He downloaded the logs Olga had forwarded to him and watched as the pages popped onto the screen. Sara had maintained a pristine reputation since leaving the palace. Over the years, he'd thought more than once that he should approach her and find out what happened in

Paris to cause her to act so out of character. Part of him longed to know whether, despite that event, she was the decent, good-hearted person he'd always believed her to be. If he could've made a mistake that afternoon outside the king's office.

When he'd stood in Queen Fabrizia's closet with his gun leveled at Sara's heart, he'd congratulated himself on his decision to stay away. Then when he'd had her in his office, she'd stated that if she'd been able to break through security there was a good reason and had gone on to insist it wasn't theft. Something deeper than the content of her speech—the note of pain in her eyes, the sincerity in her tone—disturbed him. She wanted him to believe her, but not simply to keep herself out of trouble. It mattered to her personally. Then she'd told him to report her to King Carlo, of all people. The man who'd fired her, rather than the queen...when prevailing wisdom throughout the palace was that Umberto and the queen had a strong relationship. If Sara wanted to avoid prosecution, she should know she'd have better luck with Queen Fabrizia than King Carlo.

He couldn't explain it, but his gut said Sara was telling the truth. She'd clearly broken the law, but he was missing a giant piece of the puzzle. Instinct honed by over a decade working security for the Barrali family told him that turning over Sara to the authorities—at least tonight—would be a mistake. Everything about her break-in pointed to a high-level inside job.

He tapped a few keys to display the logs from the doors closest to the king and queen's apartment. As Olga had indicated, a quick scan of the logs revealed nothing but the usual names.

Umberto reached for the small, folded sticker he'd left on the edge of his desk. He'd snagged it from the inside edge of Sara's front jacket pocket when he'd started the pat-down, but she'd been so relieved he didn't frisk the small lump he'd spied dead-center underneath her breasts that she didn't notice. He'd debated making her remove it, then decided to let it go. If it was anything of value, she wouldn't get far with it. He'd be more likely to get the full story if he let her walk away believing he'd learned nothing, when he'd already obtained the key to her co-conspirator's identity. To that end, he smoothed out the oval-shaped tag, then pulled over his desk lamp to study it more closely.

"Well, who have we here?" he muttered as he confirmed his initial assessment, that the sticker bore the loops and swirls of a fingerprint. Once he scanned it into the computer, he'd bet anything it'd match one of the keypad entries to the king and queen's wing. While he waited for the scanner to copy the fingerprint and compare it to those in his database, Umberto tapped his earpiece and called one of the women working the perimeter of the ballroom.

"Yes?" The guard's voice was low, and he could hear a single male voice in the background. Must be time for King Carlo to address the gathering.

"Is Daniela D'Ambrosio there? The queen's assistant."

A pause, then, "Affirmative."

"If she's not busy, send her my way."

"Will do."

He turned his attention to the logs again. None of the names jumped out at him, even on a closer study. All belonged to employees who worked in that wing or to members of the royal family. Then one name caught his eye at the same time his computer dinged to let him know a match was made to the fingerprint.

He hadn't entered the wing by the outside door, yet his code and fingerprint had registered. He clicked to the other screen and let out an oath.

The fingerprint on the sticker was his own.

Umberto closed his eyes and pinched the bridge of his nose as Olga re-entered from the back room. "I have her on video coming up the service stairway."

"At 10:22 pm?" he asked.

"Exactly 10:22. You've matched it to a keypad entry?"

"Yes."

"Great." A pause. "Where is she now?"

"Released. I know where she lives and works. She's not going anywhere."

He didn't look up. Olga was quiet for long moment before asking, "Are you feeling well, Umberto?"

"I'm fine. It's just been a long day." Sara Angeletti's reappearance in his life meant he'd have a long night. "I have this from here. Why don't you relieve Max so he can return to the ballroom?"

"She's very pretty."

Umberto laughed and met Olga's inquisitive gaze. "She said the same about you."

"I'm flattered. Too bad she's straight."

"And you're spoken for." Umberto frowned. "What makes you say she's straight?"

A wicked smile lifted Olga's cheeks. "I could tell when I walked in the office and saw her glaring at you."

"Excuse me? Glaring at me makes her straight?"

As she exited to the hallway, she said, "In her case, most definitely."

UMBERTO PAUSED JUST inside the double doors to the king and queen's private apartment. Morning sunshine angled in the large windows and the hum of a vacuum cleaner echoed from one of the back rooms. Adriana, the head of housekeeping for the palace, was in the midst of watering the massive Christmas tree that stood opposite the windows. When the doors clicked into place behind him, she looked up from her task and smiled in greeting.

He made polite inquiries after her health and her children, then asked, "Is Daniela D'Ambrosio still here?"

"In the queen's closet," Adriana responded. "She's expecting you."

He thanked her, then made his way through the living room before crossing the sizable bedroom. The royal apartment felt completely different than it had only twelve hours earlier. The plush rugs and furniture appeared elegant but comfortable, evergreen Christmas decorations scented the air, and framed photographs of the couple's children and grandchildren lent the space a personal touch. He wasn't creeping through in the dark as he had last night, avoiding furniture as he listened for the odd creak of floorboards or the rustle of a drawer being searched. Nor was he compelled to slink along the outer wall to get the drop on an intruder when he entered the walk-in closet.

Instead, he was faced with the queen's efficient personal assistant, Daniela, who stood to one side of the closet in front of a rod bearing dozens of designer suits and dresses. She held a tablet in her hand, ticking off boxes on the screen as she inspected each piece.

"I was wondering when you'd make an appearance. Now that I'm nearly done, may I ask what prompted this inventory?" she asked without looking away from her task. "So far, there's nothing amiss."

"You're certain?"

She logged another item, then turned to arch her brows at Umberto. "I know the queen's clothing and jewels backward and forward. I'm telling you, everything's in its place. All I have left to check are the handbags and I doubt any of those are missing." She gestured to a shelf set above the row of suits. Leather handbags stood in a line, arranged by color from darkest to lightest. "It's obvious when one is out of place."

"What about their contents?"

"Emptied after each use."

"How about the dresser?" He shot a look at the antique chest of drawers where he'd caught Sara the night before.

"It contains jewelry and accessories. Scarves, gloves, that type of thing. All accounted for."

He frowned. Daniela was thorough. She wouldn't overlook a missing ring or necklace. So what in the world did Sara sneak out of there? "Has the queen acquired any new pieces that might not be in your inventory?"

"Every purchase and gift is logged as it comes in. The queen is diligent about it, as am I." Daniela tucked a stray strand of blond hair behind her ear. "So *now* will you tell me why you called me into your office in the middle of last night's party to ask for this?"

He'd avoided the issue last night, but owed Daniela an explanation.

She'd juggled her regular duties in order to do him the favor. "It's possible an item may have been removed by a former employee."

"How former of an employee? If it was taken before my time here, then my inventory might not reflect—"

"The item would have been removed yesterday."

Surprise flared in Daniela's eyes. "In that case, I can assure you that nothing was taken. For someone to even gain access to this area without the king, queen, or I knowing would be astonishing." She let the statement float, despite the fact she knew he wouldn't give her any more information.

"Thanks, Daniela. I appreciate the effort. I had to be certain."

As he strode out of the closet, she asked, "Would you like me to speak with the queen about it?"

"No. I'll handle it from here."

His wish came sooner than he anticipated. He came face to face with the royal couple as they ascended the stairs to their apartment. In her usual light tone, the queen asked, "Umberto, how are you this morning?"

He dipped his head in deference. "I'm well, thank you. Your visit to the hospital's new pediatric wing ended early?"

"Traffic was light on our return," King Carlo said. "We decided to complete a few personal calls from the apartment before our next appointments."

"I understand Daniela is upstairs." At Umberto's confirmation, Queen Fabrizia's dark brows rose. "She said she wished to conduct an inventory of the closet before accompanying me to the Cateri Public Library's holiday celebration this afternoon. I understand it was at your request. Is something amiss?"

"Not at all, Your Highness. There was an anomaly in last night's entry log for this wing and I asked Daniela for the inventory out of an abundance of caution. I've now traced the issue, so there's no need for concern."

She placed a hand on his forearm, keeping the touch brief. Her intelligent gaze seemed to pierce him, seeking the truth even as she offered a smile. "I'm glad to hear it."

In a tone meant to reassure, he said, "I apologize for monopolizing Daniela's time."

"A confirmed inventory of all household items is useful. Perhaps I should have my closet re-catalogued, as well," King Carlo said, then turned to his wife. "Why don't you go ahead? I'd like a word with Umberto about arrangements for next week's trip to Berlin."

"I'll see you upstairs."

Once the queen disappeared from sight, King Carlo asked a few questions about trip preparations. Umberto confirmed that he would remain in Sarcaccia to accompany the queen to several local events, while Olga and a team of three others would travel with the king. The Germans had arranged for security while the king was on the ground in Berlin. "I've reviewed the plans for the meeting areas and I'm satisfied they've covered all contingencies, but I'm still waiting on their transportation information."

"Let me know if there are any issues." The king leaned forward and placed one hand on the railing, as if he were about to move past Umberto and proceed upstairs. Instead, the monarch lowered his voice. "Now about my wife's closet. She didn't notice anything out of place this morning, but you wouldn't have ordered an inventory unless you believed it to be absolutely necessary. Is there something you wish to tell me?"

Umberto acknowledged the king's perceptiveness with a brief nod. "During last night's event, there was an unauthorized entry into this wing. Measures have been taken to ensure it doesn't happen again."

"Did you identify the intruder?"

"Yes. A former employee."

The king's hand tensed, but he masked his reaction quickly. "Have you contacted the police?"

"I wish to complete my own investigation first. The individual resides here in Cateri and has strong ties to the community. If an arrest is necessary, it can be accomplished easily enough."

The king considered the information, his lips pinched in thought. "Do you believe there's any danger to members of my family?"

"No. Of that, I am confident." Sara was never a threat to their safety.

"In that case, please keep the situation between the two of us, at least until after Christmas. The police are on a holiday schedule and I'd prefer their resources remain devoted to emergencies when they're not enjoying time at home with their loved ones. No need to call upon them when you and your staff are perfectly capable of doing the job."

Despite the calm tone in which it was delivered, the mandate made Umberto uneasy. It was out of character for the king to make such a specific request; he'd always trusted Umberto's judgment when it came to matters of security. "If that's your wish, Your Highness."

"Thank you." The king turned and ascended the final few stairs toward his apartment, but paused at the top to look over his shoulder. "When's the last time you took a vacation day, Umberto?"

"Sir?"

"My family means everything to me. I take pains to arrange my schedule so I can spend Christmas with them. But as long as you've worked for me, I don't believe you've spent a holiday away from the palace. Not one that didn't happen to fall on your day off."

The change of subject caught Umberto off guard. From the queen, it wouldn't be surprising. Over the years since Umberto arrived at the palace, he'd become acquainted with Queen Fabrizia on a personal level. It was her nature to know all her employees by name and to ask after their families, and it wasn't unusual to catch her making small talk in the palace hallways or complimenting a member of the staff on a job well done when warranted. Each evening, she made it her habit to stop to chat with Umberto on the staircase before retiring to her apartment. The king, however, moved through his day with determination, his focus ever on the business of running the country. While he knew the staff, he had little time for casual conversation.

"I'm quite happy here, Your Highness. The palace is beautiful this time of year and my presence enables my staff to be with their families."

"Next year, I expect you to take time off." The king's smile was indulgent, but his tone firm. "Spend it with your loved ones. I'm sure there's a woman out there who'd enjoy sharing gifts and mulled wine in front of a fire."

"I appreciate the sentiment, Your Highness, but—"

The king raised a hand, then turned and walked away. Over his shoulder, he said, "The holiday season is a time of miracles, but only if you're available to savor them. Next year, you'll take Christmas off."

CHAPTER 6

Sara wished the last of her customers goodnight, followed the young couple to the front door, and flipped the sign to close her downtown shop.

A mixture of gratitude and exhaustion swamped her as she turned the deadbolt. By three in the afternoon, customers had occupied every single table in Angeletti Gelato. Even with three workers scooping at the counter and one more working the espresso machine, the line went out the door and remained that way throughout the dinner hour and into the evening.

Business usually wasn't so brisk this time of year, even on a Saturday, but after the previous day's rainfall kept many indoors, today's sunshine meant locals and tourists alike were making up for lost time. Shopping bags crammed every available spot beneath the tables and a lively bubble of conversation filled the air. Children pressed their faces to the display case as they made their selections, pointing out various flavors to siblings and parents. Sara had mingled with the crowd, welcoming neighbors who'd popped in for a treat and introducing herself to new customers. As evening fell, she'd greeted young adults who'd returned from college for the winter break and craved a taste of home. A healthy number of visitors inquired about sending

Christmas gifts, then went on to place orders. She and her coworkers would be up late tomorrow night, packing gelato for Monday shipments.

Sara grabbed a spray bottle to attack the glass on the front door. Thanks to increased profits from the delivery service, she'd be able to give her employees a better-than-expected bonus this year. If she concentrated on that, maybe it'd alleviate the sick feeling that'd knotted her stomach all day.

There hadn't been a peep from Umberto. No one rushed in to say they'd seen her on the news. The police hadn't appeared at her door, arrest warrant in hand. Other than the fifteen-minute trek she'd made early this morning to deliver the gold box to a local jeweler, it was as if last night never happened.

She gave the green and yellow tile-topped tables a quick wipe-down, then retreated to the kitchen to grab a few more cleaning cloths and fill the mop bucket. Davide, a teenager she employed during his after school and vacation hours, stood at one of the stainless steel counters and covered a pan of pumpkin gelato for cold storage.

"Why don't you head home when you've finished that one?" Sara said over her shoulder as she opened the closet that contained the shop's cleaning supplies.

"There are still four or five flavors out there."

"I'll get them when I wipe down the counter. I'm about to start the laundry. If you leave now, I can throw in your apron." She retrieved what she needed from the closet, then shot a look at a beige splotch she'd noticed earlier. "Looks like you were nailed with the cinnamon."

Davide lifted the front of his apron and frowned at the stain in the middle of the bright yellow, green, and white fabric. "Could be hazelnut. We went through a lot of it today."

She grinned at that. "Either way, go home. We closed late and your parents are probably wondering where you are. Tell them I said hello."

Davide thanked her, promising to drop his apron on top of the washing machine on his way out the back door.

A minute later, Sara rolled the bucket to the shop floor and left it in the far corner so she could mop her way back to the kitchen once the rest of the cleaning was complete. Though the task rarely fell to her now that she had a full staff, she didn't mind the nightly routine of closing the shop. It gave her the opportunity to savor all she'd built since leaving her employment at the palace.

She swore under her breath as she slid a clean cloth along the first section of the display case, buffing out the fingerprints and nose prints kids had left throughout the day. She'd told herself she wouldn't think about the palace. Or about its head of security.

How, after so many years, had Umberto Niro remained under her skin? When he'd started his pat-down, as horrified as she was that he'd find the small golden box hidden in her jacket, another part of her remembered exactly what it'd been like to have him run his hands along her thighs in a far more intimate manner. Between chatting with customers and employees, she'd caught herself daydreaming about those all-knowing green eyes, so bright under the dark slashes of his brows. His rich olive skin, the ridges of muscle she knew lay hidden under that tuxedo shirt. His fiercely protective nature. The way he pushed himself to be the absolute best in the world at his job.

Eight years. Shouldn't she be over him by now?

She scrubbed at a particularly greasy print and grumbled aloud, "You need to get out more, Angeletti."

She'd dated a few men in the years following the implosion of her relationship with Umberto, but the time she gave the gelato business inevitably detracted from her availability. Most men her age were ready for serious relationships. Much as they loudly bemoaned women and their ticking biological clocks, Sara had discovered that men in their thirties had inner clocks banging away, too. Sarcaccian men, by and large, held tight to Old World values. They treated women as equals in the workplace, but when it came to their home lives they secretly liked the idea of a wife who'd dote on their children during the day and whip up a fantastic dinner in the evening. The men she'd dated never would've admitted it, but when they realized she wasn't ready to scale back or sell her business to begin a family, they lost interest. Frankly, so did she.

If she were honest with herself, she'd never been interested in any of them enough for it to bother her when the relationships ended.

Perhaps if she dated more, she'd find a guy who broke the mold. One who'd respect all she'd accomplished and who'd encourage her to pursue her dreams, whether that meant children or not, the business or not. A man who'd consider her a partner in life. A man who inspired daydreams when he wasn't around. A man capable of pushing the image of Umberto Niro from her mind.

Umberto. Now that she thought about it, she should've predicted what happened outside King Carlo's office. As much as she and Umberto had enjoyed their private time away from the palace, convincing him to go had been a challenge. She'd chalked up his reluctance to a workaholic nature, but perhaps that workaholic nature existed because, despite the great adventures they'd shared, she hadn't meant enough to him to strive for a different work/life balance. Just as the men she'd dated over the last few years hadn't meant enough to her. The idea made her pause mid-swipe.

Three sharp raps on the glass door startled her. She turned to call out that the shop was closed, only to see a man with a distinct, formidable build standing on the top step, knuckles resting against the door frame. The words froze on her lips. She set down the cleaning fluid and cloth, then strode to the front door.

"I'm closed," she told Umberto through the glass.

"I know. I waited until you were alone. Let me in." He raised an umbrella, tapped it on the glass, and shot her a lethal grin.

The umbrella was hers.

So much for feeling like last night never happened.

Sara stared through the glass for a few seconds, then flipped the locks to admit him. She swept her arm toward the tables, inviting Umberto inside despite the fear shooting along her spine. Once she closed and locked the door behind him, she said, "There are only a few flavors left in the case. Everything else is put away for the night."

"I didn't come for gelato." He dropped her umbrella into the stand she kept by the door for patrons, then cast a glance at the display case. "But if that's stracciatella, I wouldn't say no. I missed dinner."

"You work too much." She made an obvious perusal of his clothing. Rather than the typical male weekend gear of jeans with a sweater, he sported a dark gray suit with a white dress shirt and silvery blue tie. "You do realize that it's a Saturday."

"Said the pot to the kettle. It's nearly ten. Most people are either relaxing in front the television at this hour or are headed in that direction. Then again, perhaps this is your most productive time of day."

She responded with a wry smile. This time last night, she was preparing to slide her umbrella through the palace's wrought iron fence. Of course he would've reviewed the surveillance video and noted the time…then realized he'd caught her without the umbrella and retraced her steps to find it. Umberto was nothing if not thorough, and now he was baiting her.

But what else did he know? Had he scoured the queen's closet and realized what she'd taken? The box was small, but had to be worth a fortune. When she'd arrived home last night and took the time to study it under her bedside lamp, she'd gasped in awe. The ornate scrollwork on its surface was the work of a master craftsman, and it didn't hold a candle to the box's interior. She'd bet anything it was one of a kind.

King Carlo promised her that no one on the staff was aware of the box's existence, so its absence wouldn't be noticed. On the other hand, Umberto wouldn't have come here without an agenda. Until he revealed it, she needed to watch her words carefully.

Sara rounded the counter, putting it between the two of them. "Weekends tend to be busy. Lots of customers. We close at nine and let the last of the table customers stay until they're done." She lifted the lid on the remaining flavors. "Cup or cone?"

"Cup."

She grabbed a large paper cup and rolled out a sizable scoop of stracciatella, then rinsed the paddle and added a smaller scoop of hazelnut. "Are you here to arrest me?"

"Hand over the gelato first, then we'll talk."

"Incorrigible. Not what I'd expect of you." She closed the lid, stuck a plastic spoon in the cup, then placed it on top of the counter. Given the racy direction her thoughts had traveled today, she didn't want to risk physical contact by placing it in his hand.

"You're acknowledging that I have a moral code?"

She let that one go. Morals were the last thing she needed to discuss with Umberto. "Are you on the clock?"

He shrugged, took a napkin from the dispenser on the counter, then strode to one of the tables with the cup of gelato. Rather than join him, Sara returned to the front of the display case and resumed cleaning.

"Removing the day's fingerprints?"

"Always."

"You must see a lot of them. Yet you haven't seen mine, not in your shop."

His odd statement intensified the trepidation she'd felt when she'd unlocked the door. She spritzed the next section of glass and continued to wipe, forcing herself to act as if nothing was out of the ordinary. "You're probably the one person in Sarcaccia, then."

"How'd you get it?"

She kept her pace steady. "Get what?"

"This."

She turned around to see him raise his hand. The sticker she'd used on her glove was attached to his index finger. Her heart dropped to her stomach as she met his gaze. She had no explanation, not even in jest.

"This was taken directly from my employment file." He withdrew his wallet from his pants pocket, then carefully placed the sticker inside.

"Your employment file." Shock ricocheted through her. Of all the people with security clearance, the thumbprint she'd been given for access was Umberto Niro's?

What was King Carlo thinking?

"While you were slinging gelato today, I recreated your little adventure. The computer system hasn't been hacked, which means someone with a very high security clearance accessed my file and gave you my print. That person also gave you my current passcode to unlock the outside doors. I suspect they were also responsible for disabling the motion detectors along Via Floriana. Who?"

"I can't tell you that right now." In a week, he'd know everything. He'd realize she could be trusted. She swallowed against the realization that she wanted him to believe her right now, and for far more personal reasons than honoring her word to King Carlo.

"Did you have a specific date in mind?" He took a bite of the gelato and raised one dark brow.

"How can you eat dessert and look menacing at the same time?"

"It's a gift. When?"

If the air in the shop grew any tenser, it'd shatter her display case. "After Christmas."

"I can't wait that long."

"It's Thursday. Less than a week. I can't explain before then."

He took another bite, then let out a low sound of pleasure. "This is delicious. I usually don't like hazelnut."

"Hazelnut is my specialty."

"Well, I've never had it this good. Perhaps I should reconsider."

His flippant tone shredded her nerves. She wanted to say, *no, you never had it as good as you did with me, and yes, you should reconsider.* Instead, she gestured to the lettering that skirted the bottom of the shop window. "Authentic Sarcaccian-style gelato, handcrafted on site."

"That explains the decor."

Using the green, white, and yellow of the Sarcaccian flag when designing the shop had been a no-brainer. "Customers should know they're getting tradition when they visit Angeletti's, even if it's on a subconscious level. Besides, I didn't want to be another froufrou pink gelato shop."

"You've never been froufrou."

"No." All the better to do her job. Well, her former job.

"King Carlo was here last month with his granddaughter, Anna, yet I don't see any photos of the event hanging on the walls. Seems a royal visit would fit in well with your decor."

"He was here for the gelato, not to promote my business." Nor was

Sara going to ask the security detail for a photo opportunity. Especially not after the monarch himself pulled her aside under the guise of complimenting her gelato to ask if she'd do a very personal favor for him. "I'm sure Anna asked him to come because she'd visited a few weeks earlier with Prince Stefano."

"You don't find it odd that the family who fired you now visits your shop?"

"No more odd than having you here. As you said, I make delicious gelato."

Umberto leaned back in the bentwood chair and considered her. "Part of me wants to send you to the police right now. Keeping your actions to myself puts me in a tenuous position and I don't like it. Each hour I don't report you will raise more questions."

"That'll help me sleep tonight."

"But the other part of me knows there's more to your visit than meets the eye. If you won't tell me how you got my fingerprint, then tell me what you took." As she turned to finish the display case, he added, "You removed something from the queen's drawer. It was the size of my hand, tucked right up in the center of your ribcage."

He *knew*? Why hadn't he taken it from her?

She kept quiet as she finished the last panel of glass. When she faced him again, his brilliant eyes glittered in challenge.

"I know you don't trust me, Umberto. When you look at me, you don't see what everyone else sees."

"Which is?"

"An honest, loyal person. Someone who loves her employees, works hard to improve the neighborhood, and who's made a good life despite challenges. Instead, you see what you want to see. A thief."

"Might have something to do with catching you red-handed."

"That wasn't the case before. You weren't in Paris. You weren't in the room when I met with King Carlo. You don't know the details of what happened." Oh, this was not where she wanted the conversation to go. She could smack herself for being so careless, letting out the words that had been lying dormant inside her for years.

Umberto merely lifted a shoulder. "Last night you were in the queen's closet, during a palace party to which you were not invited. You accessed the building illegally with a well thought-out plan in place. Even if I wasn't in Paris or in a position to know the details back then, what was I supposed to think?"

She slammed the bottle of cleaning fluid onto the counter next to the register. "We were together for over a year. You pride yourself on your observational skills. Did the manner in which I conducted myself during that time somehow escape your notice? Do you have any idea how challenging my job was, protecting Princess Sophia while she was in college in France? The balancing act I had between keeping her safe and allowing her the freedom to live and act like any other student, all while meeting the king and queen's standards?"

"That brought you into the queen's closet last night…why again?" He scraped the last of the gelato from his cup, popped it into his mouth, then dropped the plastic spoon into the container. Casual as you please.

She flexed her fingers, fuming. She couldn't tell him straight out what happened back then. She'd sworn an oath. But dammit, she wanted him to figure it out, to understand the unspoken words hovering in the air between them. He should've figured it out back then. Instead, he thought the worst of her.

Umberto stretched his long legs and studied her as if she'd crack under his perusal alone. It galled Sara that her heart ached all over again, yet his seemed blissfully at peace.

"Why are you here, Umberto? You let me go." Last night and back then.

"I don't abandon puzzles unsolved. I need to know why you were in the palace so I don't go to the police with half an explanation."

"I have an idea. Don't go at all."

"If I had all the pieces to the puzzle, maybe I wouldn't need to."

She crossed her arms and felt the familiar stickiness of melted gelato on her wrist, but ignored it. "I'll explain after Christmas."

"Explain now. You shut down the motion sensors along one of the busiest streets in Cateri and managed to scale the fence with potential witnesses nearby. You were so close to Prince Massimo you touched his dog. You had my thumbprint and current access code, a code that was changed less than forty-eight hours prior to your entry. It's a matter of national security."

She rolled her eyes. Such a cheesy, made-for-television line, even if —in his mind—it was true. She crossed the shop, grabbed the mop from the bucket, and began cleaning the floor. Since it'd been swept just before closing, it only needed a quick pass. Over her shoulder, she said, "Not that I'm confirming any of that, but you can't believe anyone else could gain access the same way."

"I didn't believe anyone could gain access, period."

When she neared him with the bucket, he rose from the chair and moved toward the door, propping his shoulder against one side of the frame as he watched her swoop back and forth.

She was within arm's reach when he asked, "What did you take, Sara?"

"Didn't you order an inventory?"

When he didn't respond, she hazarded a glance his way. His eyes narrowed. "Inventories take time. Save me a few hours' work and another trip back here to talk to you."

"And deny myself the pleasure of your company?" She skipped the area near the front door—she wasn't about to ask Umberto to move— and returned the mop to the bucket. "I need to take this to the back. Don't worry, I won't run away."

She rolled the bucket past the counter and through the swinging door to the kitchen, grabbing the bottle of cleaner and the rags as she went. Davide was long gone, his apron neatly folded on top of the washing machine with the spot prominently displayed on top. It looked like he'd taken stain-remover spray to it. Taking advantage of the moment alone, she focused on settling her racing heartbeat by locking away the cleaning supplies and collecting the laundry. All she had to do was put away the last pans of gelato and she'd be done for the night.

She needed Umberto to leave. She was expecting a phone call, and it wasn't one she could take in his presence.

"Where should I put these? I assume you don't leave them in the front overnight."

She spun to see Umberto behind her carrying two large pans of gelato, one stacked crisscrossed on top of the other.

"You shouldn't be back here. It's a restricted area."

He set the pans on one of the large stainless steel counters and braced his large hands on either side. Though his outward expression didn't change, she could feel his scrutiny so intensely, she was certain he could see right through her, could read every thought in her head.

At that very moment, her cell phone buzzed, its vibration carrying through the stainless steel counter toward his palms. It lay five feet away from him, its screen lit.

Merda.

HE WAITED. Watched the play of emotions Sara tried to keep from her face as she considered how to respond to his presence in her hallowed kitchen. Given that she'd been caught in the most restricted room in the entire country less than twenty-four hours earlier, he'd bet his gun that if he put his fingers to her wrist, he'd feel her pulse racing.

Then her phone rang, its hum coming from the countertop on his left. Her eyes flared, then she tamped it down.

He didn't look at the screen; instead, he kept a close eye on her body language as he changed position so his hand rested close to the phone. The device emitted two more low hums, cutting off in the midst of the second, before the caller could leave a message.

Sara didn't move. Her complete lack of reaction told him the call was an important one, but she didn't want him to know it. Interesting.

She shot him a look of annoyance, then turned and set the jug of laundry detergent she'd been holding on top of a lime green washing machine. "If you insist on staying back here, you need to wash your hands."

"You know me. I'm a stickler for rules." He walked to the sink, then turned on the warm water and waved his hand under the automated soap dispenser.

She pointed out the cold storage unit once he'd tossed the towel into the appropriate receptacle beside the sink. "The pans slide into the marked slots in there. Cover them with the plastic wrap first."

It was a small victory, but he'd take it. While Sara loaded the washing machine, he sealed each of the pans with plastic wrap from a large roll mounted above the counter and slid them into the cabinet she'd indicated. Rails set at precise heights held the pans. Each was labeled by flavor, with certain slots designed to hold the larger pans containing the most popular varieties. Once finished, he strode to the storefront to grab the last two flavors and repeat the process.

He hefted the pans out of the case, then took a moment to look around now that he had the space to himself. Sara's setup was impressive. From the shiny counters to the spotless floor, Angeletti Gelato was a testament to her hard work and knack for organization. He wouldn't be surprised if health inspectors considered Sara's shop a model establishment. It was the same way she'd run Princess Sophia's security team, at least until the shoplifting incident. Staff members had well-defined roles, schedules were followed with precision, contingencies were anticipated and addressed.

What took him aback, however, were the subtle touches that gave the shop heart. A Christmas tree stood in the far corner, its branches decorated in bright red beaded garlands punctuated by ice cream cones constructed of yarn. Beside the tree, a large box of toys bore a sign indicating that all donations would be given to a local shelter. Nearby, in an alcove providing access to the restrooms, a bulletin board was filled edge to edge with photographs and hand-drawn pictures from children who visited the shop.

All the characteristics Sara had exhibited during the time they'd dated were in evidence here, including her quiet artistic streak and generosity of spirit. He muttered an oath; in the few seconds he'd paused to study the shop, Umberto questioned himself all over again.

His training indicated that a non-coerced confession was rarely recanted or challenged, and catching a person in the act of stealing spoke for itself. She was guilty as sin….both then and now. Yet instinct honed by years of security work told him that a woman who lived the way Sara did, who worked these hours, who invested herself so heavily in her neighborhood, didn't steal.

Once he secured the last two pans in the kitchen, Umberto surveyed the workspace to see what other tasks needed completion. Aside from Sara's phone, the only item on the gleaming stainless steel counter was a large tray covered by an opaque plastic top. An open bakery box sat beside the tray, its sides folded as if it were ready to be used. A stack of identical flattened boxes occupied a shelf over the counter. He crossed the kitchen for a closer look while Sara finished folding rags she'd removed from the dryer. When Umberto flipped the cardboard to inspect the top of the box, he was surprised to see the same yellow and green logo and Angeletti Gelato script as was on her shop windows.

"You can't possibly use this for takeout gelato."

"We do seasonal bakery treats and put them at the end of the display case near the cash register. We also take orders." Sara closed the bifold door to the closet containing the washer and dryer, then approached and lifted the plastic lid from the tray. His mouth watered at the sight of two dozen almond-scented mini torts glazed in honey. They appeared to have been made in the past few hours.

"*Torta della Sarcaccia,*" she said, as if he didn't know. He'd once spent an entire afternoon rewiring a lamp in Sara's apartment in exchange for a slice of her wondrous holiday tort. These smaller versions were meant to be sold individually, but appeared no less decadent.

He fished in his pocket for a bill. "How much?"

"What, you'll pay for these but not my gelato?"

"I'd happily pay for both." Especially if it got him one of the torts.

She waved off the money. "No can do. These are being delivered to a reception in the morning. Otherwise, the shop's sold out."

"You're breaking my heart."

She paused before covering the torts. He cursed himself for his poor choice of words, but she covered the moment with a shrug. "There's always tomorrow."

She reached past him to flick off the light that illuminated the countertop, brushing against his arm as she did so. Distracted by the touch, it took him a second to catch her meaning. "You'll have a fresh batch?"

"Every day until Christmas. Tonight, though, I'm done."

"I'll walk you home."

"You didn't come here to walk me home."

"I came to return your umbrella. It wasn't in a spot you'd have been able to access later. At least, not on your own." Now that he was alone with her, without threat of interruption, he didn't want to leave. He grew more intrigued by her with each passing moment. The facets of her personality that attracted him all those years ago remained a part of Sara, but he was even more fascinated by the woman she'd become in the years since she'd left the palace. In the business she'd built. In the secrets she kept. "It was a brilliant method of testing the motion sensors."

"And…we're back to the beginning. I shouldn't have wasted good gelato on you if all you planned to do was circle back to where we started."

It was exactly the type of flippant answer he'd come to expect. He knew that showing up in her shop tonight with her umbrella in his hand would put her on edge. Rightfully so, given that she'd committed a crime. But to his shock, he recognized there was more to her snappy answers than cheeky defiance. It was evident in the tightness of her voice and the controlled way she held herself away from him, even if she wasn't aware of it.

She was as attracted to him as he was to her.

His chest tightened at the realization. How could he not have seen it? In the quiet confines of her shop, it felt exactly like the afternoon they'd first made eye contact.

A mandatory meeting for all palace employees had him hunched in the back row of a lecture hall at the local university, desperately trying to hide the fact he'd just pulled a double-shift and could barely stay awake. She'd pushed a bag toward him and mouthed, "Eat." He wasn't hungry, but something in her gaze made him open the bag. It contained one of the best cookies he'd had in a long time, and the sugar rush carried him through the lecture. When he'd found her afterward to thank her and to introduce himself, she'd smiled and said it was nothing.

It wasn't nothing. There'd been a definite spark, and both of them recognized it. Soon, they started bumping into each other in the palace hallways and employee parking area. Hellos said in passing turned into conversations, and he learned she'd recently been hired to work on Princess Sophia's personal detail. Within weeks, they were picking up lunch for each other during shifts.

Then she'd asked him to go snorkeling with her on one of his rare days away from the palace. He'd hesitated, knowing it might pose a conflict to date a fellow security staff member, even if they were assigned to different areas. But their connection had been undeniable. He couldn't resist saying yes. Then suggesting she join him for a hike along one of Sarcaccia's interior mountain trails the following weekend.

If he were honest with himself, that connection was the real reason he'd come tonight. He couldn't resist her.

He gave Sara a slow smile. "I'm merely here to do the gentlemanly thing. You know, return a lady's umbrella, walk her home. Compliment her on her success."

He expected Sara to grab a sweater or jacket, given the cool breeze that blew in off the Mediterranean this time of year, but she strode toward the back door without one, retrieving a set of keys from a hook on her way. Instead of pushing on the door's the metal bar to exit, she turned to face him. "I'll gladly accept the umbrella and the compliments, but I don't need you to walk me home."

He moved closer, trapping her between his body and the narrow section of wall adjacent to the door. He cut an intimidating figure and most people cowered when he cornered them, but Sara didn't. She angled her chin and met his gaze as if she'd anticipated the move. He marveled at the strength he saw in her blue eyes. Uncertainty thickened the air between them so it became palpable; the only sound in the room was that of their breathing. Then another emotion flared in Sara's eyes: fierce, fiery desire. Damn if he didn't feel it, too, as intensely as he had all those years ago. When they'd been wild for each other, but had resisted the temptation for months on end, unwilling to become the subject of palace gossip.

They'd carried out their dates with the laser-sharp planning of secret operatives. They'd thrilled to it. When they'd finally felt secure enough to make love without the fear of being discovered, it hadn't felt like an itch had at last been scratched. It was transformative. They'd known then that they were at the beginning of something momentous. At least, he had.

"What if I insist?" he asked, his voice dropping to just above a whisper.

"I doubt I could stop you."

"True. Though you do seem to be queen of this castle." He momentarily shifted his gaze to indicate the gelateria. "Given the amount of business you do and the number of employees you have, it wouldn't function well without a skilled hand running the show. You've worked very hard here."

She straightened and her hands went to her hips. They were less than arm's distance apart now. "That shouldn't surprise you. I've always worked hard."

"I know." He braced a hand beside her head. "So why did you throw it all away?"

"I didn't throw anything away."

"What was Paris if not throwing away a good career? A career you loved? It wasn't so you could open a gelato shop."

"I made a choice knowing what the consequences would be." Her expression sharpened as she looked up at him. "That's why you came here tonight, isn't it? To ask the questions you didn't ask eight years ago."

Her words shocked him as much as if she'd taken a swing at him. She'd expected him to grill her about Paris? "I wasn't in a position to ask questions then."

"Maybe not at the palace. But privately? You sure as hell were."

"You'd already said it all to King Carlo. What more could there be after, 'I did it, Your Highness,' that would have made a difference?"

"It didn't occur to you to find out."

No. Not until later, when it was too late. "You walked out."

"You didn't want to hear anything I had to say." Her shoulders remained squared and her gaze stony, but he didn't miss the slight tinge of pain in her voice.

"I came to return your umbrella and to give you another opportunity to explain what happened last night. Not to fight."

"You came for more than that or you would've sent someone. Olga, maybe."

He didn't respond. Olga wouldn't have stayed to sample the gelato, let alone helped put it away. Olga definitely wouldn't have stood this close to Sara, breathing in the scent of her or staring at the slight line that bisected Sara's plush lower lip. Olga would have made the delivery and left.

Then again, Sara didn't represent a huge piece of unfinished business to Olga.

"Admit it. You're here because your curiosity about Paris is killing you."

Now it was, but damn if he'd tell her that. "You wouldn't have answered any questions if I'd asked them back then."

For the first time all night, Sara flinched. He'd scored a hit. "Asking then would have made all the difference."

"If you wouldn't have answered, I'm not so sure it would've."

He wished he could read her mind, could delve into her secrets. As if she'd followed his train of thought, she told him, "After Christmas. If you still want to know then, I'll tell you everything I can."

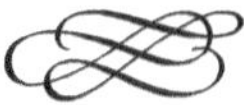

Sᴀʀᴀ's ʙʀᴇᴀᴛʜ threatened to explode from her lungs. The intensity of Umberto's green eyes pinned her to the wall. She kept her hands planted on her hips, keys dangling from the fingertips of her right hand, so she wouldn't make contact with Umberto. She was too scared to move.

Not scared of him. Scared of herself.

She had loved this man once. She'd even allowed herself to believe they had a future together. Then he'd shattered her heart into a thousand pieces. To salvage her sanity, she'd thrown herself headlong into Angeletti Gelato. The satisfaction of building her business and making new friends helped her become a new woman, one who'd reassembled the jagged shards of her broken heart to create a new, whole self. But trying to stop her reaction to Umberto now was as futile as trying to prevent fingerprints from accumulating on her display case on a hot summer day.

He wanted her. After all these years, after coming face to face with her in the darkness of the queen's closet, he still did. It was in the rough growl of his voice, in the boldness with which he planted one large hand on the wall beside her, where all he had to do was move his thumb to touch her hair. The unconscious, carnal parting of his lips called to her. Even knowing the danger he posed to her heart, her soul heeded that call as instinctively as a bloom opened to the sunshine. She had only to shift her weight, and he'd—

"I risk my job by trusting you."

His breath was warm against her face. She focused on keeping her own inhalations steady, but in doing so caught the faint sweetness of the gelato he'd eaten and something more. The rich, masculine scent she'd always associated with him. A memory swept through her: lying in Umberto's apartment one Saturday morning, the sheets halfway down his hips as he sprawled beside her. The slow spin of his ceiling fan overhead. The rumble of a bus passing on the street below. And that scent, warm and wonderful, enveloping her. She'd closed her eyes that morning, scooted closer. Inhaled. Sighed. Been rewarded with a groan of satisfaction and the weight of Umberto's bicep as he rolled to his side and curled his arm around her waist, drawing her against his chest.

That solid bicep was beside her head now, corralling her. If she budged, she'd touch him. If she touched him, she'd be lost.

"Umberto, I never intended to put you in the middle of—"

Her phone vibrated again. She'd been so distracted by Umberto's nearness she'd forgotten to grab it from the counter. The fact that its persistent buzz just cut off her line of thought made her guilty conscience even more apparent.

"That's your palace contact." His tone was hard, unyielding. "I should go look at the screen. Or answer it."

"You probably should." She hated how the words came out. Whispered. Cracked. Eight years ago, she'd made a choice she knew would cost her job. She hated that Umberto now felt he was making the same choice.

At the first opportunity, she'd call King Carlo and discuss the matter. Urge him to let Umberto in on their plans, and rely on Umberto to keep the information from the queen. She'd explain the predicament in which Umberto found himself, knowing that Sara had been helped by someone with the highest level of security clearance.

Another insistent buzz came from the phone. She saw his throat work, then hunger flared in his eyes. "Or I could trust you."

He lowered his head, brushing his lips across hers so gently she was certain he did it to tease. The rest of him didn't move—the hand on the wall, the set of his feet, the broad planes of his shoulders—only his head. She waited, refusing to close her eyes, waiting for him to pull away, to see his strategy wasn't working. He didn't. He glanced at her through his dark lashes, his mouth still grazing hers. "Until Christmas."

He kissed her again, this time as if he owned her. A feral sound came from the back of his throat as his hand slid down the wall and he shoved his fingers into her hair. This was no tactic, no calculated plan to manipulate her into telling all; this was unmistakable lust. This was the Umberto she'd loved years ago, full of fire and strength and single-minded in his passion, whether that entailed fighting criminals intent on harming the Barrali family or making love to her under a moonless night sky.

Sara's eyes drifted shut and the keys fell from her fingers. She made a half-hearted attempt to keep from dropping them, only to encounter the rock-hard wall of Umberto's stomach. Ridges of muscle palpable through the fabric of his dress shirt drew her fingertips. Common sense said to pull away, but he leaned into her palm and moved his scandalous mouth to nip her ear.

"Kiss me back." His words were low and urgent. "You wanted your mouth on mine the moment you saw me in the queen's closet. You still want it. Do it."

It was all the invitation she needed. She grabbed the end of his silk tie and wrapped it in her fist, using it to pull his mouth back to hers. She opened to him and he rewarded her with a deep grunt of triumph, one that sent a bolt of heat straight to her center.

This, she thought as he ran one hand up her ribcage, pressing her even further into the wall. This was what she'd missed in her life. No other man compared to Umberto. No one fit her so well, no one sent rivers of fire through her blood, no one deprived her of common sense the way he did. It wasn't only his skill as a lover or their physical compatibility. It was him. Even now, as he kissed her against the back wall of her gelateria, he exuded power and intelligence. Umberto was a real-life James Bond, highly trained and ready to protect the royal family and those he loved, with his life if necessary.

Unlike James Bond, however, Umberto wasn't one to leave a trail of devastated women in his wake. Only her. From the palace gossip she'd picked up over the years, he'd dedicated himself fully to the job, working hours that allowed little time for outside relationships. She refused to contemplate whether the fact no other woman had convinced him to dedicate time to personal pursuits was a good thing or a bad thing.

He tore his mouth from hers to trail kisses down her neck. She arched into his touch, reveling in the torture of his lips against her throat and the magical spread of his hand as he caressed the underside of her breast.

"Let me take you home," he said against her skin.

A choked laugh escaped her. "Too late."

He raised his head. The fervor and confusion in his eyes made her breath catch again. She angled her gaze toward the corner, to the door beside the laundry closet. "Through there. I live upstairs."

A crease furrowed his brow as he looked to the door, then back to her.

"Even you don't know everything, apparently. I own the building."

"Your name's still on the lease for your old apartment."

Had he checked on her as part of his current investigation? Or had he looked into her personal life as well as her business over the years they'd been apart? "The rent is low for the area, so I sublet it to a friend who wanted to get into the neighborhood."

"That's rather…convenient." His thumb grazed her nipple, moving in a tight circle. He kept his eyes locked with hers, as if in challenge.

"I didn't say you could take me upstairs."

"No?"

"No." She released his tie and straightened. Slowly, she covered his hand with hers, then deliberately flattened her palm so he fully cupped her breast. She searched his eyes, hoping she could convey as much with a look as with her words. "But if you're willing to trust me, I'm willing to trust you."

"That's taking a big risk."

Fire raced through her veins. Yes, it was a big risk...to her own heart.

She stretched just enough to tap the wall switch near the exit door, leaving them with only the dim security lighting by which to see. "Do it anyway."

His jaw tensed. The sheer magnitude of desire rolling off him nearly undid her. "Big risk, big reward."

Keeping his left hand where she'd placed it against her breast, he brought his right down to cage her rear and lift her against him. Before she could think, their lips met in a need-filled kiss she never wanted to end. Tasting, exploring, remembering. He lifted her higher, grinding his hips against hers, sliding her along the wall. Teasing her throat with his tongue before nipping at her ear and starting all over again. Eventually they half-stumbled, half-walked their way through the door to stairwell that led to her apartment.

It was her habit to leave on a lamp in the apartment foyer so its gleam would cast enough light under the door at the top of the stairs for her to ascend at night. Umberto's gaze lifted in the direction of the glowing sliver. "That your apartment?"

"Yes."

He spun Sara so her back was to the stairwell wall. "Any roommates? Anyone else have access to this area?"

"No and no. The apartments on the upper floors are accessed from the street. Mine's the only one that connects to the shop."

Confirmation they were alone brought a savage grin to his face, one that sent another rush of desire shooting through her. She wasn't a casual sex woman—Umberto knew that—but he also knew her well enough to know how much she wanted him to make love to her.

His arms tightened around her waist and he caught her in a deep and hungry kiss, the kind that could only occur without an audience. Her body hummed with an energy she hadn't felt in years. None of the men she'd dated since Umberto elicited this from her; now she knew no man ever could. The connection they shared was one of a kind.

Years ago, Umberto mentioned it as they'd watched the sunset from an oceanside cliff south of Cateri. He'd said he felt as if their souls could identify each other in the dark, as if they communicated with each other on a frequency only they used. Before she'd seen Umberto in the flesh last night, staring her down in the queen's closet with his gun aimed at her heart, she'd have denied that connection still existed. She'd believed it severed that afternoon outside King Carlo's office.

It defied reason, but that link had endured as surely as the ancient stone framing the building in which they now stood.

They were halfway up the stairs when her knees buckled. He eased her fall, using his hands to keep her back from hitting the treads, then knelt before her. The action wasn't one of unbridled lust, but of affection. Despite all that'd happened between them, despite the ferocity with which he wanted her, his feelings toward her remained tender and protective. He wasn't doing this with quick hookup in mind.

Sara cradled his cheeks between her hands and kissed him anew.

Umberto's position with the royal family meant everything to him. He'd worked his whole life to reach that position of trust, first in the military, then as part of the regular security staff. He'd worked long hours, even putting his life on the line for the royals. He had to believe that to be here with her, like this, could cost him his job. It was a risk she'd never imagined he'd take, particularly when he'd never grasped why she'd risked her own job.

He trusted her. And, dear God, his mouth tortured hers as if it were his mission in life.

She reveled in the moment, even as she tried to imprint the nuances in her mind. The gelato-sweet taste of his tongue. The roughened texture of his jaw. The slide of her hands over his shirt as she pushed the suit jacket from his shoulders. The pressure of his capable hands as he bracketed the outside of her thighs. She wanted this captured in her memory forever.

Umberto kissed a trail to her collarbone and released her long enough to shuck the jacket and toss it down the stairs. Sara let her head fall back, felt his fingers grasping her legs once more, and sighed her pleasure. Whatever he wanted. Anything he wanted. She would give it.

"Here," he breathed into the hollow at the base of her throat. "I want you here. On the stairs, in the dark. I want to make love to you like we've never made love before. Slow. Deliberate. Passionate. I want your legs wrapped around me and I want to see your beautiful, mischievous, mesmerizing face. I want those gorgeous blue eyes focused on me and nothing else. I want to be your only thought. And I want you to trust me."

He lifted his eyes to hers, and his gaze held her as powerfully as if he'd taken her head in his hands.

"I trust you. I want you." Her heart pounded so hard she felt it in her throat. "The stairs may not be, I mean, it's not exactly comfortable—"

"If I'm willing to take bullets for the Barralis, I can certainly take a bruise or two for this. For you."

Before Sara could think, Umberto spanned her waist with his hands and stood, lifting her into the air. He turned, switching their positions before easing himself to the stairs. On instinct, she lowered herself to straddle him as he dragged a finger down the front of her blouse.

"Oh, no, *cara*. Up. I want to watch you remove this" —starting from the middle of her chest, he finished with his index finger at the front of her waistband— "then this. Slowly. So I have the vision of you in my head forever."

He leaned back, folding his hands behind his head. She stood between his feet and did as he asked, making a show of undoing a single button at the top of her blouse.

"Now you," she whispered. "I do one, you do—"

In a matter of seconds, he undid his tie and the top buttons of his shirt, freed his wrists, then pulled both the dress shirt and undershirt over his head to reveal a chest and abs worthy of Michelangelo's chisel. "There."

Her mouth went dry as he discarded the shirt and settled against the stairs. "You said slowly."

"I want *you* to go slowly, and I refuse to be distracted by my own clothing." He angled his head. "Now…show me."

This time, her hands shook as she slipped each button free of its mooring. It'd been a long time since she'd undressed in front of a man; longer still since she'd undressed in front of Umberto. But it was desire rather than nerves that made her fingers difficult to control.

"You are breathtaking," he said as she slipped the blouse from her shoulders. The hitch in his speech and bare look of anticipation with which he watched her nearly made her knees buckle again. "Keep going."

Sara took her time removing her socks, then her pants, allowing herself the pleasure of watching his expression change as she stepped out of each leg, then used her foot to push the pants down the stairs.

"Now what?"

His chin lifted in amusement. "You take off your panties. Then allow me the pleasure of assisting you with your bra."

"You know what you're doing?"

He scowled. It was as good as saying, "You know I do," but two could play at that; she stepped out of her panties, toed them away, then inched toward him. Just as he reached for her calf, she yanked away and shook her head.

His bark of laughter filled the narrow confines of the staircase, drawing a smile from her. Bracing one hand on the railing and the other on the opposite wall, she leaned over him. "Now…your turn."

Before the words were past her lips, he lifted his hips and removed his pants. As she watched, yearning chased the amusement from his face. Navy boxer briefs were all that remained covering his perfectly sculpted body. Unwilling to wait, she bent, slid her fingers into his waistband, and was rewarded by Umberto's sharp inhalation.

With deliberate motions, she eased the waistband lower, then lower still, her gaze locked with his, until she felt his erection spring free.

Now it was his turn to shudder with desire.

"Here. I want you here," she echoed the words he'd used only minutes before. "On the stairs, in the dark. I want my legs wrapped around you. I want to make love like we've never made love before. Like you've never made love to any woman before. I want those gorgeous green eyes focused on me and nothing else. I want to be your only thought—"

His hand came to her nape and he crushed her open mouth to his. Their tongues met in a heated rush. She tried to pull away, worried he'd injure his back against the hard treads, but he refused to release her. One strong arm encircled her waist and he guided her to his lap. The length of his erection throbbed against her abdomen, causing heat to pool in her belly. Then his fingers found her center, and he drew his thumb slowly, slowly upward. A curse ripped from her as he circled, sending a jolt of pleasure through her. How had he managed to make her so hot, so sensitized, so fast?

He shifted to deepen their kiss even as he continued the exquisite torment. A frantic, undeniable craving welled within her as his mouth melded with hers. Unable to stand it much longer, she shifted and pressed her lips to his forehead while cradling his head to her shoulder.

"Umberto—"

"I want you." His breath was hot on her throat. "Please...are you...I didn't think to ask—"

"We're fine." She'd been on the pill since they'd dated, though she'd gone long spells thinking there wasn't much point, especially since she'd been extra careful with the few men she'd seen in the intervening years. She thanked heaven now that she hadn't stopped taking it.

He dipped his head lower, kissing her through her bra. She arched, feeling the soft texture of his military-short hair slip beneath her fingers as he lavished attention on her breasts. In the eight years since he'd last held her, she'd had sex, but not once had she made love. There'd been no tug at her heart, no emotional capitulation, even though she'd hoped for it. Her mind was always elsewhere...on impending payroll deadlines, on perfecting a new recipe, on ensuring her employees were well-trained and happy. On opening her new location at the marina and filling the void in her life with more work, with new goals.

Umberto was the only partner who'd ever been her match. He made her body sing like no one else, but it was far more than that. He met her intellectually. He made her heart trip every time he walked in a room. He filled her emotional void. At least he had, until…

"Trust me." He murmured the words against her breast as his fingers stroked her to the brink. "Yield to it. Trust me not to hurt you."

His rich, sexually-charged plea pushed her over the edge, sending her body into an orgasmic convulsion that radiated from deep within her. She dropped her head, muffling her cries in the smooth, strong muscle of his shoulder. Over and over, waves rolled through her. As Umberto slipped his hand from between them, her toes curled against the hard stair treads.

"No," she whispered, flexing her hips to chase his touch. She looked up in protest, but at that moment he entered her, sending another sharp jolt of lust coursing through her entire body. When he sheathed himself fully, she thought she'd pass out from the sheer pleasure of it.

He ground out a lust-filled Sarcaccian endearment, then caught her chin in his hand, keeping her gaze riveted on his. There would be no slow lovemaking, not now. Neither of them could stop the overwhelming need for release, the ache that drove them to ignore the tight confines of the staircase and unforgiving hardwood risers to take what they needed from each other. He was her only thought, and Sara knew she was his. She could hardly breathe; despite the frantic drive that brought them together, it the most intimate, soul-baring encounter of her life. He saw into her heart as no man ever had or ever would. Despite the passage of time, they fit as if they'd never been separated.

No…better. The stark appreciation in his dark, expressive gaze proved he knew the significance of this moment and relished it.

When they were spent at last, chests rising and falling with the need to recover, Umberto turned his head and planted a kiss on her wrist. Sara felt his lips curve against her skin, then his tongue darted out to lick the spot he'd just kissed.

"Gelato," he murmured before taking another taste. "Hazelnut. Best I've ever had."

His eyes squeezed shut before he gave her wrist another lingering kiss. A single tear beaded at the edge of his lashes before he turned so she couldn't see.

She kissed the top of his head and smiled.

CHAPTER 9

Sara woke to the sound of cathedral bells.

Only the faintest light crept around the edges of her curtains, despite the fact her bedside clock displayed the hour as half past seven. She sighed into her pillow, then curled her knees toward her chest and stretched her arms, only to encounter a warm, hard, masculine body behind her own. In a rush, the previous evening came back to her. Standing between Umberto and the wall of the gelateria. The caring expression on his face as he cradled her on the staircase. The feeling of his arms, tight around her back and under her knees, as he carried her upstairs after they made love the first time.

Making love a second time in her apartment, slowly, attentively.

She snuggled closer, breathing in the intoxicating scent of him. At some point in the night he must've gathered their clothes from the staircase; they were folded into two neat stacks, one for each of them, set out side by side on top of her dresser.

She grinned at the sight. It was such an Umberto thing to do.

He shifted, then eased aside the hair at the back of her neck to place a gentle kiss at her nape. "Good morning, *cara*. How do you feel?"

Her smile broadened as a sense of bliss lightened her entire being. "I haven't been this at peace in a long, long time."

He pulled the covers higher over them both, then his arm came down to mold her body more firmly against his. She cradled his forearm against her stomach, gently stroking the soft skin that covered his hard-packed muscle. They lay like that, in silence, enjoying their shared contentment for nearly half an hour before a beep echoed from across the room.

"My alarm." Umberto groaned and eased from the bed, located his phone in the pocket of his folded slacks, then silenced the beeping before he slipped back under the covers and draped his arm over her hip. In the short seconds he'd left her, his skin had chilled.

"You have it set on a Sunday morning?"

She felt his nod against her shoulder. "Unless I'm on assignment, I still go to my parents' house for breakfast, then take them to church services."

Now she remembered. She'd joined the Niros a few times, but preferred to have Umberto make the Sunday visits on his own. While his parents had always been welcoming, Sara hadn't wanted to disrupt their special family time. It was the one break he allowed in his workaholic schedule. "They'll expect you soon."

"I'd rather stay here."

She covered his large hand with hers, then raised it to her lips and kissed the roughened skin of his knuckles. Tiny scars dotted the back of his hands from years of training and, she suspected, more than one actual fight. They were capable hands, hands that protected and cared for so many people. She loved his hands.

"You can't cancel. It's the last Sunday before Christmas."

Mention of the holiday cast an immediate pall over them. So much would remain unsaid until then. She had to hope Umberto meant it, that he wouldn't call the police or report her break-in to the queen before then. It went against all his training and his personal honor code to keep such a secret. It would eat away at him. Never before had he put her before his duty; she didn't want him to second-guess the decision.

She had to convince the king to talk to Umberto. The sooner, the better.

"Will I see you again?"

Umberto's voice was scratchy with sleep and a calculated indifference, but Sara heard the apprehension there, too, as if he'd steeled himself against the emotions he'd feel in the light of day. She rolled over and propped herself on one elbow. She ran her other hand over his hair and smiled. "I think it'd be wiser for both of us if we wait until after Christmas."

"When you can explain?"

"When I can explain."

He exhaled and lifted a brow. "Would you at least tell me why you can't explain?"

"I gave my word, Umberto. I'm sorry."

His gaze dimmed, but she refused to allow him to distance himself...not yet. After eight long years, she understood the enormity of what she'd given up when she'd walked away from him. And, frankly, what he'd given up by not trusting her back then. They deserved a second chance.

She cradled one of his stubble-roughened cheeks in her palm. "Waking up with you in my bed this morning is the most glorious feeling I've had in years. I want there to be a next time, but a next time without questions or secrets between us. I want you to know, in your heart, that you don't have to choose between your job and me."

His eyes drifted closed. For a split second, she thought she'd lost him, but then he lifted his head and brushed his lips against hers. Tender and soft, it was a kiss full of promise.

After she walked Umberto through the back of the shop, she stood at her bedroom window and watched while he crossed the cobblestone street. When she'd attended college in the United States, one of her roommates looked out their dorm window early one morning and pointed to a man striding across the quad with his head down and hands jammed into his pockets. She'd announced that the guy was taking the "walk of shame." It had taken Sara a moment to grasp what her roommate meant. It wasn't a term she'd heard while growing up in Sarcaccia.

Staring out the window at Umberto now, she was reminded of that moment. His suit jacket was back in place, but he'd tucked his tie into a pants pocket and left the top button of his shirt undone. The scruff of his chin gave him a rugged, dangerous air as he zigzagged between the parked cars, but there was a liveliness in his step that characterized a man ready to take on the world. It wasn't a walk of shame; it was a walk of power.

She hugged her arms around her waist and grinned as she turned away from the window.

The light of her phone screen drew her attention at the same moment it buzzed. She'd grabbed it from the kitchen after walking Umberto to the door, but hadn't checked it. How many times had it gone off overnight? She hurried to the coffee table and clicked to answer as soon as she saw the private number.

"Your Highness. I apologize for being out of touch. I wasn't in a position to talk."

"Late night?" King Carlo's voice was low, as if he were taking care not to be overheard. A television with the morning news and the steady rumble of a treadmill could be heard in the background. Sara drew a sense of comfort from the fact that certain parts of the palace routine hadn't changed. The king rarely missed his early morning workouts. He'd once told an interviewer he did it for the mental stimulation as much as the physical, as he rarely had time alone with his thoughts. Sara knew he also used the time to have conversations he wished to keep off the record.

"Yes, sir. A few customers lingered after closing, so I wasn't alone."

She heard the beep of treadmill buttons being pushed. "I see. Umberto Niro suspects you were on the grounds Friday night."

"He does more than suspect," she admitted. Disappointment at failing the king hit her anew. "He caught me leaving the queen's closet. Luckily, he didn't see the box, so I was able to deliver it to the jeweler as we planned. How'd you know?"

"I sent the code to disable the fence for your exit and received an error message. When I tried a second time, I realized that security had changed the password in the middle of the charity ball. I managed a workaround, but when my wife and I passed Umberto in the hallway the next morning, she asked him why he'd ordered an inventory of her closet. I figured out then what must've happened."

Sara grimaced. Part of her had foolishly hoped Umberto was bluffing about the inventory. "What did he tell the queen?"

"That there was an anomaly in the entry logs for our private wing and he'd requested the inventory in an abundance of caution. He told her there was no cause for concern, that he'd since traced the error."

"That's it?"

"That's it. Since only the queen and I know the box exists, he doesn't know it's gone. Nor did he inform either of us that he apprehended you, if that's what you're asking. I find that rather...interesting."

Sara drew in a sharp breath. Umberto had lied to the king and queen? For *her*?

"However," King Carlo continued after a pause, "after the queen was out of our hearing, Umberto admitted to me that an unauthorized entry had occurred and that he suspected a former employee. I asked if he'd contacted the police. He said he wished to conduct his own investigation first, and assured me that the individual was not someone he felt posed a danger to either the royal family or the community at large."

"He questioned me for some time in his office. He suspects I stole something, but he doesn't know what. He found the thumbprint sticker and realized I had the corresponding password, which means he knows I had help from the inside. I'm sure that's why he didn't go to the police right away. And why he didn't feel comfortable telling you the full truth yet."

"You want to protect him, don't you? Umberto Niro?" Laughter came over the line, surprising her. "I happen to know the two of you were seeing each other before you left the palace. Rumor is that it didn't end well. I'm surprised you feel the need to convince me he did his duty."

She forced herself not to confirm the king's information. Instead, she said, "I don't wish to be disrespectful, Your Highness, but I wish you'd warned me that the thumbprint you provided was Umberto's. Of all the people on staff—"

"Umberto Niro is most above reproach. If the logs were seen by anyone other than Umberto himself, your entry wouldn't have raised a question. Aside from the family, he's the only person who has the complete run of the palace."

She had to give the king that point.

"When he questioned you, you must not have told him anything."

"No, sir. But he knows I wouldn't have been able to get as far as I did without help from someone with the highest level of security clearance, and that could mean a member of the family. That gave him pause."

"Even so, I'm surprised he released you."

"I think—I hope—he trusts me to some extent. I know you didn't want anyone else involved in our plan, but I promised Umberto a full explanation after Christmas. It was my only chance to leave the palace that night with the box." She heard the king take a drink and waited for him to finish before adding, "I don't know how far he'll dig between now and then. Or if he'll feel obliged to speak with the queen or call the police."

"We should be safe on that front. I asked him to keep the matter between the two of us for now, as the police are on a holiday schedule and I'd prefer they use their resources for true emergencies. He agreed to do so. I got the impression he disagreed, but he didn't voice his opinion. I doubt he'll go back on his word."

"Thank you." She knew he had to get off the phone or risk being overheard—it was rare for the monarch to be left in private so long, even during his workouts—but she had one more issue to address. "Your Highness, I know it's nearly Christmas, but I'd like you to reconsider keeping Umberto in the dark on this. He's incredibly loyal to you and your family, and he's been put in a terrible position."

She sensed the king's refusal before he spoke. "I rule the country, but my wife rules the staff. She is particularly close to Umberto. If she were to ask him for specifics about that night and why he wanted the inventory, he'd be in an even worse position. While I have the deepest respect for him and the job he does here, I can't risk having him say anything to the queen."

Disappointment welled in her chest. "I understand. I'll follow up on the box and ensure it's delivered as we planned."

She was about to hang up when the king added, "Sara? Even if no one knows it, you're the best employee we've ever had. I owe you a great debt. I wish things could've been different."

The genuine affection in his tone tightened her throat. It took effort to keep the emotion from her voice as she responded, "I've always felt that it's I who owe you the great debt. If I had to do it all over, I wouldn't change a thing. Besides, everything worked out for me in the long run, didn't it?"

She heard the treadmill slow to a stop. It was so quiet on the other end of the line she wondered if the king disconnected the call without hearing her. Then he said, "Your business is quite successful. I knew it would be. We'll talk again soon."

CHAPTER 10

Umberto read the briefing on the king's upcoming diplomatic trip to Berlin twice before the words finally started to penetrate his brain. Even then, he knew he was missing its nuances, the subtle hints that spurred him to ask the right questions to ensure he addressed security details no one else had considered.

His inability to concentrate wasn't good for the job, and he was getting damned sick of it.

He'd managed well enough last night, when he'd overseen security for the Barrali family's attendance at Christmas Eve services, but the location was a familiar one and the security protocols were completely in Umberto's control. The route was easy to lock down and cathedral employees were well-versed in Umberto's requirements. Not so with Berlin, where he was compelled to work with a foreign government.

He reached for the espresso on the corner of his desk. Olga had it delivered this morning with a homemade cannoli and a note urging him to take off New Year's Eve since he wasn't, in her words, "selfish enough to take off Christmas." Easy for her to believe, Umberto thought. Olga had a partner at home who made cannoli and loved to celebrate the holidays. He had an empty fridge and a pile of thriller novels his cousin had dropped off the previous week. Given that he could only spend so many hours reading fiction, he may as well spend the day in his office and be productive.

He certainly wasn't going to spend the day with his family, where everyone was married and acted as if he were deficient in some way for remaining single.

He downed the shot of caffeine and tossed Olga's note into his trash can before returning his attention to the Berlin report.

"Umberto?"

He glanced up as Max, a longtime security staffer, exited the control room. The glimmer in Max's eye meant he'd detected something on one of the video feeds that was exciting enough to merit delivering the news in person, rather than to Umberto's earpiece.

"What do you have?"

Max gestured toward Umberto's computer screen. A schematic of the meeting room in Berlin was displayed in one window, while the palace security feed was open in another. It currently showed a wide view of the palace kitchen. The king and queen's granddaughter, Anna, stood at one long countertop, arranging Christmas cookies on a white platter. As Umberto expanded the window, the view switched to the other end of the kitchen, where the head chef's assistant prepared salads.

"Go to the west fence. Camera six. Guy's been there for twenty minutes."

Umberto clicked to the appropriate angle. Immediately, Umberto saw what Max had noticed. What he himself should've noticed, given that it was right there in front of him.

"Early- to mid-twenties, not one of our usual fence clingers," Max said as Umberto zeroed in on the man's face and the object in his hands. "He hasn't made any moves to launch the drone, but there's a camera attached to the underside. He's been subtle, trying to keep it hidden. Doesn't appear to be armed, but—" Max shrugged. One never knew who was armed.

Umberto radioed the four security staffers nearest the area and instructed them to intercept the man, then turned back to Max. "Have the control room call the police if the drone goes up before security gets there. I don't want that over palace airspace. The guy may be nothing more than paparazzi or a college student on a dare, but don't chance it."

"They're already on it. I'll report back when I have something," Max said before leaving to follow up on the situation in person.

Umberto rubbed the back of his neck, then watched on screen while the staff approached the perpetrator, whose expression shifted to a mix of fear, awe, and desperation at the sight of the four burly, uniformed men. Within seconds, he turned over the drone and consented to a pat down.

Ten minutes later, Max called to report that the drone operator was an avid gardener with a niche website devoted to landscape design.

"A…gardener?" That wasn't what he'd expected.

"He wanted to shoot video since it's Christmas Day and the gardens are closed to tourists. We briefed him on the proper procedure for obtaining a film license, wrote out an official warning, then released him. Gave him a healthy scare first."

Umberto shook his head. "The idiot deserves a healthy scare. Besides, empty or not, who films a garden in the winter?"

"Apparently idiots who believe outdoor space should be as enjoyable in the winter as the summer," Max replied. "While we checked his identification, he waxed poetic about the proper placement of evergreens and deciduous trees with decorative bark for, and I quote, 'year-round interest.' If you make me repeat everything he said about gardening in my report, you may as well kill me now."

"If you make me read a report like that, you may as well kill me."

Umberto thanked Max, then turned his attention to the Berlin briefing to give it a final read. He cursed when he realized he'd missed a scheduling conflict, then typed a notation for Olga to rectify it when she returned to work in the morning. What the hell was wrong with him?

It was Sara. Sara clouded his judgment.

From the moment he'd seen Sara's panicked expression when he'd caught her in the queen's closet, then watched as she stiffened her spine in defiance, he'd thought of little else. Since he made love to her Saturday night, he'd thought of nothing but how much he wanted to do it again. Not in the frantic, lust-filled manner with which they'd tackled the stairs, though a wild round of staircase sex certainly held its allure. No, he craved the decadent, slow, mind-blowing sex they'd shared after they made it to her apartment. Once sprawled across her bed, he'd been able to admire the way her thigh fit to his palm. He could savor the soft sounds she'd made as she'd kissed his shoulders and chest, and enjoy the light scratch of her fingernails as she buried her hands in his hair and whispered his name.

His name never sounded as good as it had when it came from her lips. Then what she'd done with those lips...it made him hard as granite thinking about it. About *her*.

He pushed the sensual images from his mind, wrapped up his notes on the Berlin brief, then forwarded everything to Olga. His gaze went to the security feed, which showed Prince Bruno, the youngest of the Barrali siblings, jogging up the stairs to his parents' private wing. Several days' worth of beard growth dotted his jaw, a casual look he never sported outside the palace. He wore jeans and a collared blue shirt that had been left both untucked and open at the throat. Brightly wrapped packages filled his arms.

Umberto continued watching as the feed rotated through views of the palace's most trafficked areas. Soon the entire family would be ensconced in the king and queen's apartment to exchange Christmas gifts. Otherwise, all was quiet, befitting the holiday. Every post was manned, every entry and exit carefully logged. Though only a skeleton staff was on duty, they were sharp enough to handle any crisis, which was a good thing, given his own state of mind.

He cut the video feed, then took a bite of Olga's cannoli. While delicious, it didn't hold a candle to Sara's honey-glazed *torta della Sarcaccia*. His mouth had watered—literally, watered—at the sight and scent of those miniature delights in her shop.

Umberto pushed away the cannoli, suddenly craving fresh air more than he craved sweets.

He should've known going to see Sara on Saturday night would mess with his brain.

He'd spent that entire afternoon turning over events in his mind. Retracing Sara's steps had proven easy enough. He'd reviewed the surveillance footage and found the moment she'd scaled the fence. Her speed and technique were impressive; if he hadn't been looking for her at that specific location and that exact time, he'd have missed her. Then, when he'd gone to the garden to adjust the sight lines of his security cameras, he'd located Sara's umbrella. It was so easy to find, she must've planned to retrieve it on her way out, using it once again to test the fence.

Determining how Sara had accessed the palace computer systems to get his prints left him stymied. The undeniable conclusion: she hadn't. The only access to the personnel files had come from inside the palace, and only by those with clearance. Given that Umberto could count the non-family members with that type of access on one hand, his next course of action should've been to call those employees to his office and interview them one by one.

Instead, he'd gone to Sara's shop with her umbrella, telling himself that his presence might rattle the truth from her. It hadn't worked. In his heart, he'd probably known it wouldn't.

He'd gone because he'd wanted to see her again. He'd gone because she was both the best and worst thing that ever happened to him, and he didn't like things unsettled.

Umberto followed the garden's gravel path to a quiet niche in the boxwood hedge, dropped onto a stone bench, and stared into the cloudless December sky. Visiting Sara went against everything he'd been trained to do, but even now, in the cold, clear light of day, he didn't regret it. When he'd looked into her eyes and told her he trusted her, he meant it to the very marrow of his bones. But after four days with no communication, he was going out of his mind.

Whether he trusted Sara or not, the distraction had to end. He'd nearly missed catching a man with a *drone*. If the guy had been a terrorist with a bomb, rather than gardening enthusiast with the mental aptitude of a dung beetle, that drone could've made it to the windows of the private wing and taken out the entire royal family in one blast. Security threats didn't get much more in-your-face than that.

Umberto folded his hands behind his head and took a long, thoughtful breath. Sara said she'd explain herself after Christmas. Well, Christmas was here. If he didn't get answers in the next twenty-four hours, he'd go to King Carlo and tell him he needed a leave of absence. If necessary, he'd resign. His actions were going to jeopardize the royal family if he couldn't get his head on straight.

Olga could handle Berlin, if necessary. She'd grouse about it, but she'd do it. She'd headed Prince Alessandro's personal security detail for three years, so she also knew what it took to coordinate the individual family members' security assignments. The king and queen had six children—several of whom had spouses to consider—and protecting them whenever they traveled demanded attention to detail.

Before Umberto could give more thought to the particulars of handing his tasks to Olga, his earpiece crackled with the sound of Max's voice.

"There's a guest at the east gate. King Carlo wants you to give her a personal escort to the apartment. Then he'd like you to join the family."

Umberto's hands fell from his head. He frowned, straightened, then asked Max to repeat the last part. Max repeated all of it.

Umberto pushed from the bench and strode toward the palace. He didn't bother hiding the skepticism from his voice. "On Christmas?"

"As today is Christmas…yes. Right now, in fact."

Umberto had never been asked to join the family on Christmas before. No employee had, and definitely not during their morning gift exchange. Housekeeping and maintenance were given the day off, and the few members of the kitchen staff who remained on duty to prepare and serve lunch were in and out of the royal apartment as quickly as possible.

"Is this a prank for missing the drone?"

"No. I swear on Olga's cannoli."

"You took my cannoli?"

"What…wait, you abandoned your cannoli?"

Umberto scoffed. At this very moment, Max was probably hurrying out of the control room to check on the existence of the coveted dessert.

"I'm serious about the family," Max added. "King Carlo himself called down."

"If you're lying, I'm going to make you write every single detail you heard about winter gardens into that drone report." Umberto skirted the ballroom, then said, "I'm nearly to the gate. If anything comes up, you know how to reach me."

Umberto jogged down the same empty staircase he'd used on Friday night when escorting Sara from the premises, then pushed open the door to the courtyard. He took a stutter step when he saw the woman standing at the gate. She wore a pair of cropped black pants, black flats, and an ivory blouse. She'd topped it with a short, chestnut-colored leather jacket and wore a scarf loosely draped over her hair. Days ago, from a distance, he might not have recognized Sara with the scarf. After Saturday night, he'd know that lean, sensuous body anywhere.

As Umberto approached, one of the guards handed Sara a visitor's badge, instructed her to keep it prominently displayed, then waited for Umberto's nod before signaling the guardhouse to release the turnstile lock.

"Merry Christmas," she said once she entered the courtyard. A broad smile brightened her face, but her eyes remained wary. It was then that Umberto noticed the bag she'd kept near her hip, obscuring it from his view as she'd come through the turnstile.

"Dare I ask?"

"It's been screened," she assured him. "Did the guards call you down? Or did you see me on camera?"

She let the question hang in the air. While she'd asked it casually, he could tell she was hoping for a specific answer.

"King Carlo called my office and asked that I escort you to the private residence." He hesitated, then clarified, "He said there was a guest at the gate, but didn't identify you."

"I see."

He couldn't help but give her a devilish grin as he held the door for her. "I'd have come even if he had."

Her smile finally reached her eyes. She fairly flew up the staircase toward the ballroom, then rounded the corner to head for the wing housing the king and queen's apartment. Then her feet stilled and she aimed a glance down the hallway that led to his office.

"Mind if we stop in the dungeon first? It'll be quick."

"Why?"

She lifted the bag. "I brought you a present."

CHAPTER 11

His brow lifted in a mix of surprise and trepidation. "A present?"

"It's Christmas."

"I'm well aware of the date." He didn't have to add that she'd promised him answers today. She could see it in watchful way he moved, as if he expected a bludgeoning rather than a heartfelt gift.

"I'm also aware of the time," he added. "It took me a several minutes to get to the gate after the king called and I'd rather not keep him waiting. You mind holding the bag for now?"

"Seriously, Umberto? A 'holding the bag' joke?"

He grimaced as he guided her away from his office. "It wasn't intentional."

"I bet." When they reached the double doors to the royal apartment, she stopped and faced him. "I want to make sure I can find you when I'm done here. Will you be in your office?"

"The king asked that I stay and visit with the family."

Though the words were said casually, she sensed both his wonder and discomfort at receiving such a rare invitation. She had to admit it surprised her, too. As he raised his fist to knock on the door, she put a hand between his knuckles and the wood. Frown lines puckered his brow as he looked down at her. "What?"

"Thank you." She wrapped her fingers around his closed fist, then brought it to her heart. "I doubt anyone would notice it but me, but you seem off your game. I'm so sorry I've put you in this position."

He flipped his hand to squeeze her fingers. Emotion clouded his eyes; she couldn't remember seeing him so unguarded, so bare. Very quietly, he said, "Any position you've put me in is of my own choosing. And yes, I mean that in every way it can be construed. I chose to trust you. I chose to be with you Saturday night. If that means I'm looking for a new job tomorrow, then so be it. I'd do it all again."

It was the very sentence she'd uttered to King Carlo when he'd called on Sunday morning. She wanted to drop the gift bag she carried and throw her arms around Umberto's neck, but the sound of approaching footsteps caused him to release her hand and step away. As one, they turned toward the new arrival.

"Sara!" Princess Sophia's face broke into a broad smile as she reached the top of the stairs. She quickened her pace as she strode the length of the hallway. Gift bags in a rainbow of colors were looped over both of her arms, but she ignored the flapping bags and spread her arms like giant wings to enclose Sara in a hug. "I'm so happy to see you. I missed you! Did my parents invite you here?"

"Your father did," Sara replied as Sophia released her. She held up her own bag. "He engaged my delivery services."

The princess's eyes sparkled. "Gelato?"

"Wait and see."

Sophia turned the handle on the door and waved in both Umberto and Sara. "It better be gelato, because I'm nearly ten minutes late. A scoop of your cinnamon or hazelnut will make them forget to be mad at me."

The women shared a smile that spoke to a deep, abiding friendship. Given what had happened in that Paris department store all those years ago and the way it reflected on the family, it was the last thing Umberto expected. He was unaware the two had kept in touch.

Before he could consider it, he was hit full force by the tsunami that was the Barrali family. Laughter echoed throughout the room. Anna, the daughter of Prince Stefano and his wife, Megan, circled the room with the plate of cookies Umberto had seen her preparing in the kitchen. Prince Bruno held Anna's younger brother, Dario, on his lap, and made silly faces at the boy. King Carlo sat in a wing chair not far from the massive fireplace, watching in disbelief as his two eldest sons, Crown Prince Vittorio and his twin, Prince Alessandro, lay on the floor and arm wrestled, despite their mother's pleas for them to get up and act like adults. Vittorio's wife, Emily, sat on a sofa beside Prince Massimo and his wife, Kelly, making gestures with her hands as she told them a story about one of her coworkes.

"Aunt Sophia's here!" the princess announced as she stretched her arms to show off the gift bags. "Where's my favorite niece?"

"I'm your only niece," Anna said without missing a beat. At twelve, Anna was sharp as a tack and had the quick wit of her royal grandparents. She set the cookies on the coffee table, then helped Sophia add the gifts to the pile that surrounded the family's Christmas tree.

"You're late," Alessandro said through gritted teeth as he and Vittorio strained against each other, their elbows planted on the floor as they continued to arm wrestle.

"Oh, leave her alone. No one's in a hurry," Bruno said, looking Sophia's way with a grin.

One by one, the siblings fell silent as they noticed that Sophia hadn't entered alone. Vittorio and Alessandro dragged their gazes from each other to see what was happening, though Alessandro did so a split second after Vittorio, giving him the advantage needed to pin his brother's arm to the Persian rug.

"Umberto. And Sara Angeletti!" Queen Fabrizia rose from where she'd been sitting beside Bruno and little Dario and crossed the room to kiss Sara's cheeks in greeting. "I haven't seen you in ages."

"I'm honored to be here, Your Highness," Sara responded as she curtseyed in deference to the queen.

"No need for formalities. This is family time," King Carlo told Sara. To the rest of the room, he said, "I invited Sara to join us. She's helped me with a very special project."

His tone was enough to make Alessandro and Vittorio scramble from the floor and find seats. Vittorio claimed a chair near Emily, while Alessandro sat on the arm of one of the room's two sofas.

Fabrizia turned toward her husband with a look of mock irritation. "What did you do now, Carlo?"

Sophia slipped into the seat her father had just occupied. "Yes, Father, what did you do?"

The king's smile of anticipation encompassed the room. "We've had a big year. Since last December, Emily joined our family. Massimo and Kelly married. Stefano and Megan brought Dario into the world. Anna became a big sister. And you all learned about your half-brothers, Rocco and Enzo, and your half-sister Lina. It wasn't an easy year, but it was a good one."

Umberto faded back a step. While he'd been invited and knew that the king wouldn't have done so without reason, the king's speech made him feel he was intruding on a private moment.

"Through it all, your mother has been my rock." Carlo stretched his hand, inviting his wife to stand beside him. She folded her hand into his and looked up at him with such love in her eyes, Umberto felt he was bearing witness to every man's deepest desire: the undying support of a truly great woman. A great *partner*. For that was what the king and queen had been over all these years. Partners.

"I wanted to do something very special for you this Christmas," the king said, his attention now riveted on his elegant, devoted wife. "In all our years of marriage, however, I've never been able to surprise you. I've tried jewelry. I've tried to plan getaways. One year, I even updated your stationery to a new design you'd admired, but hadn't ordered."

Her laughter filled the room. "Stationery was an odd choice."

"Odd or not, you found out about it ahead of time. You've always known what was coming. And this year, I'm sure you do, too."

He sent Anna under the tree to find a gift wrapped in silver paper. Anna brought it to her grandmother, then waited while the queen pulled at the fine ribbons and delicate paper to reveal a small box. Fabrizia handed Anna the gift paper, then opened the lid. She laughed, then held aloft a set of tickets. "Cole Porter's *Anything Goes*, next month at the Royal Theater."

"That's the where the gangster has the bluebird song, isn't it? About singing even when disaster is approaching faster and faster?"

"It is." She smiled down at Anna, though with the growth spurt Anna had recently, it wouldn't be long before Anna looked the queen in the eye. "He sings until his troubles are through. I also notice that there are three tickets here. I imagine it's so your grandfather and I can take you with us."

Anna's eyes widened. "In your box? To a live musical? I've never seen one!"

The queen raised her eyes to look at Stefano and Megan. "I assume it's all right with your parents? We'll have dinner here, then take you to the show."

"That would be fantastic," Megan said. It was apparent from Megan's expression that she loved seeing the tight bond that had formed between her daughter and Stefano's mother.

"Did you know about the tickets already?" Anna asked.

The queen tried to look innocent, but it didn't work.

"She knew because her assistant had to block off the evening on your grandmother's schedule," the king told Anna. "That's why it's so hard to surprise your grandmother. I suspect it's why she mentioned the bluebird song to you. It's one of her favorites and she knew the show was coming to the theater. But I had Sara—Ms. Angeletti—bring something with her today. Something your grandmother doesn't know about. Sara?"

Sara set the bag she carried on one of the room's glass end tables, then withdrew a zippered cold pack. "For you, Your Highness."

"Oh, Carlo," the queen said as she approached Sara and unzipped the pack to look inside. Her face broke into a wide grin as she pulled a pint-sized container from the pack and showed the label to the room. "It's called 'A Bluebird's Song.'"

"Your own flavor, Queen Fabrizia, commissioned by your husband. It's made with blueberries and crushed almonds in a vanilla base." Sara spun the container so Fabrizia could read the back, which had a picture of a bluebird and a phone number. "It will be carried in our shop for the run of the show. After that, it will be kept as a custom recipe only you can order. Call that number and I'll personally arrange for delivery."

"This is so thoughtful." Queen Fabrizia handed the container to Massimo so he could take a look before passing it around the room. "I had no idea. Thank you."

"Where do I get my personal phone number?" Alessandro asked. "I'd like to place an order—"

"You have plenty of personal numbers," Vittorio retorted. "Sara's too smart to give you hers."

"Sara is a genius," the queen said, cutting off her sons. "As is my husband."

A slow, easy smile spread across King Carlo's face. "We're not finished yet. Take a seat, darling. Sara and I have one more surprise for you."

The queen's eyes widened and a happy grin lifted her cheeks. The king waited for her to sit in one of the armchairs, then surprised Umberto by asking him to do the same. "You should see this, Umberto. Then perhaps you won't feel so conflicted about failing to report a theft to either my wife or to me."

"Your Highness—"

"A theft?" the queen asked before her gaze narrowed. "So there was a reason for that inventory."

"Umberto is better at his job than even I thought," King Carlo said as he gestured for Sara to hand over the bag. "I'd arranged for Sara to take something from your closet while we were occupied at the Middle Eastern charity ball last week. Unfortunately, she was caught."

"By chance," Umberto admitted, looking from the queen to King Carlo. "The queen left her reading glasses on the coffee table and asked that I retrieve them. When I entered your apartment, I thought I heard a noise coming from the back rooms. I found Ms. Angeletti."

"You handled the situation well," the king assured him, though Umberto didn't feel reassured. Not with the queen looking sideways at him from her armchair.

"I apologize, Queen Fabrizia," he told her. "When I realized that Ms. Angeletti could only have accessed your closet with help from the inside, I thought it best to conduct my own investigation before calling the police. I mentioned it to your husband, and he asked that I keep the incident between the two of us until after Christmas."

Umberto expected the queen to react with disappointment. Over the years, they'd developed a sort of friendship...or as close a friendship as a royal could have with the head of security. She expected Umberto to tell her everything, in as direct a manner as possible. Instead of disappointment, however, she reached over and patted his arm. "My husband is the one who owes you an apology, Umberto, for placing you in a no-win situation. You have no reason to apologize to me. But if it happens again—"

"I understand," Umberto promised at the same time Sara said, "It won't. I'm not cut out for life as a thief."

"You never were," Princess Sophia said.

"It all worked out," Sara told the princess, waving off whatever else Sophia wished to say.

"And that brings me to the final part of your gift," the king said. "Perhaps Anna would like to give it to you?"

Anna crossed the room and reached into the bag Sara had handed the king. She withdrew a wrapped box. "It's heavy."

"It belongs to your grandmother. Why don't you take it to her?"

The moment she accepted the box from Anna and gauged its weight, the queen sighed and put a hand over her breast. "Oh, Carlo. I think I know what you did. You had her steal this from the hidden compartment in my dresser?"

"You know it's impossible for me to go anywhere in this palace without a set of eyes on me. Especially eyes that report everything they see to you." He grinned. "That's why I needed Sara. Open it."

The queen undid the glittering gold wrapping paper to reveal a white, lidded cardboard box. She opened it, set the lid and a layer of cushioning on the coffee table, then withdrew an elegant gold box covered in delicate scrollwork. A box, Umberto noted, that perfectly matched the size of the lump he'd spied under Sara's jacket.

"My grandmother's bird box," she said. "You had it cleaned?"

"Open it."

The queen hesitated, then ran her thumb along the front of the box to move a small, nearly invisible slider. The top of the box popped open and a tiny, blue-feathered bird rose from the interior. After a beat, it began to spin slowly, then to sing.

"You had it restored!"

"There's a jeweler in Cateri who collects antique singing bird boxes. He claimed he could get it working again. It seems he came through with flying colors."

"Grandma, it's a bluebird!"

"It is," Queen Fabrizia told Anna. "The most beautiful bluebird in the world. My great-grandparents gave it to my grandmother as a confirmation gift, then she passed it down to my mother on her wedding day. It hasn't worked in twenty or thirty years, but it's always been special to me."

"I've never seen it," Massimo said. Murmurs of agreement came from around the room.

"This was my mother's most prized possession. When she passed away, it was difficult for me to accept, so after her funeral, I put it in a hidden compartment in my dresser. Recently, I started taking it out each year on her birthday. Now that it sings, I think I'll leave it on display." She lifted her gaze to smile at her husband. "It's the perfect way to end a year of new beginnings. I love you."

"And I you." The edge in the king's voice emphasized the tight bond he and his wife shared. Umberto couldn't help but glance at Sara. Her eyes were filled with unshed tears, showing that she, too, had heard the emotion in the king's response.

"Now, on to the rest of the gifts!" Carlo declared. "Anna, would you hand out what's under the tree?"

As Anna dove under the tree, Sara leaned close to the king and said something Umberto couldn't hear. Then she turned and smiled at the queen. "Have a very merry Christmas, Your Highness. I'm going to take my leave, but I do hope you'll call for more gelato soon."

"Only if you promise to make the delivery yourself."

"Of course."

"It's been a pleasure to see you. You've done more for our family over the years than anyone will ever know, and we are eternally grateful." The heartfelt words and the expression on the queen's face twisted Umberto's gut.

It took a beat for him to grasp that the queen meant the words for him as much as for Sara.

Suddenly, the pieces started to fall into place. The ramifications were enough to send a wave of nausea to his throat.

Sara took the bag she'd brought with the queen's gifts and looped it over her arm, then hugged Princess Sophia goodbye before wishing a happy holiday to the rest of the family.

Umberto stood to address the king and queen. "I should escort Ms. Angeletti from the building. Thank you for including me in your family time."

The queen smiled up at him. "We're glad you could come. Have a wonderful holiday, Umberto."

"Yes, it was important to me to have you here," King Carlo added. "Once you've accompanied Sara to the gate, you're welcome to take the rest of the day off. I'm quite certain the rest of the staff can cover for you if necessary."

"Thank you, Your Highness. I will." He didn't miss the gleam in the king's eyes as the monarch shot a pointed look from Umberto to Sara. Suddenly, Umberto wanted nothing more than to be alone with her. With every passing second, more pieces of the puzzle clicked into place.

More pieces that pointed to the eight years he'd spent without Sara being entirely his fault.

CHAPTER 12

"I THINK it was just pointed out to me that I'm the world's most colossal ass."

Sara paused on the stairs to look at Umberto. His rich olive skin looked as pale as the white marble of the staircase.

"You had no way of knowing that I'd broken in as a favor to the king or why. It was supposed to be—"

"Not that. Paris. It was Sophia, wasn't it?" Umberto's hands were shaking as he reached out to place them on her shoulders. "You were with the princess and her friends in Printemps. Friends she'd finally made that semester after having a rotten freshman year."

Sara felt tears pricking her eyes. She fought to control them, only to feel a knot form in her throat. Finally, *finally*, he understood. "Umberto, I can't talk about that day. I swore never to discuss it."

"Come with me."

He took her hand and guided her down the stairs and through a series of hallways until they were in the palace library. A long, narrow room filled with books and Impressionist paintings, it was one of Queen Fabrizia's favorite places in the palace. It was also completely empty.

"No one can hear us," Umberto said as walked her to the far end of the room, then urged her to sit beside him on one of the room's sumptuous, high-backed sofas.

"Still, I can't tell you—"

"Let me take a stab at it. Sophia had just turned twenty. She'd moved out of her university's residence halls and into a rental apartment with a new group of friends. Friends who'd lived life out in the world at large, free to go and do as they pleased. Friends she'd made for herself, not friends who entered her social orbit because they had connections to the royal family. You and I both know that the princess was sophisticated in many respects, but socially…she wasn't like other twenty-somethings. She hadn't experienced the social struggles other teens face. She wanted to impress them."

Sara remembered it like it was yesterday. She'd been dressed like a college student herself so she'd blend in with the crowd as she watched over Sophia. After a morning of shopping to celebrate the fact they'd finished their fall term exams, Sophia and her roommates went to lunch at a trendy restaurant not far from the Paris Opera. Afterward, they decided to do more shopping and wandered through the Galleries Lafayette, then made their way to Printemps. Sara had a bad feeling about the afternoon from the moment the girls had finished lunch; the others had been in a mischievous mood, and several of them had stolen glances at each other behind Sophia's back as they'd entered the high end store. She heard one of them urge Sophia to, "do it." Another girl kept saying, "it's not a big thing… everyone does it…it's just for fun."

The girls spread out on one of the store's upper floors. Sara pretended to shop and kept an eye Sophia as the princess shifted blouses along a rack, searching for one in her size. The princess set the brown bag that contained her pre-lunch purchases on the floor, then continued studying the blouses. Sensing what was about to happen, Sara approached Sophia from behind, moving within arm's reach of the princess just as a blouse fell from one of the hangers into the open bag.

Sophia picked up the shopping bag and turned toward her friends, completely unaware of Sara's presence.

A thousand curse words were on the tip of Sara's tongue as she gave Sophia space, hoping the princess would think better of what she'd done and replace the blouse. Eventually, Sara followed the group downstairs, toward the street-level exit.

Sara's only task was to ensure the princess wasn't physically harmed as she attended school in Paris; under no circumstances was she to act as a parent and discipline her in any way. It had been made clear that she was to stay in the background and allow Sophia her independence. But at the last minute, as Sophia approached the exit and showed no signs of removing the blouse from the bag, Sara dodged around a cosmetics counter and plucked it from the princess's fingertips.

The alarm sounded less than a second later. Sara had—literally—been holding the bag, standing at the main exit of Printemps with a blouse that cost a week's salary.

"You took one with an anti-theft tag?" one of the girls hissed at the princess.

"What's that?" Sophia's eyes grew wide and her entire face went bright pink. She spun to look at Sara, only then realizing that Sara had taken the shopping bag.

"Say nothing," Sara told Sophia before the princess could protest. Mustering every ounce of authority her position and their age difference afforded her, she added, "I stole a blouse. You had no idea. You and your friends were shopping and didn't find anything and decided to leave. Got it?"

"Sara, you can't!"

"Are the receipts for this morning's purchases still in this bag?"

"Yes, but—"

"Then I must have put this blouse in with your purchases when you weren't looking. What you bought this morning cost more than this blouse." She kept her voice hushed, aware the store security guards had nearly reached them. "It wouldn't make sense for you to steal it when you're perfectly willing and able to buy it."

"I didn't want to steal. I-I just thought—" Tears welled in Sophia's large, dark eyes. In that moment, Sara knew she'd made the right choice.

"I know you didn't. And you never will again. These girls are not your friends. If you're asked, you'll say exactly what I told you. Understood?"

The security guards had hauled Sara into their office then. She'd been questioned, arrested, then released on bail. She'd gone straight to the princess's apartment to ensure that Sophia and her friends would stick to the story she'd given them, then took Sophia to a bedroom where they could speak in private.

"I can't let you do this," Sophia had said. "It's gone too far already. It's my fault. My parents will kill me, but I just can't—"

"It's already done. I'm in a much better position to handle this than you are. If you go to the police now, it'll make it much worse. But in exchange, you need to do a few things for me."

The princess was in tears by that point. "I'll do anything you want."

Sara had ticked off her requirements on her fingers. "First, you move back into student housing immediately. I'll ensure you're matched with a better roommate for the spring semester. You'll stay away from these girls."

Sophia opened her mouth to argue, then thought better of it. "All right. I can do that."

"Second, the alcohol is getting out of hand. You had two glasses at lunch. Those girls took advantage of the fact you were feeling less inhibited, and others will, too, if given the opportunity. Cut back or, better, cut it out entirely. I know it's not fair, but you have to live life to a different standard than others."

"Oh, Sara. I'm so sorry. You've been so good to me since I've been here—"

"Third, you will tell your mother and father what you did. I'm taking the fall in public, but you will tell your parents everything. Then you'll tell them what you're doing to prevent an incident like this from happening again. If they tell you to transfer back to Sarcaccia for the rest of your college years, you'll do it. I'll tell them I think you've learned your lesson and that you're better off in Paris, but the decision will be theirs."

Sophia agreed, and both of them flew to Cateri the next day. By then, Sara had met with the store ownership and the local police. A deal was worked out that allowed her to pay a fine rather than face criminal charges, and she was forbidden from entering Printemps again.

She'd been lucky. Or so she'd thought until she faced Umberto outside the king's office that afternoon.

His expression tightened as he faced her now. "She was desperate to be liked by students she thought were cool. She stole that blouse, not you."

Sara looked into Umberto's eyes as he waited for her response. Choosing her words carefully, she said, "When we're young, don't we all care too much about what others think of us?"

His thumb rubbed hers. "You risked your job when you realized Princess Sophia was in trouble. That's why she looks at you the way she does. It's why King Carlo was forced to fire you. Privately, you'd exceeded the scope of your duties, and publicly, you were a shoplifter."

"I'd do it again. I've always believed in putting people first, and that day—" She grimaced, realizing she'd admitted what she shouldn't. "Not that I'm confirming anything, you know."

"I understand."

"Once I convinced the king that he shouldn't go back to the Paris police—which wasn't easy to do—and that he had no choice but to fire me, he made it right."

"But he—" Umberto's fingers tightened around hers and he shook his head. "The shop. I wondered how you managed to get it up and running so quickly. I should have known."

"My severance package was very generous. He's been wonderful to me, Umberto, all this time. The whole family has been wonderful."

"But I wasn't." Umberto's brows knit and lines formed at the edges of his eyes. "When you walked out of his office, I was too focused on my own anger to see what was right in front of me."

The pain etched on his face proved she wasn't the only one whose heart was broken that afternoon. "You can't blame yourself. I didn't give you a chance. I was so overwhelmed with what had happened, with the idea that I had to start over, and with the enormity of what the weeks would be like for me after the shoplifting incident became public knowledge." She raised Umberto's scarred knuckles to her lips, then met his gaze. "I wasn't expecting to see you in the hallway when I left the king's office. I'd intended to call you from home that night. I thought that if I invited you to my apartment, I could give you enough information that you'd figure out what must've happened without actually having to tell you. You've worked the same job. You know the challenges we face. But when I saw you there—"

"I may as well have been an executioner."

Sara sighed. She hated hearing the guilt in Umberto's voice. "I snapped."

"I should've come to you that night. I should've apologized and heard you out."

She leaned forward until her forehead touched his. "I don't think I would have listened. I was emotionally spent. It might've been the right choice to give up all I'd worked for at the palace, but I was angry and frustrated. I turned that anger toward you and blamed you for not trusting me."

"I didn't trust you. Not the way I should." He let out a deep breath. "All these years, I've wondered what happened. I'm sorry I hurt you, Sara. You can't imagine."

"No more sorry than I am for hurting you. After a few days had passed, the media attention was so intense I couldn't risk trying to see you. I knew that our coworkers must have had questions for you. People knew we were close. A lot of them suspected we were seeing each other. I didn't want to risk your reputation."

"I wouldn't have cared."

"Easy to say in retrospect. You were moving up the ladder quickly then. You were focused on your career, just as I was."

"True, but I should've done what you did, and put people first. I should have prioritized you over my duty." Umberto exhaled in frustration, then grew quiet. They'd both made mistakes. They'd both suffered.

After a long moment, she raised her head so she could study his face. "We each swore an oath to protect the monarch and his heirs, no matter the cost. Protecting the Barralis safeguards our country and our way of life. By rejecting a thief in your ranks, you believed you were doing what was necessary to uphold your oath, much as I made my decision in Paris to uphold mine. We hurt each other, but it does no good to judge ourselves now. We can't go back to undo what was said and done."

"No, we can't." His jaw tensed, then he let go of her hand. For one wild moment she feared he was going to say goodbye, but then he smiled and cradled her cheeks in his hands. "But we can try again. We can move forward."

Her heart leaped in her chest. She'd give anything for a second chance with this man, though if it didn't work out, she wasn't sure she could stand the pain again. "A new beginning?"

He grinned. "Yes. If you're willing to risk it."

"Are *you* willing to risk being hurt again?"

With one hand, he smoothed back her hair. "When I was very small, my mother told me that no one escapes life unscathed. We all have our wounds. Thankfully most wounds are like bruises or paper cuts. They're painful in the moment, but soon healed and forgotten. Other injuries take longer. A broken wrist. A sprained ankle. Those wounds require more care and linger in our memories. But if we keep our heads held high, we endure."

"Wise mother."

"Yes, she was. What she didn't warn me about are those rare wounds that refuse to heal properly."

Umberto released Sara and pointed to his forearm. "Say metal fragments are left in an arm following a car accident. The skin may heal, even if the wound is jagged or deep, but underneath the surface, it festers. It throbs or itches when you least expect it. While the arm may bend and function, it's not the way it used to be. It's not *right*. The only way to heal a wound like that is to reopen it, clear away what wasn't properly treated the first time, then monitor it to ensure the skin and bones knit properly. It's a risk. You could cause more harm, rendering a functional but suboptimal limb useless. Or you could have a complete recovery."

Umberto's hand dropped to her knee. "Sara, you're the wound that never healed. I may appear functional, but I'm far from optimal. Without you, my life isn't *right*. I'm willing to risk further injury to make it right. Permanently right. Even if that means starting over slowly and rebuilding trust."

As Umberto looked at her, the love in his gaze made her heart swell. He was such a good man. Such a thoughtful man. Never in a million years would she have thought to equate what happened in their relationship to a car accident, but the healing analogy was an apt one. She covered his hand with hers, knitting their fingers together. "You trusted me enough to wait for Christmas, even though you believed your job was at risk."

"You trusted me enough to let me stay with you Saturday night."

That drew a smile from her. "It was the best night of my life. Waking up beside you felt like waking up in heaven. Then when I watched you walk across the street with that cute little bounce in your step—"

"You watched from your window?"

"I couldn't help but watch you."

A broad grin spread across his face. "Then I'd say we're off to a good start."

Unable to resist any longer, Sara closed the distance between them to kiss him. Tenderly, at first, then with more ardor as his mouth did wondrous things to hers. Finally, he eased back and put his index finger to her lower lip. "I've always loved this crease in your bottom lip."

"I split it falling out of a tree when I was a girl. Never healed properly."

"A project for me, then." He kissed her again. She felt his smile against her lips, but more than that, she felt the love he carried in his heart. Having Umberto in her life again was a miracle, one too fragile to believe.

When he finally broke the kiss, she said, "Rebuilding a relationship takes take time, you know. And patience."

His smile didn't falter. "I've lived with the pain of losing you this long. I'm willing to be patient and deal with setbacks if there's a chance at having you in my life permanently. If it will help, I'm willing to take a leave of absence from the palace."

"You're needed here."

"You're a distraction. I've been awful at work all week."

"You caught me."

"You're a terrible thief. I heard you rustling through the queen's drawers all the way from her living room."

"True." She ran her hand down the front of his shirt. "Carlo knew, I think. About us. I think it was why he chose me to help him with the queen's Christmas gift."

"He couldn't have asked any of the staff. Queen Fabrizia has ways of finding out what everyone is doing. And you know the layout. That being said…it's possible. I think he was hoping to give us a second chance."

"I saw the look he gave you when you offered to escort me out of the apartment." She grinned. "Think he knows what we're up to now?"

"If Max is paying attention to the video feed."

Sara jerked back in horror. "We've been watched this whole time?"

"This end of the library is the furthest from the camera, and the view is of your back. You can't be identified. That's *if* Max is paying attention and noticed that there's anyone in the library at all. I imagine he's busy eating the cannoli I left on my desk if he hasn't taken it already."

"You had cannoli? For breakfast?" It was so unlike Umberto. The man loved his sweets, but not first thing in the morning. He was the espresso-and-go type.

"Olga's partner, Filomena, made it. She sent it over this morning. I wasn't going to refuse."

Sara stretched to thread one finger through the top of the gift bag she'd carried out of the king and queen's apartment. She held it in front of Umberto. "Then maybe you don't need this. I tried to give it to you earlier, but—"

Umberto took the bag and set it between them. His expression changed from curiosity to gratitude as he looked inside and saw the green and yellow box she'd tucked beside the queen's gift before leaving her apartment this morning.

"This better not be a tease."

"It's not."

He withdrew the box and opened the lid to her homemade *torta della Sarcaccia*. "This smells amazing."

"I made it last night. Merry Christmas."

He leaned across the box to give her yet another kiss, then said, "I haven't gotten you anything yet."

"You've already given me the perfect gift. You told the king you'd take the afternoon off, and I bet you don't do that very often. How about you come back to my place and we celebrate the holiday together?"

"That's another gift for me, *cara*."

She wrapped his tie in her fist and pulled his mouth back to hers. "It's a gift for us."

Eighteen months later

"Good job getting your gown through the gap in the evergreens."

"You're never going to stop teasing me about overhearing you with Prince Massimo that night, are you?" Sara asked with a laugh as Kelly stood before her balancing a glass of champagne and a plate with a slice of wedding cake in one hand while holding a fork in the other.

Sara and Umberto had nearly skipped a cake in favor of *torta della Sarcaccia*, but in the end, she'd convinced him they should have both. Of course, they'd also ended up with cannoli from Olga and Filomena, along with two trays of miniature chocolate cheesecakes that Anna made with help from the palace chef. The variety suited the group in the garden just fine.

"I understand that Prince Vittorio came out here and widened the entrance himself, just for the occasion," Kelly replied. "Of course, I didn't tell him that I'd once tested the entrance during a charity ball."

"I don't want to know, either," Prince Vittorio said as he walked up behind them. "The branches will grow back quickly. No sense in having a secret garden for the family if it's not a secret. But I couldn't figure out how Sara would possibly get through the evergreens without ruining her gown."

"It was very kind of you to do," Sara told the crown prince. "I'm honored that your parents offered the garden for our wedding."

It had been the perfect location for their celebration. Only their immediate families, a few members of the security staff, Sara's employees, and the royal family had been invited. Keeping the event small enabled Sara and Umberto to exchange their vows in front of the fountain while their guests watched from nearby benches. Afterward, everyone wandered through the garden while they enjoyed prepared desserts and gelato from Sara's shop. Sara had even made a tub of the queen's special 'A Bluebird's Song' for the occasion...at the queen's request.

"We're elated that you accepted." Queen Fabrizia approached on her husband's arm. "Everything is in bloom, the air smells sweet, and I can't think of a better place to celebrate such a special occasion. Of course, you also look stunning."

Sara welcomed the queen's heartfelt hug, then a kiss on each cheek from King Carlo. She'd known their royal duties would take them away from the festivities early; even so, they'd lingered longer than she'd imagined. "Thank you, both of you. You've made Umberto and me very happy."

"Umberto's a lucky man," the king said. "But he's still not taking enough time off. I hope you'll convince him to use more of his vacation days."

"I promise." Whether the king realized it or not, Umberto's workaholic tendencies had eased. While he kept long hours during the week and insisted upon manning the staircase at the end of each day when the king and queen retired to their apartment, he rarely spent time at the palace on weekends. In fact, it was over a long weekend this past April that he'd surprised her with a trip to Malta. They'd enjoyed an overnight ferry from Sarcaccia, then watched the sunrise over Valetta's Grand Harbor from St. Barbara's Bastion. Just as the sun filled the sky with an array of oranges and blues, Umberto knelt before her and proposed marriage.

It was the perfect way to begin the weekend and the rest of their lives together.

"Do you have plans for a honeymoon?" Kelly asked.

"I'm going to surprise her." Umberto's arm snaked around Sara's waist and he pressed a loving kiss to her temple. "I told her to pack for warm weather and to have the staff at both her shops ready to take over operations for two weeks."

"Wow. That's very trusting. I'm not sure I'd have been able to let Massimo plan a holiday without telling me where we're going," Kelly said, though the loving smile aimed at her husband made it clear she'd trust him with anything.

"The harder part is leaving Angeletti Gelato for two weeks in the middle of the summer tourist season." Sara looked from Kelly and Massimo to Vittorio. "You've seen how long the lines can get."

"The marina location was packed when I visited last week," Vittorio said.

Sara gave the crown prince a broad smile of thanks. Frequent, unannounced visits by members of the royal family had added to the gelateria's reputation. It also helped rehabilitate Sara's reputation in the eyes of the press. These days it was rare to see reference to the fact that the Barralis once fired her for shoplifting.

She wondered what the press would make of the fact she'd married the head of palace security. When she'd expressed concern for his reputation, Umberto insisted it wasn't an issue. Much as she wanted to protest, her arguments died every time she looked at him. Finally, she'd found an intelligent, compelling man who was her partner in every sense of the word. A man who loved that she had aspirations to build on her gelateria's success. A man whose opinion mattered to her and who cared about her opinions in return. A man with whom starting a family felt like the greatest adventure of all.

Olga and Filomena approached to thank them for the invitation to the wedding, then promised to visit after Sara and Umberto returned from their honeymoon. One by one, Sara and Umberto's coworkers and members of the Barrali family did the same, with Princess Sophia giving each of them teary, heartfelt good wishes. Finally, Sara's and

Umberto's families helped clean up, taking home leftover desserts as a thank you before leaving the newlyweds alone in the garden.

"I'm tempted to take you out over the Via Floriana fence," Umberto said, aiming a deliberate glance in the direction of the spot where he'd found her hidden umbrella a year and a half earlier.

"We might not make our flight if you do that. This gown was not designed for climbing fences."

"We'll make it." He wrapped her in a warm embrace, then twirled her through the flowers until they stood near the fountain. "If for some reason we don't, we'll just take the next flight. We'll make it worth the wait."

"Everything with you has been worth the wait. And the risk."

His green eyes sparkled with a combination of love and laughter before he framed her face in his capable hands.

"This from the world's worst thief," Umberto said before drawing her to him for their first private kiss as husband and wife. "Though you've stolen my heart. Forever."

Thank you for reading *A Royal Scandals Christmas*. If you enjoyed this book, please consider leaving a review at your favorite bookseller or book club website.

There are several full-length novels in The Royal Scandals series. Read on to enjoy a sample of the first title, *Scandal With a Prince*.

ACKNOWLEDGMENTS

Many thanks to my wonderful partners in crime, Christina Dodd, Emily March, and Susan Sizemore. Your insights have been invaluable. If you're ever asked about my research for *Christmas With a Palace Thief*, I urge you to plead the fifth.

Certain men possess voices so richly captivating, so drenched in sexuality, that they can bring a woman to her knees with a few simple syllables.

In a crowd of hundreds, it was the sound of one such voice that caught Megan's attention first.

Her stomach seized the instant her ears picked out the distinct timbre amongst the din of merry voices echoing through the packed rotunda of the newly-renovated Barcelona Grandspire Hotel. Around her, men and women went on sipping *cava* from crystal flutes as they discussed upcoming business deals or renovations to their vacation homes. Tuxedoed waiters continued their discreet circumnavigation of the room, gathering used hors d'oeuvre plates and refreshing drinks. On the surface, all appeared unchanged. It was a perfect late spring night in a perfect city, and thus far the hotel's grand reopening celebration was a resounding success.

Then she heard it again. Only three or four indistinguishable words, but they hit her gut with the same force as a sucker-punch from a male twice her size. A well-built male like Prince Stefano Barrali, whose third-in-line claim to the throne of Sarcaccia meant he enjoyed immeasurable wealth and connections without the pressures that usually accompanied them, while possessing the Mediterranean good looks and sultry charm that often did.

A few feet away from Megan, a gray-haired gentleman and his much younger wife cast subtle glances toward the hotel's side entrance, the one used when high-profile guests needed to make an inconspicuous arrival or exit. Megan resisted the urge to follow suit, but a breath later the overall volume in the lobby rose even as men tall enough to see over the crowd leaned closer to their companions to whisper into diamond-studded ears.

It's not possible. Not here, not on the biggest night of her career to date.

Without allowing her smile to drop or the cadence of her speech to change, skills honed by years of professional banter at events such as this, Megan continued her conversation with Mahmoud Said, the CEO of a large Egyptian telecommunications company, giving him an overview of the beachfront hotel's state-of-the-art conference and special event facilities. At the same time, she strained to catch the familiar sound once more. Perhaps the voice existed only in her mind, a stress-induced result of the months of work that had gone into tonight's soiree or a trick caused by the rotunda's domed roof.

No, even as Mahmoud asked a question about the hotel's business center, she accepted that she'd ceased imagining Stefano's flirtatious, luxuriant voice years ago. In all probability, the sound emanated from one of the televisions mounted over the bar in the cocktail lounge adjacent to the lobby. Though the bartender had been instructed to keep the sets muted in keeping with the formality of the night's celebration, with so many people crowding the lobby it wouldn't take much for a remote control to get bumped the wrong way or for a guest to assert herself and tune in to a report about a celebrity—or hot young royal—who caught her eye.

The Grandspire's manager, Ramon Beltran, circled through the crowd near Megan, patting shoulders, shaking hands, and accepting congratulations as he went, before he ascended the lobby's grand staircase to cascading applause. With a sweeping gesture, he sounded a ceremonial gong calling the guests to attention.

"Ladies and gentlemen," he announced as the reverberation faded, "thank you for attending our celebration tonight. We're honored to have so many friends and family of the Grandspire share this important evening. Dinner will now be served in the Gaudi Ballroom. I hope you enjoy both the meal and the view."

A pair of waiters opened the doors to reveal the ballroom's all-new floor to ceiling windows, which overlooked an immaculate beach and the Mediterranean Sea beyond. Modern tables topped with white-on-white orchids and Gaudi-inspired place settings filled the room. The resulting spike in conversation obliterated any chance Megan had of pinpointing the source of Stefano's voice.

Mahmoud excused himself to check on a friend, providing Megan the opportunity to conduct a discreet surveillance of the expansive marble lobby. Keeping her demeanor pleasant and professional, she scanned the faces of the well-heeled men in attendance, most of whom now escorted exquisitely gowned women past the lobby's large floral arrangements and into the ballroom.

The face that matched the voice didn't materialize. She exhaled, directing her nervous energy toward smoothing the silk fabric of the honey-colored cocktail dress she'd purchased especially for tonight, but her stomach remained unsettled.

At a signal from Ramon, Megan made her way against the tide of guests to encourage the attendees still clustered in the sunken bar area on the far side of the lobby to join the rest of the crowd in making their way to dinner. Progress was slow. All around her, air kisses were exchanged, lunches suggested, and holidays arranged as guests mingled. Gossip snaked its way through every conversation.

It was exactly the type of event where one expected to find Prince Stefano being courted by the movers and shakers of major corporations and high society, all of whom hoped that making inroads with the Barrali royal family would help them gain access to the family's vast financial and social network. However, as the Grandspire's head of business development, Megan had combed through the guest list for tonight's soiree more than once and Prince Stefano's name wasn't on it. It would not have escaped her notice.

As she descended the wide steps leading to the lounge area, Megan's gaze flicked to the bank of televisions mounted high over the sleek granite bar. Five soundless screens carried sporting events, but the sixth flashed the latest celebrity gossip. The bartender, a sociable young Catalan with a knack for attracting female attention, watched alongside a curvaceous blonde guest who gasped at the blaring announcement of a popular Spanish soap star's pregnancy with twins.

A sense of relief washed through Megan. That must've been it. It wouldn't be the first time Stefano spoke to her from a television.

The bartender glanced from the buxom blonde to Megan, shooting Megan a disarming *what can you do?* grin before fiddling with the remote to mute the sound and return the television to its usual sports station.

Megan arched a mischievous eyebrow at him, then at the blonde's back, before stretching her toes inside her new gold heels to release the tension of the last few hours. She couldn't blame herself for being on edge. Tonight's event was the culmination of five years of hard work. Given that investment of time and energy, together with a shortage of sleep this past week while the final preparations were made, she should've expected her nerves might get the better of her. She needed to take a cue from both the bartender and the guests lingering nearby and relax. The best way for her to showcase the refurbished hotel to the potential business clients in attendance would be to visibly enjoy the Grandspire herself—tonight's dinner, the art exhibition, the rooftop fireworks, all of it—and consider it a reward for a job well done. After all, she'd already booked eight major conferences and over two dozen smaller events for the coming months, enough to kick-start the hotel's income stream and gild her resume before she sought her next position.

Invigorated at the thought, she made her way to each of the seating areas in the lounge and introduced herself to those guests she didn't already know before directing them toward the ballroom. One by one, empty glasses filled the bar top as the partygoers progressed to dinner. However, a cluster of people remained near the fireplace, their attention riveted on a male seated in their center. Megan hated to interrupt, but couldn't see past those who were standing to identify the speaker. Only his highly polished shoes were visible between the high heels and wingtips of those surrounding him.

A man making his way toward the stairs glanced toward the fireplace when he thought no one was looking, though his partner, a woman whom Megan recognized as the owner of a major shipping company, stared openly, apparently unconcerned that others would notice her fascination with the conversation taking place.

The knot returned to Megan's stomach, twisting tighter than before. Everyone in attendance tonight was accustomed to the trappings of money and fame. Whoever sat near the fireplace held a special allure, even amongst the social elite, the kind often reserved for royalty. And *always* reserved for good-looking royalty.

A familiar rumble of laughter cut through the lounge, confirming her fear. Low, sexy, and even more inviting than Megan remembered, if such a thing were possible. Her knees softened and the floor seemed to sway beneath her.

After their last face-to-face meeting, she'd spent weeks trying to contact Stefano, using every means at her disposal, but now she needed nothing more than to escape. Seeing him in the flesh would make her want everything she knew she could never have, and she did not want to *want*. Especially not him.

Wanting Stefano could mean losing everything.

She took a step backward and started to turn away. She'd ask the bartender to send the group to dinner, then figure out how she could possibly avoid the prince for the rest of the evening so she could keep her attention where it needed to be: on work. Stefano's presence wouldn't distract her unless she let it.

"Megan." The telecommunications CEO she'd spoken with earlier appeared at her elbow, propelling her back toward the fireplace. "Have you had the opportunity to meet my guest? I didn't wish to say anything until I knew he'd arrived." Mahmoud's voice dropped to a whisper as he added, "You know these types. You cannot always count on them to appear when they say they will."

Before Megan could protest, the group parted in front of her to reveal a broad-shouldered man sitting on the far edge of the cocktail table, his face turned away as he laughed at a comment from a statuesque, cat-eyed brunette wearing the most arresting red gown Megan had ever seen.

Mahmoud cleared his throat. "Prince Stefano, may I present Megan Hallberg, the Grandspire's director of business development? Megan, this is Prince Stefano Barrali of Sarcaccia. His father and I have hosted a number of charity events together over the years, so I wanted Stefano to see the Grandspire's new facilities. I'm certain he'll give King Carlo a favorable report on the hotel's suitability for our future events."

The brunette tried to hide her disappointment at the interruption as Stefano spun and stood in one easy motion. Megan's mouth went dry as sand. She'd forgotten how tall he was, how fluidly he moved. As Stefano stepped toward her, the memory of their first meeting returned in a rush that threatened to flatten her. He'd moved in that same easy manner when he'd approached her a decade ago, offering to carry a length of pipe for her as she struggled to maneuver it through an alley in the congested Venezuelan village where they both worked as volunteers. She'd joked that he was her hero when he'd hefted it onto one shoulder as if it were no heavier than a loaf of bread.

But there were changes in him, too. While the celebrity gossips frequently commented on Stefano's athleticism, his playful nature, and even his dimples, no report could accurately convey the ways he'd matured in the years since Megan had last seen him. Television and magazines failed to capture the masculine line of his shoulders as they filled his tuxedo jacket, the texture of the skin along his sunkissed cheekbones, or the utter charisma he exuded.

Megan forced herself not to flinch as he came within arm's reach. She hadn't thought it possible his appearance could improve over the years, but it had. He'd become broader, stronger, more confident...more *him*.

Of course, his most distinctive physical characteristic could never change. His eyes were a clear sea green with a distinct ring around each iris, as if Picasso himself had taken up a narrow paintbrush to edge the green in black. She remembered all too well the last time she'd looked into those eyes. She'd been twenty-two, as had Stefano. They each sported grubby clothes that evening, having worked the entire day to finish installing a water system, but they'd been unwilling to use a single precious moment to change, knowing it was their final night together before returning to their separate lives. Their *real* lives.

He'd threaded his long fingers through her hair as they stood on a secluded beach not far from the village. Even in the waning light of the setting sun, she'd seen the deep passion in those green eyes. "I will never, ever forget you," he'd whispered before pulling her into a heart-stopping, explosive kiss. "These have been the best days of my life."

It felt surreal to look into those same eyes now, knowing she'd been forgotten within weeks, perhaps even days, relegated to what would become a long, long line of disposable women. A decade's worth of women, starting with the one to whom he'd become engaged less than a month after leaving Venezuela. The one to whom he'd run, barefoot, across the palace courtyard in a photo that appeared around the world, intriguing even those who'd never heard of the Barrali royal family.

Yet she couldn't have forgotten Stefano Barrali, even if she'd wanted to forget. Emotion threatened to overwhelm her as he stood before her, reaching out to take the hand she extended as if she were on autopilot. Before he could speak, undoing her with his whiskey-rich voice, she managed a calm, "Prince Stefano, it's an honor to have you here at the Grandspire. I hope you're enjoying your time in Barcelona."

He wrapped his large hand around hers, the touch shaking her very center. Searching out any excuse to break eye contact, she glanced toward Mahmoud and thanked him for the introduction. It was an act of sheer self-preservation out of fear Stefano could see to her soul, revealing both the wild lust coursing through her and the secret she'd kept hidden for so long.

Twenty floors above them, in the expansive suite that served as Megan's residence while she worked on the hotel's revitalization, a young girl with sea-green eyes and the same dark, wavy hair as Stefano sat at a desk, under the supervision of Megan's parents, finishing her homework.

A young girl conceived that very night on the beach.

A ROYAL SCANDALS WEDDING

More Royal Scandals titles will be available soon. For updates, please visit nicoleburnham.com, where you can subscribe to Nicole's Newsletter.

Subscribers receive exclusive content, including the short story *A Royal Scandals Wedding*, an inside look at the wedding of Megan Hallberg and Prince Stefano Barrali from the novel Scandal With a Prince.

ABOUT THE AUTHOR

Nicole Burnham is the RITA award-winning author of over twenty novels, including the popular Royal Scandals series.

Nicole graduated from an American high school in Germany, then obtained a BA in political science from Colorado State University and a JD/MA from the University of Michigan. She lives near Boston, spends as much time as possible at Fenway Park, and travels abroad whenever she can score cheap airfare.

Readers may visit Nicole's website and subscribe to her newsletter at nicoleburnham.com.

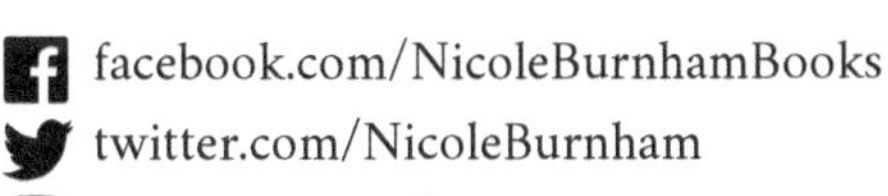

facebook.com/NicoleBurnhamBooks
twitter.com/NicoleBurnham
instagram.com/nicole.burnham

www.ingramcontent.com/pod-product-compliance
Lightning Source LLC
Chambersburg PA
CBHW061532210726
48287CB00006B/1916